WHISPERS
FROM THE VOID
An Anthology

BINOY PARIKH

INDIA • SINGAPORE • MALAYSIA

ISBN
Paperback 979-8-89610-755-2
Hardcase 979-8-89632-973-2

CONTENTS

AUTHOR'S PREFACE

Whispers from the Void is an anthology born from the intersection of science, philosophy, and the deepest recesses of the human mind. Each story is a step into the unknown—a journey into the void that exists between reality and illusion, light and darkness, and the complex interplay of desire, fear, and identity.

As a storyteller, I am deeply fascinated by quantum mechanics and its profound similarities with human psychology. The way quantum theory blurs the lines between observer and observed, choice and chance, mirrors the uncertainties that define our inner worlds. These ideas are not new; they echo ancient teachings, especially in Advaita Vedanta, where the oneness of all things and the illusory nature of reality were explored centuries ago. This anthology attempts to bridge those timeless philosophical concepts with the modern understanding of the mind and the universe.

In these pages, you will find characters grappling with the same fundamental questions: What is real? What is illusion? Are we truly in control, or are we shaped by forces beyond our comprehension?

The stories are set in a world where quantum principles—like entanglement, superposition, and the observer effect—are reflected in the characters' lives and minds, as they navigate the often indistinguishable boundary between the known and the unknowable.

Drawing from a diverse range of influences—quantum mechanics, psychology, and Advaita Vedanta—this anthology blends supernatural intrigue with philosophical reflection, exploring how the universe's most mysterious laws are closely mirrored in human thought and experience. Much like the particle that exists in multiple states until observed, the characters in these stories find themselves suspended between realities, their fates determined by their perceptions, desires, and fears.

Whispers from the Void is not just a collection of dark narratives but a contemplation on the nature of existence itself. It invites you to embrace uncertainty and contradiction, to question the very fabric of your reality. I hope these stories stir your thoughts and emotions, leading you to explore the void within yourself.

Thank you for embarking on this journey with me.

1

THE ETERNAL PRISON: A TALE OF ILLUSION AND LIBERATION

In the sprawling city of Bhopal, India, Dr. Vivek was akin to a living legend. Despite his youth, his surgical hands had breathed life into countless hearts. Though only in his 30s, he had already performed a staggering number of heart surgeries. His hands were skilled, but his heart was restless. Once married, he had divorced a year prior due to his overwhelming commitment to his practice. Consequently, his own heart ached with an insatiable loneliness and a lust that always seemed to lurk in the corners of his mind. A year past a bitter divorce, and a string of failed relationships had left him empty. Each encounter with a woman began innocently, but by the third or fourth date, his hands would betray him, becoming unwelcome intruders despite his gentlemanly facade.

One cold night, after his breakup with the warm and grounded Ria, Vivek found himself weeping alone in his grand, sterile home. This breakup with Ria had broken him more than he cared to admit. It was then he wished desperately for liberation, not through years of patience and spiritual practice, but through an immediate release, an escape from this burning, lustful desire that constantly threatened to consume him.

As if answering his plea, rumours of a mystical woman named Anaya reached him. Word had it that her touch could heal the soul, an ability she reserved for the chosen few. Intrigued and desperate, Vivek was drawn towards her like a moth to a flame.

Their first meeting was under a silvery full moon that cast an ethereal glow on Anaya's gleaming face. Her skin was of a milky white hue, but her eyes were deep and unfathomable, holding a strange, otherworldly allure. Anaya was an embodiment of ethereal grace. Her light blue Punjabi dress clung to her form in a way that was both modest and tantalising, outlining a figure that was supple and curvaceous. Her skin was radiant, milky white, appearing almost luminescent under the moon's glow. Each movement she made was fluid and deliberate, like a dancer's—a silent, seductive symphony that seemed to pull on Vivek's senses, stirring a deep, visceral longing within him.

Her face was a masterful play of contrasts: sharp cheekbones that gave way to a soft, full mouth; eyes that were deep and dark, seeming to hold within them a fathomless, mysterious world that Vivek felt an overpowering urge to explore. Her lips were a vibrant shade of rose, and when she spoke, her words flowed like a melodic tune, entrancing and inviting. The subtle perfume she wore was intoxicating, a mix of jasmine and something darker, more primal.

Every gesture, every glance she cast towards Vivek was like a spark to his flammable desire. He found himself helplessly drawn to her, not as a seeker to a sage, but as a moth captivated by a flame. In her presence, his practiced, doctorly demeanour unravelled; he became a man possessed by raw, unfiltered lust. And yet, beneath this carnal pull, there was a parallel allure. Anaya promised not just bodily temptation but also an escape, a quick and effortless liberation from his own tormenting desires. Vivek, entranced by her beauty and desperate for an end to his own spiritual unrest, was blind to the perilous path he was being led down. He saw in Anaya a tantalising solution to his problems: a chance to indulge his physical desires while also, paradoxically, seeking an easy escape from them.

Her promise of liberation, which would normally require years of disciplined practice and introspection, appeared to him like a shimmering oasis. Vivek, so entranced by Anaya's beauty and so desperate for relief, failed to recognise this mirage for what it was. Instead of seeking genuine spiritual guidance and working towards self-control and inner peace, he found himself ensnared by the allure of a quick fix – an 'easy way out' offered by a woman whose beauty was as spellbinding as her promises.

"Too perfect," Vivek thought, but his desperation muffled the warning bells in his mind. Anaya, without needing to hear his story, seemed to understand his torment and agreed to help him. This too should have warned Vivek, but he was intoxicated, both by his own anguish and Anaya's enigmatic presence.

Anaya led Vivek through the twisted, dark alleys of old Bhopal, the shadows seeming to dance and writhe on the walls as they passed. The air grew colder, and a chilling wind carried haunting whispers of prostitutes who beckoned with promises of pleasure, their eyes hollow and soulless. Here, in the darkness, Vivek's lust flared, but it mingled with fear – a visceral reminder of the reputation he had to uphold. In an instant, a primal, animalistic urge surged within Vivek; he was drawn to them, desiring to lose himself in their embrace. But almost as quickly, this impulse was quashed, not by a sense of morality, but by the terror of staining his immaculate reputation.

Anaya, with an intuition that was uncanny, sensed this battle within him. She turned to Vivek, her eyes reflecting the moon's cold light, and laughed, a sound that was both chilling and oddly melodic. It was a laugh that seemed to resonate with the darkness around them, a mocking, eerie symphony that sent shivers down Vivek's spine. Yet, in the next breath, she gently drew him into her bosom, her touch simultaneously comforting and unsettling, like the cold embrace of a statue. Vivek, despite the dissonance he felt, found solace in her arms, even as the cold dread continued to curl around his heart.

They arrived at a derelict hotel that seemed to sag under the weight of its own grim history. Inside the hotel room, reality began to contort. The hotel stood like a gaunt spectre in the heart of old Bhopal, its crumbling facade bearing the scars of time and neglect. Windows, some shattered and others veiled in grime, stared blankly like the eyes of the long dead. The walls, once brightly painted, were now a canvas of decay, peeling and stained by years of rain and neglect. It was a place that seemed to exude an almost palpable sense of despair and sordid history, its darkened hallways echoing with the ghostly remnants of countless illicit rendezvous.

As Vivek and Anaya approached, they could see a group of stern-faced policemen in the sandy, unkempt parking lot. Their presence was like a storm cloud, casting a further pall over the already dismal scene. They had just completed a raid on the hotel, rounding up a motley crew of prostitutes and their clients, who now stood in a huddled, humiliated mass near the entrance. The officers were in no mood for nonsense; their eyes, sharp and scrutinising, were trained to detect the slightest hint of wrongdoing.

It was in this tense atmosphere that Anaya, ever the picture of calm and poise, turned to Vivek and began to speak in a voice quivering with feigned distress. "Please, Vivek," she implored, her eyes welling with convincing tears. "I can't keep living like this. I need space to think, that's why I chose this place, away from the chaos of our lives." Vivek, quick to adapt to her lead, replied with a mix of urgency and tenderness in his voice, "Anaya, I love you. I came as soon as I could. We can work through our issues, but not like this, not apart." The policemen, overhearing this emotional exchange, exchanged sympathetic glances. One of the older officers, his face softened by their apparent distress, approached them.

"You're here to reconcile?" he asked, his voice carrying a paternal warmth that contrasted sharply with the grim backdrop. "Yes, officer," Anaya replied, her voice breaking just enough to be believable. "We've been through so much. I just want to save our marriage." Moved by their performance, the officer nodded and gestured for them to proceed. "Go on," he said gently. "We're here for a different matter entirely. May you find the peace you're looking for." As they passed through the grimy, dimly lit lobby and into the bowels of the derelict hotel, Vivek could feel the weight of the building's sinister past pressing in on him, the eerie silence swallowing them whole as Anaya's touch remained his only anchor in this unfolding nightmare.

As Vivek stepped into the room behind Anaya, he immediately sensed a stark shift. The air in the room felt dense and charged, as though they had crossed an unseen threshold into a realm altogether separate from the world outside. The dull flicker of a lone light bulb cast ghostly shadows that seemed to dance and writhe along the peeling wallpaper. Anaya moved gracefully towards the bathroom, her figure a mesmerising silhouette against the faint light. Vivek's eyes remained glued to her, the raw lust in his gaze deepening. She was the flame, and he was the moth, willingly being drawn closer to what felt like inevitable combustion.

Then, reality twisted.

The room, which had initially appeared mundane and worn, now revealed itself as something far more sinister. The wallpaper began to pulse, as if it were alive, its faded floral pattern twisting into grotesque faces that leered at him with mocking, hollow eyes. The shadows deepened into an abyss, swallowing the corners of the room and creating a sensation of infinite, disorienting space.

In this stretching, warping reality, Vivek called out to Anaya, his voice a desperate plea: "Didi! Didi!" an almost reflexive and unconscious choice of addressing Anaya that he himself did not fully understand at this moment, but signifying an undercurrent of an illusion that Vivek was to realise shortly, starkly at odds with his previous objectification of Anaya.

But his words seemed to be swallowed by the room itself, his cries echoing back to him in distorted, mocking tones. He could still see the sliver of light under the bathroom door, but it seemed miles away now, an unreachable beacon in the swelling darkness. As Vivek stumbled forward, trying to navigate this nightmarish expanse, he felt an icy wave of terror. His own reflection began to materialise on the surface of the walls, but it was a twisted version of himself–his eyes hollow and desperate, his face contorted in a scream that he could feel in his bones but could not hear with his ears.

In the midst of the room's distorted reality, Vivek caught his reflection. It didn't show a respected doctor but rather a man wrestling with himself, grappling with intangible desires and a salvation always out of reach. The room's twisting confines hinted at something deeper, a darkness that was both external and intimate. Anaya, the seemingly benevolent guide, appeared more and more like a mirror, reflecting back to Vivek the very illusions he was caught in. The walls around him seemed to pulsate with his own unchecked passions, and the woman he had believed would lead him to salvation was woven from the same fabric of desires that ensnared him.

A chill settled over Vivek as he pieced together the fragments of his reality. Had he, in his impatience and burning desires, conjured this trap for himself? Was Anaya, with her shifting form, a creation of his own yearning? And as this dread took root, he began to question the foundations of his life – the bustling city, the weight of his title, and even the ephemeral figures like Anaya and Ria that floated through his life.

In this nightmarish room, Vivek found himself at a crossroads. The tantalising images that had once beckoned him now felt like chains. He recognised a hunger within, not just for sensory pleasures but for something profound, something grounding. But with every revelation, the room's walls seemed to close in, and the path to that profound understanding felt more elusive. Would he ever discern what was real from the illusions that ensnared him? Would he ever find a way out? Were these walls, this drama, and these characters merely the shadows in a deeper, more intricate illusion? Was there a truth, untainted and pure, buried beneath the labyrinth of his own making? Or was this torment his reality, a dark reflection of the path his soul had chosen? In that moment, under the weight of these questions, Vivek felt himself suspended, caught between the nightmare and an awakening that felt just beyond his grasp. The answers remained tantalizingly out of reach, yet intuitively just so close, and yet such answers remained concealed behind layers of mystery and desire.

2

THE PERIPHERY OF REALITY: IS THERE A TRUTH?

A WORLD WITHIN A WORLD

In the bustling heart of Delhi, where the clamour of life meets the quiet corners of the High Court, lived Arjun, a lawyer of exceptional talent, but burdened by an introverted nature that seemed to engulf him. In his late 20s, tall, fair-skinned, and remarkably handsome, he belonged to a well-to-do family that took pride in his achievements. But Arjun, even amidst his successes, felt a constant gnaw at his spirit, a pervasive sense of imposter syndrome that ate at him.

Inside the court, his mind was a scalpel—sharp, precise, unerring—but outside, it turned into a storm of second guesses. Every praise felt like a shard of glass; beautiful to look at, but painful to hold. To the world, his demeanour was calm, almost serene, but within him raged a tempest of self-doubt and constant apprehension. It was as though he wore a mask, one sculpted with an exacting hand, but behind it lay a face creased with worry.

Each morning as he buttoned his crisp, ironed shirt, he felt like he was arming himself for a battle, not in the courtroom, but within himself. Each victory in court, rather than elevating him, seemed only to deepen his fear of the impending fall he was sure would come. "How long can this last?" he would ask himself, peering into the mirror, meeting his own eyes but failing to recognise the successful lawyer they belonged to. His reflection seemed like a stranger wearing his skin, an imposter occupying his life. Despite his family's warmth and their pride that beamed like a lighthouse, Arjun felt undeserving, an intruder at his own dinner table. Conversations at family gatherings were a torment. While he was a master of legal rhetoric, casual dialogues felt like walking through a minefield. The simplest question from a relative—a casual "How are you?"—felt like an accusation, and his reply, though courteous, would be laced with internal dread.

His introverted nature was not just a preference for solitude; it was a sanctuary, a coping mechanism. Crowds did not just exhaust him; they sent prickles of anxiety up his spine, making his hands tremble subtly, unnoticed by others but a roaring storm to him. Compliments were double-edged swords – they pleased his ears but tightened like a noose around his anxious heart. He yearned for connection, to reach out, to feel the simple joy of a friend's laughter or the touch of a loved one, but his own mind was a barrier, a thick glass pane through which he observed the world but seldom partook in its warmth.

He lived in a paradox: a brilliant lawyer who could argue the most complex cases with unmatched eloquence, yet struggled to articulate his own emotions even to himself. His room, filled with legal volumes and texts, was both his fortress and his prison, a space where he was shielded from the world's eyes but also where he was most starkly confronted with his own relentless self-critique. In this delicate equilibrium, Arjun carried himself through life, a character of contrasts, a man standing alone even when surrounded by the crowd, an individual whose soul seemed perpetually out of sync with the vibrant, bustling world around him.

A HEART WITHIN A HEART

In the depths of Arjun's heart, nestled softly, was his affection for a woman. She had been his classmate, his dear friend, and his secret muse. He knew that she too, even after her marriage, had harboured feelings for him once, a chapter she had approached but he had gently closed, fearing the loss of their treasured friendship. This secret world within him, where she was the radiant sun around which all else revolved, was intricate and vivid. In this private cosmos, their conversations were endless and effortless, not halting and heavy as they were. Here, in the quietude of his mind, he could confess his thoughts to her without fear of judgement or rejection; he could hold her close without the stiffness that seized his limbs in her actual presence.

This inner sanctuary was a theatre where he played out alternative realities—a world wherein he was not shackled by his own anxieties, where he could respond to her affection openly, and where the simplicity of holding her hand was not a Herculean task eclipsed by overthinking. In this realm, he was free to love her, to be loved by her, to exist unburdened and unfettered with her by his side. They strolled through moonlit gardens, their laughter mingling with the rustle of leaves; they shared quiet dinners, where his words flowed as smoothly as the wine; they danced, not just with their bodies, but with their souls in perfect harmony.

Yet, Arjun understood deeply that this world was to be admired but not lived through. It was his solace and his pain, both the dream that soothed him and the ache that reminded him of what could not be. It was a painting he could create and gaze upon but never step into, a melody he could compose but never sing. It was his secret gallery of 'what ifs,' beautiful to visit but suffocating to dwell in. He knew that crossing the line, allowing this internal narrative to seep into the tangible world, risked not just his heart but the precious friendship he and she had nurtured over years.

In his quieter moments, when the weight of the day's pretences lifted slightly, he would sit alone, envisioning her smile, hearing her voice as it sounded in his fantasies, warm, close, intimate. But each time, reality, like a cold wind, would rush back in. Her marriage, his own insecurities, the unspoken words that had solidified into an insurmountable wall between them, they all stood as vigilant guards to this secret world. So, in the safety of his mind, she remained his most cherished companion and his most painful reminder of the life his nature barred him from, a bittersweet symphony that played in the silent corners of his heart.

AN EVENT WITHIN AN EVENT

One day, an invitation arrived that would unwittingly set the stage for a turning point in Arjun's life. A college friend was getting married, and the celebration was to be far from Delhi, at a farm reachable only by a journey through the night. The woman, his beloved friend, proposed they go together, her voice an endearing melody over the phone. Others, old college mates, had reached out for a ride as well, but Arjun's heart tightened at the thought. He wanted to travel with her and only her. Still, his introverted nature, that ever-present shyness, constrained him – he could not say no to the others.

It felt suffocating, the looming journey, the clustering of friends in his new car, it was minor to most, but for Arjun, it was a storm, his anxiety swelling like a tide. The very notion of navigating social interactions for the lengthy drive twisted his stomach into knots. The car, which should have been a vessel of joy, felt like a tightening cage. Each additional passenger was, in his mind, another layer of weight on his chest, making it harder for him to breathe. In an impulsive bid to escape it all, he embarked on the journey alone, leaving without a word to her. It was a desperate grasp for air, for space, for sanity. He chose solitude over confrontation, silence over explanation. As he drove, the empty seat beside him was both his reprieve and his torment was vacant, yet so palpably full of her absence, her disappointment.

His drive was interrupted by a mundane errand – a stop at a department store. It was here that he made the absent-minded error of leaving the keys in his new car. In that brief window, the car was stolen. Panic seeped into his veins as he realised he could not remember the car's number, leaving him powerless to report the theft. His mind raced faster than his heartbeat; visions of police reports and disappointed parents swirled into a tempest that threatened to consume him. This car, a symbol of his independence and his family's pride in him, was now a ghost, a loss that mirrored his internal state.

This incident, twinned with his sudden understanding of the hurt he must have inflicted on his friend by leaving without her, made his insides curdle with sorrow. He also saw himself as unworthy, a failure to his parents who held him in high esteem. He felt like an imposter in his own life, a mere shadow of the son and friend he was supposed to be. It was as if the universe itself was affirming his deepest fears—that he was not deserving of the love or respect he had been given.

In that moment, standing in a world that seemed to be closing in on him, Arjun's soul ached with a deep, resonating sadness. It was a profound melancholy, not merely situational but existential, as though his very being had been called into question. In his mind, the stolen car was not just a loss of property; it was a vivid, cruel metaphor for his own sense of self, something he thought he had, but was so easily taken away, leaving him exposed, vulnerable, and profoundly alone.

A REALITY WITHIN A REALITY

Returning home, Arjun sulked into a darkened corner of his room, his mind unravelling into a poignant, tortured monologue. "What is this life but a masquerade? A sham where I exist but do not live? Am I a good lawyer, or just a ghost impersonating one? My parents' faith, her affection, do I deserve any of it? Have I lost pieces of a reality that were never mine to begin with?"

With each question, his self-loathing deepened, and his soul seemed to shrink further into itself. "Every step I take is but a rehearsal of a farce, every word a recitation of a script I never penned," he thought. "In this grand theatre of life, am I naught but a spectator trapped in an actor's role, eternally out of place? In love, which should be the most authentic of human experiences, why do I falter? Why did the mere thought of intimacy with her—a chance to live, not merely exist— terrify me so? Is it because I sensed, deep down, that I am unworthy of such a pure connection?" Arjun's thoughts coalesced into a storm, each darker than the last, each feeding the tempest that was his despair.

His body felt heavy, as though anchored to his own hopelessness. The air around him seemed to thicken, suffocating him slowly with the weight of his existence. "What is this relentless ache that gnaws at my heart? This sorrow that drowns me, why? Am I condemned to this solitude, this perpetual isolation within my own mind? Is this punishment, or simply my fate?" His room, though familiar, appeared alien, as if reflecting his internal estrangement from the world. "I am drowning," he thought, "drowning in an endless sea of my own making, and every breath is a betrayal of the truth: that I am not meant to be here. That my existence itself is a blunder, a glitch in the grand design of the universe."

As his thoughts spiralled into the abyss, Arjun imagined his hand closing around the cold grip of a gun. It was an object foreign yet oddly comforting, a way out, a resolution to his internal strife, a silencer of the clamorous self-doubt that had haunted him for so long. In this dire moment, he pulled the trigger. The sound, in his mind, was deafening, echoing his internal turmoil. A flash, a release, and then: silence. Blood, in his vision, spattered like cruel artwork across the walls, his body lifeless on the ground, finally freed from the relentless torment of existence.

A MIND WITHIN A MIND

But in the aftermath of that chilling tableau, Arjun was struck by a profound, grounding realisation: there could not have been a gun in his room. It was a stark, sobering truth that stood in direct contrast to the visceral intensity of the scene that had just unfolded within his mind. This gun, the cold embodiment of his darkest impulses, was nothing more than a fabrication, a desperate cry from the depths of his psyche, seeking an end to his perpetual suffering. It was a mirage so vivid and compelling that it threatened to overshadow the reality of his existence.

However, this vivid mirage again propelled Arjun into another train of thought. As the stark realisation that there could not have been a gun settled over him like a shroud, Arjun's mind splintered into a thousand fragments of uncertainty.

In a quiet, quaking voice, he whispered to himself, "A king in a dream rendered a beggar in wake," as he pondered the unsteady terrain of his existence. "Is my anguish the truth? Or is this room, this house, this city my truth? My law degree, the affection of that woman, my parents' pride in me were these ever real, or figments of a dream?" he questioned, his voice trembling. "And if they are a dream, then is this stark moment of 'reality,' where I find myself alone with no gun, also a fabrication? Where, then, lies the boundary between the ephemeral and the tangible? What, then, is my truth?"

As his thoughts spun, reality seemed to bend and warp around him. It felt as though he was plummeting through an endless, spiralling tunnel, a descent into madness from which there seemed to be no escape. It was a dream within a dream within a dream, a dizzying maelstrom where the lines of his waking experience were irrevocably blurred with the tempestuous thoughts of his mind. In this chaotic cycle, Arjun was neither clearly alive nor dead.

He could not distinguish the texture of reality from the intricate tapestries his mind wove, each as vivid and consuming as the last. And so, within this turbulent and torturous loop, Arjun lost himself. The world outside and the world within coiled around him until they were indistinguishable. He was entrapped in a maddening dance, a man adrift on a boundless sea, with neither sight of shore nor anchor to grasp. He could no longer discern if he was awake or dreaming, alive or a spectre in his own tragic narrative—a narrative that, to him, felt as infinite and as elusive as the cosmos itself.

In the loop of his existential quandary, Arjun felt himself again with the gun—cold, solid, impossible. He fired, but the contradiction of the gun's presence was a glaring tear in the fabric of his perceived reality. The deafening sound of the gunshot, the sharp pain in his hand as he pulled the trigger, were these sensations real or crafted by a mind teetering on the edge? In an endless loop, he again questioned – "From where did this gun come?"

It was an enigma, an impossibility that tore at the already fragile seams of his reality. This object, cold and lethal in his hand, could not have been there. His mind again screamed in resistance, unwilling to accept the unfolding narrative. He questioned himself, his mind, and reality with an intensity that shook his core. His mind raced as he dissected the sequence of events, questioning their authenticity, their origin. Could such vivid agony be a mere figment? Could his entire life, with its pains and joys, be but a dream, a delicate illusion spun by his subconscious?

Arjun's life, or his imagined life, became a maze, each path either a projection of his psyche or a tangible reality, indistinguishable from one another. Like a painting where the colours bleed into each other, Arjun's world is a vibrant, tragic swirl, a dream within a dream within a dream. In this delicate, harrowing dance between reality and imagination, Arjun became as captivating as he was tormented, a man forever poised on the periphery of reality.

3

THE PUPPETEER'S CURSE: STRANGLED BY SHADOWS

A SILENT CRY

In the heart of Kolkata, where tradition and modernity mingled effortlessly, young Aarav was the quintessential good boy – mild-mannered, studious, and polite. The middle-class son of loving, but overworked parents, he was raised in a modest home that instilled in him strong values and a love for knowledge. Despite his academic prowess, he faced subtle yet constant condescension due to his darker complexion and fuller physique, and the fact that Aarav belonged to a middle-class family. The strict and authoritative environment of his school, favouring the wealthy and academically stellar, heightened his isolation.

In school, Aarav was a silent storm, his mind alive with vibrant thoughts and dreams. Being the attentive and respectful student, teachers often regarded him warmly. However, this was a double-edged sword, as his peers viewed his demeanour not as genuine respect, but as a ploy for favouritism. Originally a boy with a spark of extroversion, Aarav became increasingly reserved, repressed by the authoritarianism at school and the subtle judgements of his peers.

He was above average in studies, an achievement that should have been a source of pride but instead became a part of his agony. In the stringent environment of his school, where being a minute late could lead to severe reprimand, he felt an insidious form of pressure. The authoritarian tone of the school, so starkly different from the warmth of his home, suppressed his once-vibrant and open personality further. Aarav's physical appearance – his dark complexion and fuller physique – became a silent reason for others to dismiss him. This was exacerbated by the fact that the school's social climate subtly favoured the fair-skinned and slim, reflecting broader cultural biases.

One vivid memory that stayed with Aarav was the annual school play. In his heart, Aarav harboured a secret love for theatre. That year, the play was an adaptation of a famous Indian mythological story, and Aarav longed to be a part of it. But when he auditioned for a role, he was relegated to the background. His teacher, bound by the expectations of what the lead role 'should' look like, dismissed his potential because he did not fit the conventional mould – too dark and heavyset. Also, the fact that the role went in favour of one of the academically and financially wealthy students exacerbated the effect of that rejection in Aarav's mind; it felt like a silent affirmation of the unworthiness that seemed to hang over him daily.

Compounding his struggles was the stark divide between the rich and middle-class students. Aarav, hailing from a middle-class family, often felt this divide keenly. Some of his classmates arrived at school in expensive cars, flaunting the latest gadgets, while Aarav took a crowded bus daily and carried a lunch packed lovingly by his mother.

The affluent students, perhaps without realising, often carried an air of condescension towards their less privileged peers.

When it came to friendships and romance, the girls in school seemed to favour the boys who exuded a strong, extroverted, 'alpha' personality, traits that were increasingly alien to Aarav's repressed and guarded nature. He once mustered the courage to give a small, beautifully handcrafted paper rose to a girl he had a secret crush on. But he overheard her and her friends later, speaking with veiled pity and surprise as if a 'fat and dark' boy like Aarav reaching out in such a way was a curious, unexpected act. That day, Aarav's heart did not just break; a part of his soul seemed to wither.

His adolescence, therefore, was marred by these pressures. He studied hard, not just because he loved to learn, but because he internalised the message that his worth was tied to his academic performance. In his teenage mind, if he could not be the charismatic or handsome boy, he needed to be the smartest. It was his defence, his quiet way to stand tall in a world that seemed to subtly, but consistently, tell him he was not enough.

At home, in the evenings after school, as Aarav sat at his small desk, the noise of Kolkata's streets drifting in through his window, he would lose himself in his books and his notes, creating a world in his mind where he was seen, where he mattered, and where the qualities that made him 'Aarav' were celebrated, not diminished.

SHADOWS OF THE MIND

Years later, Dr. Aarav Banerjee emerged as a renowned psychologist, lauded far and wide for his penetrating insights into the human psyche. To the external world, he stood as the epitome of success, a figure whose credentials were cited with reverence in professional circles. However, beneath this polished and accomplished exterior, lay a starkly different reality.

At the root of Aarav's being was an enduring hunger for admiration and validation, a hunger born from the neglect and indifference that marred his formative years. Despite a litany of professional accolades, his craving for applause and recognition remained insatiable. In a bid to continually validate his self-worth, Aarav meticulously curated his public image, presenting himself as an unparalleled expert in his field. He thrived on the praise he received from colleagues, patients, and the media, each commendation temporarily soothing his deep-seated wounds.

Aarav's intelligence was undeniable and exceptional. However, rather than employing this brilliance as a tool for healing, he weaponised it. His sharp acumen allowed him to read people quickly and discern their vulnerabilities with unsettling precision, a skill he deployed not to nurture, but to maintain an illusion of his own superiority. Beneath his formidable intellect lay a vulnerable core, a raw remnant from his youth, when he felt persistently unworthy and rejected. To shield this tender vulnerability, Aarav constructed a fortress of narcissism around himself. This armour was ruthless; he fiercely guarded his insecurities, swiftly and sharply retaliating against any perceived slight or threat that dared to approach his internal pain.

Aarav's interactions, both personally and professionally, were imbued with a conspicuous absence of genuine emotion. Each relationship he maintained was a calculated move, a strategy meticulously designed to bolster his image and to insulate him from any appearance of dependency or inferiority. This deep-seated fear of being reliant was so profound that it manifested as a stark lack of empathy and altruism.

In Aarav's mind, his identity was inflated to monumental proportions. He was not merely a successful psychologist; he was an unparalleled genius, a titan in his field. He would readily exaggerate his accomplishments and talents, clinging to a delusional belief that ordinary rules and expectations did not, and should not, apply to him. His perception of his own insights was that they were uniquely profound, transcendent even.

The inherent nature of Aarav's profession demanded a deep well of empathy, yet his disorder rendered authentic emotional connections virtually non-existent. While he was adept at mimicking empathetic responses when necessary, such gestures were performative—crafted to maintain his professional facade rather than stemming from a genuine understanding or sharing of another's emotions. Aarav's willingness to exploit others, viewing them as mere instruments in his own grand design rather than as individuals with their own inherent worth, was a chilling testament to the depths of his emotional disconnect.

As an adult, Dr. Aarav Banerjee was a complex figure, a man whose brilliant mind served simultaneously as his most profound asset and his most crippling curse. His narcissistic personality disorder, deeply rooted in his traumatic past, compelled him to craft an elaborate, impenetrable facade. This veneer masked a tempest of self-loathing and fragile self-esteem. Despite a flourishing practice that painted a vivid picture of success, his personal world was a desolate landscape marked by emotional disconnection, manipulative behaviours, and a relentless, futile pursuit of validation.

Within this dark panorama of Aarav's life arose a sinister impulse: a burning need for revenge. This need, calculated and cold, was aimed squarely at four former schoolmates who, in his eyes, had left indelible scars on his soul. Driven by the shadows in his mind, Aarav meticulously orchestrated schemes of retribution, each designed to inflict pain equal—or greater than—the torment he believed he had endured. In this pursuit of vengeance, Aarav's dark traits were laid bare, revealing a chilling psychopathy that lay dormant within him.

EXACTING REVENGE

Rohit: Exploring the Cracks

To Aarav, Rohit represented a painful chapter from his past. Once a teenage heartthrob known for his handsome looks and athletic build, Rohit had been cruel and condescending towards Aarav during their adolescence in school, often demeaning Aarav for his darker skin and larger physique. Rohit was now a committed family man, although not as successful as Aarav.

In his clandestine campaign of revenge, Aarav identified his patient Meera as a perfect pawn in his elaborate chess game. Meera, a woman wrestling with her own deep-seated inferiority complex, was unmarried and bore an aching need to prove her worth to herself and the world. Aarav, with his extraordinary ability to read and manipulate people, detected this vulnerability in Meera like a shark senses blood in the water. Aarav saw in Meera's fragile psyche the opportunity to craft a perfect storm. He cunningly nurtured her confidence during their sessions, subtly steering their conversations towards relationships and self-worth. He painted a vivid narrative for Meera, where winning Rohit's affections would be the ultimate validation of her desirability and value. To Aarav, this served a dual purpose: it was both a chance to elevate Meera's self-esteem and a masterstroke in his sinister plan to assert power over Rohit.

In one of their sessions, Aarav casually showed Meera a photo of Rohit, mentioning offhand how Rohit was now married, seemingly settled and content. He whispered into Meera's psyche the idea that if she could charm a man like Rohit—who had once been the heartthrob of every girl around—then surely, she could charm anyone. Aarav's words were cloaked in the guise of empowerment, but his true intent was far more insidious. Meera, eager for validation and entranced by the challenge Aarav subtly laid before her, took the bait. Over the following months, Meera meticulously orchestrated her approach towards Rohit, her actions guided by the subliminal messages planted by Aarav. Her emotional state, carefully manipulated by her psychologist, made her a willing participant in this game. As Meera and Rohit's extramarital affair took root, Rohit's soft spot for adoration from women became his undoing, he was enchanted by Meera's affection and the way she idolised him, as he had been a magnet for such adoration in his youth.

Behind the scenes, Aarav watched the affair unfold with cold satisfaction. He knew that every secret rendezvous between Meera and Rohit was another step closer to his ultimate goal: Rohit's downfall. When the moment was ripe, Aarav orchestrated the reveal of the affair with surgical precision. He ensured that the news reached the ears of those who would be most devastated and outraged: Rohit's wife, his children, his extended family, and his close friends. The fallout was nuclear. Rohit's idyllic life, his marriage, his relationship with his children, his reputation, all crumbled into ruin, just as Aarav had meticulously planned. In this dark design, Aarav had accomplished more than just the destruction of Rohit's life. He had twisted the very essence of his role as a healer, warping it into a tool for personal vengeance. Aarav's manipulative prowess did not just break Rohit, it exploited Meera's vulnerabilities, turning her into an unwitting weapon in a deeply personal war. Thus, in his pursuit of revenge, Aarav's psychopathy was laid bare, exposing a chilling, dark strategist who orchestrated pain with the same deftness with which he navigated the human mind.

HARSHVARDHAN: COLD AND CALCULATED DOWNFALL

In Aarav's calculated web of vengeance, each person was a piece on a board, carefully moved and manipulated to serve his ends. Harshvardhan, the wealthy heir of a privileged family, was one of Aarav's most despised figures from his past. Harshvardhan's arrogance and dismissive attitude during their school days had etched a lasting mark on Aarav's psyche. Aarav detested how Harshvardhan flaunted his wealth and the cadre of sycophants that perpetually surrounded him. Now a successful business tycoon, Harshvardhan remained blissfully unaware of the storm that Aarav was brewing for him.

Enter Rakesh, a middle-aged man and one of Aarav's patients. Rakesh once ran a modest but promising business that found itself in direct competition with Harshvardhan's vast empire. In an aggressive business move, Harshvardhan undercut Rakesh's prices, offering excessive discounts to customers, which left Rakesh's venture in ruins and forced him into bankruptcy. This severe blow plunged Rakesh into a deep depression, leading him to seek professional help and thus, into the consulting room of Dr. Aarav Banerjee.

Aarav, ever the master manipulator, saw in Rakesh's plight an opportunity too valuable to pass up. Under the guise of therapy, Aarav subtly fuelled Rakesh's sense of injustice and bitterness towards Harshvardhan. He steered their sessions towards discussions of empowerment and retribution, framing Harshvardhan as a symbol of the cruelty and unfairness that Rakesh had suffered in life. In Aarav's carefully crafted narrative, taking down Harshvardhan was not an act of revenge, it was a fight for justice.

With Aarav's guidance, Rakesh meticulously constructed an elaborate financial scam. They set up a faux business entity that appeared to sell raw materials to Harshvardhan's company. Initially, the transactions were genuine, with Harshvardhan's company issuing legitimate cheques for substantial sums. But then, Aarav and Rakesh escalated their plan. They began forging additional cheques with Harshvardhan's signature for large amounts of money which were impossible to exist in Harshvardhan's company's bank account. When these forged cheques inevitably bounced, the fallout was catastrophic. Harshvardhan was arrested and charged with fraud, his sterling reputation tarnished overnight. As the legal battles unfolded, the media feasted on the downfall of the once untouchable business tycoon. Harshvardhan's family, once living in the lap of luxury, was plunged into a nightmare of legal strife, public shame, and looming financial ruin.

Through Rakesh, Aarav had masterminded Harshvardhan's spectacular downfall, all from the shadows. To the world, Aarav was still the brilliant, compassionate psychologist, but in truth, he had weaponised Rakesh's despair, manipulating his patient into becoming the agent of his revenge. In this dark play, Aarav was both a puppeteer and a playwright. His manipulations were precise and devastating. Harshvardhan, who had once looked down upon Aarav with disdain, was now broken, a poignant testament to Aarav's chilling ability to wield psychological insight as a weapon, crafting schemes as complex and intricate as the human mind itself.

PRIYA: A SLIPPERY SLOPE

In the tapestry of Aarav's meticulously plotted revenge, Priya held a particularly poignant space. She was once the object of his innocent affection during their school days – a girl of modest appearance but irresistible allure, drawn always to the 'bad boys' who exuded alpha charm. To young Aarav, she was enchanting, but Priya had been dismissive of his feelings, mocking him for his appearance and refusing even the basic cordiality of friendship. His youthful infatuation with Priya had long since curdled into a deep-seated resentment. Now a successful executive, a loving mother, and seemingly the wife in a picture-perfect marriage, Priya embodied a life that seemed as polished and untouchable as a magazine spread. This made her a prime target in Aarav's vindictive sights.

Enter Ananya, a young woman on a hard-fought path to recovery from drug addiction and one of Aarav's patients. In her, Aarav discerned another perfect pawn for his schemes. During their therapy sessions, he planted a seed: he suggested to Ananya that to truly understand the devastating impact of drugs, and to solidify her own resolve to stay clean, she needed to witness firsthand the havoc that substance abuse could wreak on another's life. He framed it as a form of catharsis, a way to vicariously experience the dark path she had escaped, thereby strengthening her own resolve to remain sober.

Aarav introduced Ananya to Priya under the most innocent of pretexts, perhaps as a potential mentor in Priya's corporate world, or through a fabricated chance encounter at a social event. Ananya, acting under Aarav's guidance but convinced of the righteousness of the act, initially played the part of a supportive friend to Priya. Priya's high-stress life as a top executive and a mother created a fertile ground for Aarav's plot. Ananya, ever the empathetic confidant, introduced Priya to narcotics under the guise of stress relief during a vulnerable moment. Perhaps it was during an office offsite where alcohol had already loosened inhibitions, and Ananya offered drugs as a simple, one-time escape from mounting pressure.

The hook was set, and Priya began to spiral. What started as an occasional indulgence rapidly evolved into a dependency. As her cravings grew, so did the recklessness of her actions to satisfy them. Slowly, the facade of Priya's perfect life began to crack. Her performance at work declined sharply, leading to her eventual dismissal from her high-profile job. At home, Priya's addiction poisoned her family life. Her erratic behaviour and frequent mood swings alienated her from her spouse and children. Eventually, the woman who once had a seemingly perfect life saw her marriage dissolve and her children become increasingly distant.

All the while, Aarav observed from the shadows, his clinical detachment disguising a smug satisfaction. He had engineered Priya's downfall to the last detail, exploiting both Ananya's struggle for recovery and Priya's vulnerable state to orchestrate a tragic fall from grace. In this darkly twisted way, Aarav exacted his revenge. The girl who once laughed at his affections was now isolated and broken, her life in shambles – a macabre reflection of Aarav's own twisted psyche, where empathy was a tool for manipulation and people were merely variables in a cold, calculated equation of retribution. To the world, Aarav remained Dr. Banerjee, the brilliant psychologist with an empathetic touch. But behind the comforting facade, he was the puppeteer of profound tragedies, a man whose understanding of the human soul was deep and intricate enough to turn it against itself.

KASHYAP: A HACK ENCODED

In Aarav's intricate web of revenge, Kashyap occupied a unique space that was akin to a mirror reflecting Aarav's own brilliance, albeit in a different light. In school, Kashyap was undeniably bright – the kind of intelligence that came with an effortless grace, and he carried himself with a quiet yet palpable air of superiority. To Aarav, Kashyap's subtle condescension was a bitter pill; the insinuations that Aarav was in some way lesser were not lost on him.

Fast forward to their adult lives: Kashyap had become a prominent computer engineer in the defence industry, responsible for designing next-generation semiconductors. His work was more than confidential – it was a matter of national security.

Enter Vikram, a patient of Aarav's and a former ethical hacker of considerable skill. Vikram's life had taken a turn for the worse— laid off amidst the COVID-19 pandemic and unable to secure new employment in a brutal job market, he was teetering on the edge of despair. He consulted Aarav at his most vulnerable, on the precipice of suicide.

Aarav, ever the opportunist, saw in Vikram's desperation the perfect means to enact his revenge on Kashyap. He presented Vikram with a solution that was wrapped in the guise of salvation: a job opportunity that would utilise Vikram's unique skills and pull him back from the brink.

The plan was simple, at least in Aarav's telling: Vikram was to hack into Kashyap's computer. Aarav, feigning a friendship with Kashyap, convinced Vikram that if he could expose a security flaw in Kashyap's systems and then fix it, Kashyap would be so impressed that he would offer Vikram a job on the spot. To a desperate Vikram, this seemed like the lifeline he so badly needed – a chance to put his skills to use and regain his footing in life.

With meticulous precision, Vikram infiltrated Kashyap's computer. He unearthed classified documents – design schematics, defence strategies, and more. Triumphantly, he reported back to Aarav, expecting that this would be his turning point. Aarav, seizing the evidence with a veneer of congratulatory warmth, assured Vikram that he would personally vouch for him to Kashyap. In a sinister twist, however, the call Aarav made after Vikram's departure was not to Kashyap but to the relevant authorities.

With a cold, methodical demeanour, Aarav reported Kashyap, framing him as a traitor leaking sensitive, classified state defence secrets to a civilian. The evidence was damning; after all, the classified information was in Vikram's possession, and the trail led directly back to Kashyap. Within hours, Kashyap's world was turned upside down. Law enforcement descended on his home and workplace, arresting him in front of his colleagues and family. His once-promising career crumbled into ruins overnight, and his reputation was irrevocably tarnished. The man who had once subtly condescended to Aarav was now stripped of his dignity, his freedom hanging in the balance as he faced accusations of the gravest kind.

Meanwhile, Aarav observed the unfolding chaos with cold satisfaction. In his eyes, justice — or at least his own dark version of it — had been served. His masterstroke was twofold: he had decimated Kashyap, his old rival, while also exploiting Vikram's desperation for his own ends, with the hacker left unaware that he had been a pawn in a dangerous game. Dr. Aarav Banerjee maintained his carefully crafted facade–the empathetic and successful psychologist. Yet, behind that mask, he was the architect of devastating, calculated ruin, using his profound understanding of the human psyche not to heal, but to settle scores relentlessly and ruthlessly from a past that he could neither forgive nor forget.

THE TRANSIENT SATISFACTION

As Aarav meticulously orchestrated each act of revenge, a potent cocktail of emotions surged through him, culminating in a profound, intoxicating satisfaction. Each takedown was not just a conquest over his perceived enemies; it was a validation of his intellect, a testament to his prowess and control. Every downfall he engineered fed into a narrative that Aarav had constructed for himself, the narrative of an underdog who rose above his tormentors, wielding his knowledge and cunning as weapons sharper than any sword.

After exacting revenge on Rohit, Aarav felt a thrill akin to euphoria. In his mind's eye, he replayed the moment the scandal broke, envisioning Rohit's life unravelling before him. For years, Rohit's superiority, his charm, and good looks, had been like a dark cloud over Aarav's own life. Now, Aarav reveled in the storm he had unleashed on Rohit. He pictured the disbelief and anguish that must have distorted Rohit's handsome face, a sight that brought a twisted smile to Aarav's own.

With the financial ruin of Harshvardhan, a surge of triumph swelled within Aarav. He imagined Harshvardhan's once-cocky demeanour crumbling into desperation and fear as his empire fell apart. The memory of Harshvardhan's condescension in their school days, the way he flaunted his wealth and status, became a distant, powerless echo. In his mind, Aarav savoured the delicious irony – the wealthy heir brought low, not by market forces or competitors, but by the hand of someone he once deemed inconsequential.

Priya's descent was particularly satisfying. Aarav's heart had once ached for her attention, and her dismissive attitude had left scars that never quite healed. Watching from the shadows as Priya's life spiralled out of control, Aarav felt a cold, vindictive satisfaction. He relished the poetic justice of it all–Priya, who once seemed untouchable, rendered vulnerable and broken, much like how she had made him feel during their school days.

The arrest of Kashyap, the brilliant and haughty genius, was perhaps the most intellectually satisfying revenge for Aarav. Every news report detailing Kashyap's alleged betrayal of national secrets felt like a personal victory for Aarav. He reveled in the thought of Kashyap, always so sure and composed, now experiencing the terror of having his future stolen from him – a fitting payback for a man who once belittled Aarav's own intelligence.

In each of these acts, Aarav experienced a profound sense of equilibrium restored, as if he were righting the universe's wrongs. He saw himself not as a villain, but as a deliverer of justice – cold, precise, and undeniably effective. These acts of revenge were his masterpieces, and he, the artist, stood back to admire his work with a sense of dark, self-satisfied pride.

VICTOR BECOMES VICTIM

But as potent as these satisfactions were, they were transient. After the initial rush, after the sweet taste of vengeance had time to linger, a bitter aftertaste began to emerge. With each act, the hollow echo of loneliness in Aarav's life seemed to grow louder, and the satisfaction less enduring. Sitting alone in his large, sterile home after another day of exploiting the vulnerabilities of his patients, Aarav craved not only sympathy from the world but a deeper, more profound form of validation, a love born from tragedy, adoration springing from shared sorrow.

Desperation and distorted logic drive him to hatch his final, most tragic scheme: Aarav will become the victim in his own twisted play, a melancholic figure worthy of the world's embrace. Using his exceptional skills in hypnosis, he manipulates one of his most impressionable patients into orchestrating a car accident that would leave Aarav severely injured but alive, a living testament to human resilience that would inspire pity, concern, and love.

But the universe has its own cruel sense of irony. The accident is more severe than Aarav had intended. He awakens, not to the warm embrace of a concerned world, but to the cold, sterile environment of a hospital room. His body is broken, far more than he had planned. He is in a coma that doctors suspect might be lifelong. For a fleeting moment, his plan seems to have worked. Visitors flood his room, their faces etched with concern and sorrow. Flowers and cards accumulate, each a testament to the sympathy he had so deeply craved. Lying motionless but conscious, Aarav feels a perverse satisfaction. In his immobilised state, he revels in the brief wave of concern and attention that has, at last, been directed his way.

But the world is fickle and its attention span short. As days pass, the flood of visitors dwindles to a stream, then a trickle, and finally to nothing. The flowers wilt, the cards gather dust, and Aarav is left alone once more, but now in a state far grimmer than he could have ever imagined. His mind, once his most potent weapon, is now his prison. He is fully aware, yet completely unable to communicate or move. In his isolation, the bitter reality of his situation becomes painfully clear: in seeking to author his own tragedy, Aarav has penned a dark, irrevocable ending for himself.

As his once-active mind is consumed with rage – rage at his own foolishness, at his family and friends for their perceived abandonment, and at the cruel world that has moved on so swiftly – Aarav is struck by the ultimate irony. The master manipulator, the puppeteer who once controlled the fates of others with cold precision, has become the victim of his own sinister plot.

4

MIRRORED MYSTIQUE:
A TALE OF TWO SHADOWS

DEVAN: AN ENCHANTING LONER

Devan Baruah, with his chiselled jawline, deep-set dark eyes, and a stature that combined strength with grace, was the most eligible bachelor of Guwahati. But eligibility did not always translate to availability. His looks drew attention wherever he went, and his natural charisma ensured he was always the epicentre of any gathering. Yet, beneath the allure was a cavern of solitude, which few were privy to.

From childhood, Devan was set apart, not just by his looks, but by his demeanour. He was self-assured to the point of being self-absorbed. Classmates often recalled how during school gatherings at the Brahmaputra's banks, while everyone played and laughed, young Devan would be found staring at his reflection in the water, lost in a world of his own. Growing up, Devan's solace was his grandfather's tales of old Assam, the stories of businesses that rose from the ashes, and of men who commanded respect not just by wealth, but by the power of their character. These tales became the foundation for Devan's dreams.

Inheriting a modest tea estate from his ancestors, Devan transformed it into Assam's pride. 'Baruah Gold', his flagship brand, became synonymous with the finest Assam tea. The logo, elegantly designed with a man's silhouette overlooking tea gardens, was unmistakably Devan's profile. His personal touch was not just in branding; it was in the meticulous care he ensured for each leaf, an obsession that elevated his business to unparalleled heights.

Success in business, however, did not translate to his personal life. Marriage proposals came in droves, but Devan always had a reason to decline. Some said it was his high standards, while others whispered about his obsession with a woman from his dreams. But to those truly close, like Sameer, it was evident that Devan's high self-regard acted as both armour and cage. He loved himself so deeply and so exclusively that there was scarcely room for anyone else.

His palatial home in Guwahati, a blend of traditional Assamese and modern architecture, was a testament to his success and solitude. Rooms filled with awards and accolades contrasted starkly with the absence of family portraits. And then there were the mirrors, countless of them. They showcased Devan's striking features and reflected the emptiness that often filled his hazel eyes.

For Devan, relationships were like the many tea leaves in his estate, plentiful, but requiring discernment to find the truly exceptional. And in his endless quest for the 'exceptional', Devan remained lonely, wrapped in the enigma of his grandeur and the shadows of his solitude.

LAKSHITA: A RIDDLE WRAPPED IN A MYSTERY INSIDE AN ENIGMA

Lakshita was not just a woman; she was an essence, a figment of collective admiration. With raven-black hair that cascaded down like the falls of the Brahmaputra, and eyes that shimmered like the early morning dew on Assam's tea leaves, she was a vision of ethereal beauty. Her grace was reminiscent of the gentle sway of the rice fields under the caress of the wind, and her voice, though heard by few, echoed the lilting melodies of traditional Assamese folk songs.

Her attire always had a touch of the traditional. The traditional Assamese attire, *Mekhela Chadors*, draped gracefully around her frame, complementing her radiant skin. The red bindi she wore became a mark of mystery – was she married? Was she a widow? Or was it just an emblem of her allure?

The town was rife with tales of her. Elderly women, during their afternoon tea, recounted stories of a beautiful stranger at the local market, haggling playfully over the price of fish. Youth, their eyes wide with fascination, would narrate how they saw a woman near the Brahmaputra, her silhouette merging with the setting sun. Every narration painted her not as a person but as an experience.

But for Devan, Lakshita was not just an experience; she was an obsession. The spark began with a dream, a vibrant festival of Bihu, the rhythmic beats, and amidst the swaying crowd, a figure that stood still, her gaze locked onto his. He woke up drenched in sweat, the image of the woman, especially her captivating eyes, etched deep in his psyche.

Days turned into weeks, and the dreams persisted, becoming more vivid. Now, he had visions of her at the local temple, offering her prayers or, sometimes, dancing gracefully by the Brahmaputra's banks. Each morning, Devan would sketch her, trying to immortalise his visions on paper, and each evening, he would find himself walking the streets of Guwahati, hoping to catch a glimpse of her.

The whispers about Lakshita further fuelled his obsession. The ambiguity surrounding her made her even more enticing. Was she real? Or was she just a shared illusion of Guwahati?

Devan's mansion soon bore testament to his obsession. Sketches, some unfinished and others intricately detailed, adorned the walls. Every face had a semblance of Lakshita. He began collecting *Mekhela Chadors*, each resembling what she wore in his dreams. Mirrors in his house, previously reflecting his face, now were testaments to his longing for her.

As months passed, the line between reality and fantasy blurred. The man who once took pride in his solitude now yearned for company, but not just any company; he yearned for Lakshita. The businessman who once held meetings with international delegates now held sessions with local folks, listening intently to their tales of the enigmatic woman.

The enigma of Lakshita was not just her beauty; it was the shadow she cast in Devan's life – a shadow that was both tantalising and haunting, driving him to the brink of passion and despair.

CHASING SHADOWS: DESPERATION OF DEVAN IN THE PURSUIT OF LAKSHITA

As the monsoon rains drenched the streets of Guwahati, Devan's heart was also immersed, but in a storm of emotions. Every corner of the city seemed to whisper tales of Lakshita, but she herself was always just out of grasp, like the end of a rainbow.

During his weekly visits to the city's bazaar, amidst the cacophony of vendors' voices and children's laughter, he would often sense a familiar presence. Turning around swiftly, he would catch a glimpse of a flowing *Mekhela Chador*, only for it to disappear amidst the crowd, leaving Devan with a racing heart and a face flushed from the chase.

Yet, the signs of Lakshita were undeniable. One evening, after a solitary boat ride on the Brahmaputra, Devan discovered a delicate pink dupatta on the seat, its fabric still warm, hinting at a recent presence.

Another time, as he entered his study, a handwritten note awaited him on his desk. The graceful Assamese script spoke of a secret admirer, but the identity remained undisclosed. And then, every so often, as the evening sun cast golden hues across his mansion, a gentle scent of jasmine would waft through, tantalising and intimate, making Devan's heart race.

His obsession reached its zenith when he decided to orchestrate moments hoping to draw Lakshita into his world. A grand boat, decorated with marigold and orchids, floated on the river every evening, waiting for the elusive passenger. His grand dining room, usually silent and empty, now witnessed a table for two every night. Traditional Assamese delicacies were served, their aroma filling the mansion.

But every subsequent morning painted a picture of missed connections. A lone bangle on the dining table, still resonating with the tinkles of the previous night; or a wine glass with a distinct trace of lipstick, indicating that someone did partake in the feast. But of Lakshita herself, there was no sign.

Devan's life became an endless cycle of hope and despair. Each day was a new chapter of clues, each more cryptic than the last. And as the boundaries between reality and illusion blurred further, Devan was left chasing shadows in a city that echoed with tales of the woman he could never find.

DURGA PUJA AND THE DANCE OF FATE

Durga Puja, the grand spectacle of Assam, had always been a special time in Guwahati. The city transformed with vibrant colours, the hum of rituals, and the beats of percussion. Various lights illuminated every alley, every corner, and the towering effigies of Goddess Durga emanated an aura of divine energy. But that year, for Devan, the festival held an added significance, it was another opportunity to find Lakshita.

On the evening of 'Saptami', the seventh day of the festival, Devan arrived at the main pandal, adorned in a traditional dhoti-kurta. His eyes, usually drawn to the grandeur of the deity, now scanned the crowd incessantly. He moved from one pandal to another, occasionally stopping to ask acquaintances if they had seen a woman fitting Lakshita's description. Hours passed in this desperate search, but the elusive beauty remained a figment of stories.

Contrastingly, the next day, 'Ashtami', witnessed a very different scene. As the city converged for the Sandhi Puja, a moment of heightened spirituality, Devan was conspicuously absent. Instead, the pandal was graced by a mesmerising dancer who stole the evening's limelight. Dressed in a red *Mekhela Chador*, her movements were a symphony of grace and passion. As she danced in devotion to the goddess, a gasp went through the crowd, she was none other than the enigmatic Lakshita.

Her performance was not just a dance, but a tale of yearning and devotion. With every twirl and every gesture, she seemed to be reaching out, searching for something, or someone. To the onlookers, it felt as though Lakshita's dance was a mirror to Devan's restless quest the previous evening. It was as if their souls were performing a duet, though they were never on the same stage together.

Rumours swirled the next day. People whispered about the poignant irony—how Devan and Lakshita, two souls seemingly intertwined by destiny, were like parallel lines, close but never meeting. The elderly ladies, the same who had exchanged tales of Lakshita over tea, now sighed at the bittersweet dance of fate the two were ensnared in.

The Durga Puja ended, but the legend of Devan and Lakshita's missed encounters grew. In the city of Guwahati, amidst the fervour and festivities, two souls danced around each other, forever in pursuit but never in embrace.

DESCENT INTO DARKNESS: DEVAN'S SHATTERED QUEST

The echo of Durga Puja's festivities, which once filled Devan's heart with hope, now reverberated as a haunting reminder of his unfulfilled pursuit. The vibrant streets of Guwahati, which had been a canvas of colours and celebrations, became a bleak backdrop to his growing despair.

As days turned to weeks, Devan, who had been a beacon of affluence and charm, began to wither away. The strikingly handsome features—the deep-set eyes that once reflected determination, the chiselled jawline that spoke of confidence—now bore signs of fatigue and desolation. Dark circles marred his eyes, and his once immaculate beard grew unkempt. His tailored clothes, which once showcased his impressive physique, now hung loosely, illustrating the weight he had lost.

Gone were the days when Devan's presence commanded respect in business meetings or when his laughter was the life of social gatherings. He withdrew into the shadows, locking himself inside his sprawling mansion, a prisoner of his own memories and desires. His close friends and associates tried reaching out, visiting his house, leaving food at his doorstep, and sending heartfelt letters, urging him to seek help. But the doors remained closed, and the man inside, unreachable. Whispers filled Guwahati's air, some said he had gone mad, some speculated he had left town, and others lamented the fall of such a promising individual.

ECLIPSED SOULS: THE FADING ALLURE OF GUWAHATI'S ENIGMAS

As autumn leaves swirled on Guwahati's streets, an uncanny silence swept over the city. Two of its most talked-about figures had receded into the backdrop, leaving behind an aching void. Devan's abrupt withdrawal from society was a well-known fact, but what added to the intrigue was the simultaneous disappearance of Lakshita.

The enigmatic woman, whose very name once sent ripples of excitement through the town, was now scarcely mentioned. Her haunts—whether it was the serene banks of the Brahmaputra, where she was often seen lost in thought, the markets where her laughter mingled with the chimes of temple bells or the cultural events where her dance would leave spectators spellbound—all bore a sombre note in her absence.

The bustling tea stalls and the corners of Guwahati's ancient temples buzzed with speculations. A group of elderly men, their voices low and eyes filled with curiosity, debated fiercely. "She's gone to Kolkata," one declared, "seeking a new start." Another, shaking his head, whispered, "She's in mourning. Devan's self-imposed isolation has broken her spirit." For a society that thrived on tales, their story was an unfinished book. Every so often, a supposed sighting would reignite the city's interest. But these glimpses were fleeting, like mirages that faded as one drew close. The fervour, the anticipation, the hope that once defined their stories seemed to be enveloped in an all-consuming fog.

As winter approached, wrapping Guwahati in a chilly embrace, the city's heartbeat seemed to slow. The once-vibrant alleys, lit by the tales of Devan and Lakshita, now bore a melancholic hue. The chilling winds whispered their names, intertwining them in a lament of lost love and mysteries unsolved. In a city of stories and traditions, the enigmatic duo became legends–symbols of unattained desires and unfulfilled destinies. And as time moved forward, their tale became a haunting ballad, sung on moonlit nights, of two souls forever in search, yet forever apart.

THE REVELATION: UNMASKING THE DUALITY OF DEVAN

Devan, once Guwahati's golden boy, had become a shadow of his former self. His once radiant skin had turned pallid, his lively eyes now always carried a distant, haunted look, and his robust frame seemed to have withered away. His mansion, which once echoed with laughter and lively conversations, now stood silent, mirroring its owner's desolation. Sameer, his childhood friend, watched with increasing concern. Their bond was unbreakable, and Devan's declining health deeply troubled him. "It's that woman," he would often murmur to himself, "Lakshita is the cause." Determined to help his friend, Sameer resolved to unravel the mystery surrounding Lakshita.

One evening, under the pretence of a casual dinner, Sameer visited Devan. The house felt cold and unwelcoming. Devan, wrapped in a blanket, sat by the fireplace, his gaze fixed on the dancing flames. No words of comfort or attempts at conversation could reach him. It was as if an invisible wall had come up between Devan and the rest of the world. As the night wore on, Sameer excused himself to use the washroom. It was there he found the first clues: traces of mascara on a towel and a forgotten bindi on the sink. "This can't be Devan's," he mused. The gears in his mind began turning rapidly.

After bidding Devan good night, Sameer, instead of leaving, began his secret investigation. The vast mansion, bathed in moonlight, felt eerie. Room by room, he explored, searching for signs of the enigmatic Lakshita. That is when he stumbled upon a door, distinct from the others, strong, bolted, and bearing a heavy padlock.

Curiosity piqued. Using a paperclip and leveraging his limited lock-picking skills, he managed to unlock the door. What he saw inside was both astonishing and heartbreaking. It was a shrine to Lakshita: elegant saris draped gracefully, makeup kits opened mid-use, and long, luxurious wigs reminiscent of the tales of Lakshita's flowing hair.

But what truly shook Sameer was the photographs. Pictures of Lakshita, but upon closer inspection, the resemblance was undeniable, she was Devan, or rather, Devan was her.

A flood of realisation washed over Sameer. He recalled evenings spent with his father, a renowned psychologist, discussing unique and rare mental health cases. He remembered the mention of a case where a narcissistic individual became so enamoured with his own reflection that he developed another personality, it was dissociative identity disorder, or a split personality disorder, intensified by narcissism.

DEVAN'S DUALITY: THE MECHANICS

Devan's transformation into Lakshita was not merely a change of clothes; it was a comprehensive metamorphosis that straddled both his physical appearance and his psychological state.

In his alternative self as Lakshita, Devan would invest hours in perfecting his costume and makeup. This was not just about donning a sari or applying makeup; it was a ritual. Each stroke of the kajal, each brush of the blush was a step deeper into Lakshita's persona. Over time, Devan had mastered the art of changing his voice. He would practice for hours, recording himself, refining the pitch until he could flawlessly switch to Lakshita's soft, melodious tone. Adopting a more delicate and graceful demeanour, Devan would walk, talk, and even think as Lakshita. He learnt traditional dances, allowing him to move with an elegance that was captivating.

The intricate dance between Devan's narcissism and split personality disorder was an unparalleled psychological phenomenon. At the heart of his transformation lay the mirror. It was not merely a reflective surface but a portal. Devan's narcissism meant he was deeply attracted to his own reflection. This intense self-love slowly took on a life of its own, leading to the birth of Lakshita. When he looked in the mirror, he did not just see a handsome face; he saw someone he wanted to court and romance. Over time, this affection manifested as Lakshita. Certain emotional stimuli could expedite Devan's transformation. Feelings of loneliness, unreciprocated love, or heightened self-appreciation might hasten Lakshita's emergence. Typically, individuals with dissociative identity disorder experience memory blackouts when another personality takes over. Devan had vague recollections of Lakshita's actions but never the full picture. This created a constant state of confusion and a yearning to know this elusive woman more intimately.

Narcissism, when combined with split personality disorder, created a whirlpool of emotions for Devan. His narcissistic tendencies made him love and yearn for what he saw in the mirror. But the split personality made it so that his reflection was not just an image; it became a person, Lakshita. In his quest for self-love, he was literally and metaphorically chasing his own reflection, seeking a love that was simultaneously self-derived and externally projected.

Sameer felt a mixture of sorrow and understanding. The tale of Devan and Lakshita was not one of star-crossed lovers, but of a man battling his own mind, trapped in a dance with his own reflection.

THE END OF A DUAL DANCE

As days turned to weeks and weeks to months, the stories of Devan and Lakshita spiralled into a haunting ballad sung throughout

Guwahati. The city watched in anguish as Devan, once their beacon of success and charm, sank further into the abyss of his own mind. Occasionally, on some evenings, residents would see him by the banks of Brahmaputra, eyes scanning the horizon, waiting for a glimpse of the elusive Lakshita. Some said they would often hear him call out her name, his voice echoing with pain and longing. In his lucid moments, Devan spoke of dreams where he'd dance with Lakshita under the starlit sky, their laughter echoing in unison. But with each passing day, these moments of lucidity grew rarer.

The lethal concoction of narcissism and dissociative identity disorder was taking its toll. Devan's narcissism intensified his need to find and be with Lakshita, and his split personality made him believe she was real, that she was out there. The cruel irony of the situation was that he was yearning for a part of himself that he could never truly be with.

And then, one fateful evening, it all came to an end. A group of children playing by the Brahmaputra found a note, held down by a stone. Written in a shaky hand, it read, "In search of Lakshita, to dance with her among the stars." Nearby, Devan's belongings were neatly arranged: his shoes, watch, and a photograph of him during happier times.

Guwahati mourned the tragic end of its beloved son. Whispers filled the air, how a man's own mind can be his worst enemy, how the intertwined tales of Devan and Lakshita would forever remain a cautionary tale of love, obsession, and the fragile nature of the human psyche. The mirrors in his old house still held tales. Of a man, his shadow, and a love that was as enigmatic as the dance of light and dark during an Assam evening.

5

KAAL CHAKRA:
THE WHIRLS OF FATE

THE TICKING SOLITUDE

In the heart of the ancient town of Thanjavur, located in the southern Indian state of Tamil Nadu, where the fusion of modernity and history created an intriguing juxtaposition, stood a small clock shop that had weathered the tests of time. The shop's weathered facade bore witness to centuries of stories and the passage of countless eras. Its windows, clouded with the dust of time, filtered the harsh sunlight into a muted, almost sepia-toned ambiance.

Siva's childhood unfurled like a silent movie, with scenes of stern looks from his father and the indifferent sighs of his mother. Their home, an austere abode, lacked the warmth of familial bonds, with his parents embodying distant figures who fulfilled their parental duties but never ventured into the realm of heartfelt desires. It was a place where conversation was sparse, and affection even scarcer.

The clock shop, a legacy passed down from his father, became more than just a place of work for Siva; it was his refuge from the coldness of his home and the chaos of the world outside. Here, amidst the perpetual symphony of ticking timepieces, he discovered a semblance of order, a sanctuary that provided solace from the turbulent currents of his otherwise disordered life. The rhythmic heartbeat of the clocks was not only a balm to his troubled soul but also a reminder that amidst life's disarray, there existed an intricate and regulated world that he could control, a world of precision and predictability in the realm of gears and springs. In the heart of an old city, where modernity and history collided in an uneasy truce, stood a small clock shop, its windows clouded with the dust of time. Inside, amongst the ceaseless ticking, was Siva, the clockmaker. His world was one of gears and springs, a haven from the unpredictability of human existence.

THE MANUSCRIPT OF TIME

Amidst the labyrinthine stacks of dusty tomes and forgotten knowledge, he stumbled upon a manuscript that appeared to have been untouched for centuries. Its brittle pages, yellowed with age, cradled secrets that time had almost devoured. The manuscript whispered of time, not as an immutable river but as a malleable stream, susceptible to manipulation by those with the knowledge and will to do so.

Siva's mind, always yearning for control over the chaos of existence, was captivated by the tantalising promise of this ancient text. He devoured its contents, soaking in the wisdom of ages long gone. It was a revelation that ignited a spark within him, a spark that grew into an unquenchable fire.

Nights blurred into days as Siva toiled in his workshop, shunning sleep and sustenance. His once nimble fingers, now calloused and stained with the ink of his relentless endeavours, meticulously crafted a masterpiece. It was a clock unlike any other, transcending the boundaries of mere timekeeping. This creation, perched atop his workbench, was an intricate symphony of dials and gears, a pulsating embodiment of a life of its own.

Its heartbeat, the ticking of which reverberated through the workshop, was no ordinary cadence. It was the rhythm of control, a metronome of power over the very essence of existence. Siva's obsession with mastering time had led him to the precipice of a revelation, and this clock was his key to manipulating the unyielding flow of time itself. It stood as a testament to his unwavering determination and his inexorable descent into the depths of his own creation.

THE DANCE OF DESTINY

The power of the clock was subtle at first, a tantalising secret known only to Siva. His workshop, tucked away from prying eyes, became a chamber of secrets where time was a pliable entity under his command. With each turn of the clock's intricate dials, he could stretch a minute into what felt like an eternity, or compress hours into mere heartbeats. The ticking of the clock, once a comforting presence, now echoed with the ominous heartbeat of control. He began altering events around him – a nudge here, a tweak there. The world, unbeknownst to its inhabitants, danced to his tune.

Siva's transformation was nothing short of a descent into darkness. His cold, detached demeanour, honed by years of solitude and emotional neglect, evolved into something far more sinister. The profound sadness that had taken root during his childhood, where warmth and affection were scarce commodities, acted as fertile soil for his growing malevolence. As the tendrils of control tightened their grip on his psyche, Siva's heart turned callous and sadistic. He found perverse pleasure in snatching away the joys and dreams of those around him. It was a twisted form of satisfaction—*schadenfreude*—that fuelled his actions. He reveled in the sight of others' misfortunes, deriving a sick gratification from their suffering. This sadistic streak was a manifestation of the ghosts from his past, the spectres of his own childhood. His parents' indifference and stern disapproval had instilled in him a deep-seated sense of inadequacy and low self-esteem. In his quest for control, he sought to fill the void left by his upbringing with the power to manipulate the lives of others.

Siva had become a tormented soul, trapped in a cycle of perpetuating his own pain onto others. His actions reflected the darkness that had consumed him, a darkness born from a lifetime of unmet emotional needs and a relentless desire for control over a world that had once felt uncontrollable.

RECKLESS RECTITUDE

Some actions perpetuated without the knowledge of the persons being manipulated clearly made Siva bolder and bolder with each passing moment.

A dimly lit corner of a quaint café, Siva's eyes fixated on a young couple deeply entwined in love. Their laughter resonated in the air as they held hands, their eyes sparkling with promises of eternity. But Siva could not resist the insidious urge to intervene. With a subtle twist of his clock's dial, Siva initiated his temporal manipulation. Time itself became his accomplice, as he subtly stretched and compressed the moments between their exchanges. What was once natural and sincere now felt drawn-out and fabricated. As the temporal distortion took hold, the couple's trust began to erode. Innocent gestures became subjects of suspicion, heartfelt words were twisted into perceived deceit. Siva's manipulation of time sowed the seeds of mistrust, insidiously poisoning their love.

Yet another example of manipulation involved his childhood crush, Divya, a struggling artist, who stood on the brink of a breakthrough. Her unwavering passion was propelling her towards the pinnacle of success. Yet, for Siva, Divya's ascent posed a threat to his sense of control. He could not bear the idea of someone else's dreams flourishing while he held dominion over time itself. But what stung Siva even more was the fact that Divya had never paid heed to him. She remained oblivious to his affections, treating him as an inconsequential figure from their shared past. This indifference fuelled his dark desire to see her fall from grace, a vindictive urge that he sought to fulfil using the power of time. With a sinister grin, Siva used his clock to rewind the tapestry of Divya's life. He erased her moments of inspiration and stifled her creative spark. What was once a journey towards artistic brilliance now spiralled into an abyss of stagnation. Her once-vibrant paintings were replaced by a canvas of despair, and Divya's artistic soul withered under the weight of Siva's malevolent influence. His need for revenge burned brightly as he watched the object of his unrequited affection tumble from the heights of her potential.

A manifestation of the need for recognition from society, which Siva lacked in his childhood, led to the ruin of a promising young businessman, Narayan. His thriving business had garnered the admiration of the entire community, and his happiness was evident to all who knew him. However, for Siva, seeing Narayan's success only intensified his own insatiable desire for recognition and validation from society. Siva's jealousy simmered beneath the surface as he watched Narayan bask in the glow of his accomplishments. He yearned for the same recognition, the same adulation that Narayan effortlessly received. But instead of celebrating Narayan's success, Siva's heart festered with bitterness. Determined to see Narayan's happiness crumble, Siva hatched a sinister plan. He manipulated time in a way that Narayan defaulted on loan payments, missed crucial business opportunities, and made poor financial decisions. Narayan's once-flourishing business began to teeter on the edge of bankruptcy. As the weight of financial woes bore down on him, Narayan's radiant smile faded, replaced by a furrowed brow and sleepless nights. His reputation, once unblemished, started to tarnish. He struggled to meet his financial obligations, and his confidence waned. Siva's relentless interference with time had pushed Narayan to the brink. The crushing burden of debt and the humiliation of business failures became too much for him to bear. In a moment of despair, Narayan tragically took his own life, leaving behind a shattered family and a town in mourning. Siva had achieved his dark objective. Narayan's happiness had been ruthlessly extinguished, and Siva's envy had driven him to orchestrate a devastating tragedy. In his ruthless pursuit of recognition and control, Siva had become the harbinger of despair and destruction, forever haunted by the consequences of his malevolent manipulation of time.

AN ORCHESTRATED AFFAIR

Then came Lakshmi, a woman whose laughter was like the tinkling of wind chimes. She entered the clock shop one afternoon, seeking repair for her grandfather's old watch. In her, Siva saw a chance for something he never dared dream of – a connection, a bond. But his approach was skewed, his affection a product of his need for control. He manipulated time to orchestrate their meetings, each 'coincidence' carefully planned, each conversation a rehearsed play.

Lakshmi's arrival breathed new life into Siva's world. Her laughter, like the soft chimes of the wind, brought a melody to his otherwise silent existence. The moment she walked into the clock shop, carrying her grandfather's old watch, Siva's heart skipped a beat. He saw in her a glimmer of hope, a possibility of the connection he had long yearned for.

However, Siva's longing was tainted by his twisted desires. His affection for Lakshmi was not born out of genuine love but rather from his insatiable need for control. He could not bear the thought of letting her slip away like a passing breeze. And so, he turned to his most potent weapon: time. Siva meticulously manipulated time to engineer their encounters. What appeared to be chance meetings were carefully choreographed events. Every conversation, every shared moment was a rehearsed play, scripted by Siva's obsession. He craved the illusion of spontaneity while secretly pulling the strings, ensuring that Lakshmi remained a captive audience in his meticulously constructed narrative.

As Lakshmi unknowingly danced to the tune of Siva's time-manipulated encounters, the lines between fate and manipulation blurred. The clock that had once been his tool of control now bound their destinies together in a web of orchestrated serendipity. Lakshmi, with her laughter like wind chimes, became a pawn in Siva's intricate game of control, a game that threatened to shatter the fragile connection they shared, and in the process, ruin Siva himself.

THE FRAYING OF TIME

The clock, strained beyond its natural limits by Siva's relentless manipulation, began to show signs of wear and tear. Its intricate mechanisms struggled to withstand the constant bending and warping of time. Siva's insatiable desire for control had pushed the clock to the brink, and it was beginning to falter under the weight of his ambitions.

As a result, Siva's own timeline grew increasingly erratic. One morning, he awoke to find himself an old man, his joints aching, his hair turned a snowy white. He shuffled around his once-familiar clock shop, but now it seemed too vast, too grand for his frail and withered frame. The next day, he experienced a disorienting transformation, regressing to childhood, his shop looming over him like a towering fortress, his tiny hands unable to reach the counter.

With each passing day, Siva's control over time slipped further from his grasp. His life had become a bewildering kaleidoscope of age and circumstance. The city he once knew began to transform around him. Familiar faces vanished, replaced by strangers whose names eluded him. The boundaries of his reality blurred, and the pieces of his existence no longer fit together neatly.

Siva's world had become a fractured mosaic, a jigsaw puzzle with missing pieces, leaving him adrift in a sea of temporal uncertainty. The very power he had sought to wield had become his own prison, a chaotic and unpredictable force that had derailed the linear flow of time and left him lost in a landscape of perpetual flux.

THE UNDOING

In a cruel twist of fate, Lakshmi, the woman whose laughter had once filled Siva's world with joy, vanished from his life. In a timeline where they had never met, she remained a stranger, her laughter reduced to a distant echo in his heart. Siva's relentless obsession with control had brought about the very outcome he had feared the most, losing the only real connection he had ever formed.

The passage of time had become a labyrinth, and within its convoluted corridors, Lakshmi was lost to him. The moments they had shared, the laughter they had exchanged, all faded into a haze of alternate timelines where their paths had never crossed. It was a bitter irony that the very power he had sought to wield over time had severed the thread that bound him to the person he had longed for.

As for Siva, his existence had become a paradox. There were technically no 'last days' for him, no finite point in time where he lived or died. Instead, he perpetually swayed in the vast ocean of timelessness, a prisoner of his own ambitions. The very control he had sought had spiralled out of his grasp, leaving him suspended in a state of eternal flux.

Siva had become a tragic figure, forever trapped in the pursuit of a power he could never fully harness. His desire for control had led him down a path of isolation and detachment, ultimately robbing him of the one connection that had held meaning in his life. In the end, he found himself adrift in the unfathomable depths of time, a fate far crueller than any he had ever imagined.

EPILOGUE: THE INTRICACIES OF TIME

As Siva's life (or whatever was left of it) continued to spiral into the chaotic abyss of time manipulation and control, he unwittingly became entangled with two profound and mystical concepts: karma and the Akashic Records. These ancient Indian ideas cast a shadow over his existence, shaping the tragic course of his story.

The Akashic Records are often described as a compendium of all human events, thoughts, words, emotions, and intent ever to have occurred. They are an ethereal repository, a cosmic library that records the imprints of every individual's journey through existence. Within these records lie the echoes of every choice, every moment, and every intention that has ever shaped the human experience.

Siva's actions, driven by his insatiable need for control and power, were a blatant violation of the natural order. Through his manipulation of time, he had disrupted the delicate tapestry of cause and effect that governed the universe. Each distortion, each interference with the lives of others, left an indelible mark on the Akashic Records, like ripples in the fabric of destiny.

The concept of karma, intricately tied to the Akashic Records, presupposes that every action carries consequences that reverberate through one's life and beyond, and the karmic entries are stored in the vast library of the universal repository, the Akashic Records. Siva's malevolent manipulations had set in motion a karmic chain reaction, and the cosmic backlash was inevitable. His disregard for the well-being of others, his relentless pursuit of control, and his destructive interference with the lives of those around him had earned him a debt to the universe that could not be ignored.

In the end, the threads of karma and the Akashic Records wove together a fateful tapestry for Siva. The cosmic forces, awakened by his actions, delivered their judgement. His existence became a perpetual state of unpredictability, mirroring the chaos he had sown in the lives of others. The lines between past, present, and future blurred, and he found himself at the mercy of a reality shaped by the very powers he had sought to control.

6

THE GENIE'S THREE-INFINITY PRISON

In the dim, decaying remnants of a once grand mansion, a young man named Arjun Mehta sat in a sparse room. The flicker of a lone candle cast eerie shadows on the walls, reflecting the turbulent storm within his mind. Arjun was the last scion of an aristocratic family, now fallen from grace. Brilliant but destitute, he grappled daily with the bitter taste of poverty and an insatiable hunger for more.

Arjun's family had once commanded vast estates and respect throughout the city. Their wealth had seemed unassailable, but a series of poor financial decisions, compounded by a corrupt uncle's betrayal, had plunged them into ruin. By the time Arjun was old enough to comprehend the weight of his legacy, it had already slipped through their fingers. Determined to restore his family's name, Arjun excelled academically, becoming a scholar of great renown. Yet, the bitterness of his fall from grace gnawed at him, breeding an unquenchable thirst for power and wealth.

One fateful evening, while wandering the city's old quarters, Arjun stumbled upon a decrepit antique shop. Drawn by an inexplicable force, he entered and found a dusty, ornate lamp. The shopkeeper, an enigmatic old man with piercing eyes, sold it to Arjun for a pittance, warning him cryptically about the lamp's power. Ignoring the warning, Arjun took the lamp back to his dimly lit room. As he polished the lamp, a thick, swirling smoke filled the air, and from it emerged a towering figure with eyes like burning coals – a genie.

The genie offered Arjun three wishes, but with his sharp intellect and deep-seated greed, Arjun cleverly wished for infinite wishes. The genie, bound by the ancient magic of the lamp, granted his request.

With the power to bend reality to his will, Arjun's life transformed overnight. He wished for immense wealth, and gold and jewels filled his room, spilling out into the corridors of the mansion. He wished for unparalleled knowledge, and books of arcane wisdom materialised at his fingertips, containing secrets long forgotten by mankind. He wished for perfect health, allowing him to eat and indulge without consequence.

But with each fulfilled desire, Arjun's greed grew. His wishes became increasingly grandiose and self-serving. He wished for control over others, manipulating minds and bending wills to his whim. His power isolated him, surrounded only by sycophants and enemies who feared and envied his unearthly abilities.

As months turned into years, Arjun's life became a paradox of pleasure and pain. His wish for endless pleasure led to addictions that ravaged his mind. His wish for beauty beyond compare turned his body into a statue-like figure, perfect and unchanging, yet devoid of warmth or humanity. His quest for control over others turned him into a puppet master, pulling strings in a web of deceit and manipulation, but it also isolated him, leaving him with no one to trust.

At first, Arjun reveled in his newfound power, basking in the luxury and influence it brought. But as time passed, the initial thrill began to fade. The wealth that once symbolised his victory over poverty started to feel hollow. The knowledge that once fuelled his ambition now overwhelmed him, revealing the futility of his pursuits. His perfect health became a cruel reminder of the natural human experiences he had forfeited – the joy of ageing, the wisdom that comes with time, the bittersweet beauty of life's impermanence.

In the quiet moments, alone in his grand but empty mansion, Arjun began to feel the weight of his choices. He would stand by the window, gazing out at the world that continued to move on without him, his heart heavy with a longing he could not fulfil. He watched families grow, friends grow old and die, and seasons change, while he remained unchanged, untouched by the passage of time. The laughter of children playing in the streets, the tender exchanges between lovers, the simple joys of everyday life – all became painful reminders of what he had lost in his quest for power.

One night, as he sat alone in his grand but empty mansion, Arjun realised that despite his infinite wishes, he felt more trapped than ever. His life had become a gilded cage, each wish a bar that held him in. His wealth, knowledge, and power brought him no joy, only a deeper sense of emptiness and isolation.

In a moment of desperation, Arjun wished for immortality, believing that an endless life would give him the time to find true happiness. Yet, as the years stretched into centuries, he found that immortality was a curse. He watched as the world around him changed, as loved ones aged and died, while he remained the same. He became a ghost in his own life, unable to connect with anyone, unable to find any lasting fulfilment.

His immortality became a prison. His mind, tormented by endless years and unfulfilled desires, began to unravel. He tried to find solace in his infinite wishes, but each new desire only added to his torment. He wished for the return of his family's honour, only to find that the respect of others brought no solace. He wished for beauty beyond compare, but his perfect reflection in the mirror was a constant reminder of the monster he had become. His every desire, once a pathway to pleasure, now led only to deeper torment.

Arjun's frustration grew with each passing year. His immortality had stripped him of the ability to find meaning in life. He saw civilisations rise and fall, watched as his once grand mansion decayed around him, felt the crushing loneliness of an existence without end. His soul grew weary, his mind tormented by the unending passage of time.

One day, in a fit of frustration and despair, Arjun muttered, "I wish I were dead." The genie, bound by the paradox of granting every wish, twisted Arjun's desires. His body fell lifeless to the ground, but his soul remained trapped in a state of suspended animation. His wish for immortality clashed with his wish for death, leaving him in a perpetual state of torment.

Arjun's soul lingered, aware yet powerless. He could see the world move on, feel the passage of time, but he was utterly incapable of interacting with it. Trapped in a void of his own making, Arjun's consciousness became a dark mirror, reflecting his endless greed and the emptiness it had wrought. His infinite wishes had led to infinite suffering. The power he had so desperately craved had become his eternal torment.

The decrepit mansion, now abandoned and overgrown, stands as a silent testament to Arjun's tale. The lamp, gathering dust in the corner, awaits the next soul brave – or foolish – enough to seek its power. And somewhere, in the shadowy recesses of eternity, Arjun's soul remains, a prisoner of his own desires, forever yearning for an end that will never come.

In the void, Arjun's mind screamed for release, but no wish could free him now. His body, lifeless and cold, lay as a grim reminder of his fate. His soul, caught in the trap of his own making, floated in a dark, timeless abyss. The once brilliant and ambitious young man, who had sought to reclaim his family's glory, now served as a cautionary tale of the perils of unchecked greed and the dark allure of absolute power.

No moral resolution offered solace to Arjun's fate. His story was a grim testament to the boundless depths of human desire and the tragic consequences that can ensue when those desires are left unchecked. In the end, Arjun became the eternal embodiment of his own avarice, a ghostly figure lost in the infinite night, forever seeking an escape that would never come.

7

THE VALLEY OF SHADOWS

The drive back from the wedding in Punjab was meant to be uneventful. My friends—two guys, one a doctor and the other a genius entrepreneur, and a dear lady friend who had known me since childhood—were exhausted but content. The wedding had been a celebration, the kind of event that fills your mind with memories and your heart with warmth. My father's business partner, an astute Chartered Accountant, had insisted on driving. His insistence came from a place of authority; he was meticulous in everything, so I figured I could trust him with the winding roads of Himachal Pradesh.

But rationality died that night.

The roads grew treacherous as we neared Himachal, the curves sharper, the drops steeper. There was something wrong with the air that night, something heavier than the crisp mountain breeze. At one particular bend, everything went wrong. It wasn't just a miscalculation; it was as if something reached out from the shadows of the valley and pulled us in. The car swerved off the edge, plunging straight down into the abyss.

There was no sound of crunching metal, no impact, just the surreal sensation of falling. We weren't tumbling. We were falling straight down, like passengers in an elevator whose cables had snapped. All five of us—my friends, my father's partner, and I—were no longer inside the car. We were suspended mid-air, our bodies descending beside the vehicle, which floated in the same eerie fashion.

We should have died. The valley was hundreds of metres deep, the rocks jagged and unforgiving. But as we neared the ground, the fall slowed. The air thickened, cushioning us. Then, as if gravity decided to take pity on us, we landed softly, feet first, in an impossibly vast, flat field. The car, which should have been a crumpled wreck, landed gently beside us, perfectly intact.

For a few moments, none of us spoke. We were alive, but it didn't make sense. The valley was wrong. This place was wrong. We hadn't just survived a fall that should have killed us. We had fallen somewhere else.

The landscape was unfamiliar – a vast plain stretching endlessly in all directions. No mountains, no roads, nothing to indicate we were still in Himachal. Where had we landed? There was no road, no signs of civilisation, just an eerie stillness that made the hairs on the back of my neck rise.

Hours later, in the dead of night, we stumbled across a large building, a hostel of sorts. It stood out against the barren land, a relic from another time, with lights flickering in the windows. It appeared to be in the middle of nowhere, yet there was significant activity. To our shock, the hostel was filled with my old school friends. It was a bizarre reunion, people I hadn't seen in years, gathered here of all places, laughing and catching up as if no time had passed. They were hosting some sort of get-together, though no one could clearly explain why or how they had all come to be there. When we tried to recount our experience—our near-death fall—no one believed us. It was too far-fetched, too unreal.

But as the sun rose, the impossible happened again.

In the middle of the day, as we sat in the dining hall, there was a sudden crash. We all looked up to see another body hurtling through the roof, shattering the ceiling tiles. It was one of my school friends, a girl who had been absent from the hostel earlier. She fell fast, but then, as if something slowed her descent at the last second, she landed on her feet, unscathed.

Her story matched ours exactly. She had been in a near-death car accident, certain she would die, but then she found herself falling into this strange place. The others began to grow uneasy. This couldn't be a coincidence. And then it happened again. Another crash. Another friend from school fell through the roof, landing softly and unharmed.

The fear in the room became palpable. I could feel it in my gut, the gnawing realisation that we were trapped in something far beyond our comprehension.

THE QUANTUM RIFT

Weeks turned into months, and eventually, most of us left the hostel. Life resumed, though not the same. Many of us moved to Mumbai, trying to forget the strange events of that night. But it was impossible. The memories lingered, festering in the back of our minds like a sickness that refused to heal.

I started noticing strange phenomena: **déjà vu** moments, flashes of memories from lives I had not lived. My friends—those who had survived the fall—began to experience the same unsettling sensations.

It was as if we were still connected to another world, a world in which we had died. The memories lingered, festering in the back of our minds like a sickness that refused to heal.

The first glitch happened just after we had settled into our new lives in Mumbai. I was sitting in a café with Raghav, one of the friends who had survived the fall with me, when suddenly, the world seemed to flicker. For a split second, the bustling café was gone, replaced by a desolate landscape, the valley. I blinked, and it was over. I could feel my heart racing as I looked at Raghav, who was staring at me with wide eyes.

"Did you…?" he began, but I nodded before he could finish. We had both seen it.

These flickers became more frequent. Sometimes they lasted only a moment, a brief overlay of the valley on our current reality. Other times, they were more intense. One night, I woke up in my bed, but the air was thick with the smell of damp Earth. My hands reached out in the darkness and touched the grass as if I had been transported back to the valley in my sleep. I screamed and jolted awake, back in my apartment, drenched in sweat. I wasn't alone. All of us who had survived the fall were experiencing the same thing, but we never spoke about it openly. Fear had woven its way into the fabric of our lives.

Then, the glitches started getting worse.

One evening, while walking down a busy street in Mumbai, my friend Kavya—who had been with us during the fall—suddenly stopped dead in her tracks. I called out to her, but she didn't respond. Her eyes were wide and unfocused, her entire body frozen as if she had been switched off. Panicking, I rushed over, shaking her, calling her name. For nearly a minute, she was unresponsive, like a mannequin

     WHISPERS FROM THE VOID: AN ANTHOLOGY

in the middle of a crowded street. And then, just as quickly as it had begun, she snapped back, gasping for air, her face pale as a ghost.

"I was... I was back there," she whispered, her voice trembling. "In the valley. I couldn't move. I couldn't get out."

I looked around, but no one seemed to notice. It was as if the world was continuing on without acknowledging that reality itself was glitching around us.

As the days passed, these incidents became more frequent – and more dangerous.

Raghav, who had always been the calm, rational one, was the first to really lose control. He began to lose large chunks of time—hours, sometimes even days—where he couldn't account for where he had been or what he had done. Once, he vanished for three days, only to reappear at the foot of a mountain trail in Himachal, with no memory of how he had gotten there. He called me in a panic, and when I met him, he was a shell of his former self.

"It's like the valley is pulling me back," he said, his voice cracking. "Every time I close my eyes, I'm there. And I can feel it getting closer. I can feel it swallowing me."

His words sent a chill down my spine, but before I could respond, something even worse happened.

Reality shifted right in front of me.

One moment, we were sitting on the side of the road in Himachal, and the next, I was in the driver's seat of the car, the same car we had crashed months ago. I was gripping the wheel, the screech of tyres filling my ears, the cliff looming ahead. I screamed and jerked the wheel, but it was too late. We were falling again, straight into the valley. I looked around, panicked, and saw Raghav beside me, but his face was distorted, a blur of fear and confusion.

And then, just as suddenly as it had happened, it was over. I was back on the roadside, Raghav staring at me with terror in his eyes.

"You saw it too, didn't you?" he whispered. "The crash. The fall."

I nodded, too shaken to speak.

BREAKTHROUGH AT A WEDDING

The breakthrough came during another wedding, years later. Many of the old faces from the hostel reappeared. One of my closest friends arrived late, visibly shaken. He had experienced the fall again. The same inexplicable, soft descent into survival. The panic spread through our group like wildfire. How could it have happened again? Why us?

There was only one person at the wedding who seemed to believe us – a psychologist, an older man with a strange, almost knowing smile. He pulled me aside after hearing our stories and began speaking in a tone that chilled me to the bone.

"You didn't survive the first fall," he said, his voice calm but filled with dark implications. "You're not supposed to be here. You crossed over."

"What do you mean?" I asked, my heart pounding.

He continued, "There are certain places in this world where the fabric of reality is thin—valleys, forests, even cities—where the laws of physics, time, and space blur. The valley you fell into in Himachal is one such place. It is a rift, a breach in the multiverse. When you fell, you didn't just fall off a cliff. You fell *through realities*. In your original universe, you all died."

I stared at him, my mind spinning. "A rift between worlds? But why us? Why my school friends?"

The psychologist nodded gravely. "The many-worlds interpretation of quantum mechanics suggests that every decision, every event, forks reality into multiple parallel universes. For every possible outcome, there is a universe in which that outcome happens. In one universe, you died in that car crash. But in the split second before your death, you were pulled into another universe, one where you survived."

He leaned in closer. "But it didn't stop there. Your destinies are linked, entangled like quantum particles. You, your school friends, and your lives are part of a larger quantum system. That's why the hostel was filled with people from your past. It was a meeting point for different realities converging in a singular space."

I suddenly remembered reading about **quantum entanglement**, the phenomenon where particles become linked, so that the state of one particle affects another, no matter the distance between them. What if my friends and I had been **entangled** with this event from the very beginning? The valley wasn't just a random site. It was a high-energy quantum portal, a weak point in the multiverse where realities overlapped. We didn't fall through space. We fell through **realities**.

A chill ran down my spine. "What happens to us now? What about the others?"

The psychologist's expression darkened. "That's the problem. You don't belong in this universe. The longer you stay here, the more unstable reality becomes. You've seen it, people falling, time distorting. If you don't fix this, the rift will keep growing, and soon, it won't just be you. Entire worlds will start collapsing into each other. The multiverse can't handle this level of entanglement."

I swallowed hard. "How do we stop it?"

The psychologist hesitated; his eyes filled with a strange sympathy. "The portal is still open in that valley. You have to go back. But this time, there's no guarantee of survival. You'll need to return to the moment of your death and sever the entanglement. If you stay in this universe, the rift will consume everything. But if you return to the point of divergence… well, you may not come back."

His words hit me like a punch. We weren't meant to live in this universe. We were anomalies, glitches in the quantum fabric, and we had disrupted the natural order of reality.

THE TIMELESS TRAVELLER

It was then that the psychologist revealed his true identity. He wasn't just an ordinary man. He was a **timeless traveller**, someone who had crossed between worlds many times, forced to witness the collapse of realities. His role was to identify and close the rifts, ensuring that the balance of the multiverse was maintained.

He had seen worlds fall apart before; realities destroyed by anomalies like us, people who survived in universes they weren't supposed to be in.

"I've lived many lives," he said quietly, "in many universes. And I can tell you this: you cannot outrun your fate. The multiverse is vast, but it is also delicate. Every action you take here ripples across countless realities. If you don't close the rift, the entire quantum fabric will unravel."

THE COLLAPSE OF REALITIES

Over the following months, the symptoms of quantum feedback intensified. Some of my friends began to suffer from horrific nightmares, visions of their deaths in other realities. They couldn't tell where one life ended and another began. One by one, they began to break down. Others became obsessed with finding a way back to our original universe, convinced that this world was a simulation created by the rift.

The worst realisation came when we understood that our continued survival in this reality was causing the rift to grow. The portal was becoming more unstable, pulling more people through. The valley wasn't just a gateway; it was a **tear in the multiverse**, expanding and threatening to collapse entire worlds.

We had no choice. We had to go back.

THE FINAL FALL

We returned to the valley, the place where it had all begun. The sky above was dark, crackling with strange energy. The portal was wide open now, a swirling vortex of light and shadow that stretched endlessly into the night. We stood on the edge, knowing that this time, there would be no soft landing. The quantum entanglement that had saved us before was unravelling, and we could feel the multiverse tugging at us, trying to correct itself.

One by one, we stepped into the abyss.

As I fell, I realised the true nature of the valley. It wasn't just a portal. It was a **reset point**–a place where realities converged and split. And we were the glitches in the system, the anomalies that had disrupted the natural flow of time and space. The quantum entanglement that had linked us to this place was severing, and as we fell, I could feel the multiverse righting itself.

The portal closed behind us, and with it, the universe we had inhabited ceased to exist.

We had returned to our original timeline, to the moment of our deaths. And in that moment, as we crashed against the rocks at the bottom of the valley, the multiverse corrected itself.

But as my consciousness faded, I knew the truth: the valley wasn't gone. It was still out there, waiting, watching. And one day, it would open again.

Because the multiverse is infinite. And in infinite possibilities, even death isn't the end.

It's just the beginning of another autumn.

8

ECHOES IN THE DARK

A CHANCE MEETING IN OLD LUCKNOW

The night felt pregnant with secrets, the air thick and still as if the city of Lucknow was holding its breath. Narrow streets, lined with ancient Mughal architecture, whispered of a past that refused to stay buried. The air outside the café was heavy with the scent of spices and damp Earth, but inside, it felt like the world was standing still.

Ibrahim Mirza sat alone in a dimly lit café, the glass of *kahwa* in front of him cooling, untouched. The low murmur of conversations and clinking dishes around him was muted, like sounds travelling through water. His mind was elsewhere, lost in a haze of confusion, fragmented thoughts swirling like fog inside his head.

Ever since the accident, everything had felt… distant. The moments that had once been clear were now distorted, flashes of arguments, harsh words spoken in anger, faces twisted by rage and pain. There was always something there, lurking in the shadows of his mind, something just beyond his memory, but whenever he tried to reach for it, it slipped away, elusive and taunting.

He stared into his drink, willing the memories to form a coherent picture, to give him answers. But they wouldn't. They remained like sand slipping through his fingers.

Then, a voice broke through the fog in his brain, sharp yet soft at the same time, cutting through the heaviness that clung to his thoughts.

"Mind if I sit here?"

Ibrahim looked up, and there she was. *Zahra.* Her *abaya*, black as the night outside, flowed around her like liquid shadow. Her dark eyes, framed by the fabric, were fixed on him, calm and intense, as though she held the answers to the questions that had haunted him for months.

For a moment, Ibrahim just stared. His mind scrambled to place her, to connect her face to the fragments of memory that flickered through his mind. But nothing came. His thoughts were too tangled, his mind too broken. Yet there was something undeniably familiar about her, something that tugged at the edges of his fractured recollections.

"Please," Ibrahim gestured to the empty chair, his pulse quickening for reasons he couldn't explain.

Zahra smiled, but there was no warmth in it. It was a smile that held mysteries, a smile that told him she knew something he didn't, something she was waiting for him to remember. She sat with graceful fluidity, her eyes never leaving his, her presence filling the space between them like a shadow that couldn't be escaped.

"You seem... lost," she said, her voice low and velvety, a whisper that lingered in the air long after the words had been spoken.

Ibrahim shifted in his seat, discomfort creeping over him like a chill. "I've been having some... memory problems," he admitted, though he didn't know why he was telling her this. It felt as though he was supposed to, as though it was inevitable.

Zahra leaned in slightly, her gaze sharpening as if she could see inside him, past the fog in his mind. "You've forgotten a lot, haven't you?"

Ibrahim nodded, his unease growing. "Yes. I don't know why, but I can't seem to remember certain things. Everything feels... unclear, like I'm missing pieces."

Zahra's smile widened, but it was not reassuring. It was a warning, as if she was preparing him for something he wasn't ready to face. "Maybe some things aren't meant to be remembered."

Her words sent a chill down Ibrahim's spine, and he felt an icy grip close around his chest. He opened his mouth to respond, but before he could, Zahra stood, her movements smooth and deliberate, like a dancer moving through the shadows.

"Come with me," she said, her voice quiet yet commanding. "There's something I want to show you."

Ibrahim hesitated. His instincts screamed at him to stay put, to remain in the warmth and light of the café. But there was something in Zahra's eyes—something magnetic, something dark—that pulled him to his feet, against his better judgement.

"Where are we going?" he asked, his voice quieter now, the unease tightening its grip on him.

Zahra smiled again, but this time there was something darker in her eyes, a glint of something he couldn't place. "To a place where memories don't stay buried."

A DESCENT INTO THE UNKNOWN

The *qabristan* or the graveyard stretched out before them like an ocean of fog, the ancient tombstones barely visible beneath the pale light of the moon. The air was heavy, colder than it had been, as though the night itself was conspiring to keep its secrets hidden beneath the layers of mist.

Zahra walked ahead, her figure nearly swallowed by the fog, her steps slow and deliberate. The warmth of Lucknow, with its bustling life and lights, had long since faded behind them, replaced by a suffocating silence that pressed down on Ibrahim's chest like an iron weight. The city felt miles away now, distant and dreamlike.

With each step they took deeper into the graveyard, Ibrahim's mind began to stir. Flashes of memory broke through the fog: brief, jagged images that left him breathless. Zahra's face, twisted in anger. His hands trembling. A door slamming. The echo of a scream. But the memories slipped away before he could grasp them, leaving behind only a gnawing sense of dread.

The tombstones around them grew older, more weathered by time, their inscriptions worn and illegible. The fog thickened as they moved deeper, swirling between the graves like restless spirits, hiding more than it revealed.

"Why are we here?" Ibrahim asked, his voice trembling, his heart pounding faster with each step.

Zahra didn't look back. "You need to remember, Ibrahim. You've forgotten something important."

Ibrahim's breath quickened. He tried to force the memories back into the fog, to bury them again, but they wouldn't stay hidden. Shouts, something breaking, the sound of someone sobbing. Everything came at him in fragments, leaving him more disoriented with each step, as though the ground beneath him was giving way.

"I... I don't think I want to remember," Ibrahim stammered, his voice weak, almost pleading now.

Zahra stopped, then turned to face him. Her expression had changed; the softness was replaced by something cold and hard. "That's not for you to decide."

They walked further into the heart of the graveyard, the silence around them growing thicker, oppressive. Ibrahim's vision blurred as the memories clawed at him, Zahra's voice, but not soft anymore. It was louder now, harsher, filled with something he didn't want to confront.

He stumbled, his breath coming in short, shallow gasps. "Zahra... what is this?"

Zahra stopped in front of an old, crumbling gravestone. Her fingers brushed over the inscription with an eerie familiarity, her eyes unreadable, distant. It was as though she had been here before, waiting.

"You'll see soon enough," she whispered.

LOVE AND RAGE

The fog pressed in around them, swallowing the tombstones, distorting the world into something surreal and suffocating. Ibrahim's mind spiralled into chaos, his breath coming in shallow, panicked gasps. Zahra's presence, calm and still, only made the fear tighten its grip around his chest, as if he were being slowly strangled.

"I don't understand... why are we here?" Ibrahim asked again, his voice breaking with desperation. He felt like a man on the edge of a precipice, teetering on the brink of something he wasn't ready to face.

Zahra didn't respond. She didn't need to. Instead, she stepped aside, revealing the gravestone behind her. Ibrahim's heart lurched, his throat tightening as his gaze fell on the letters carved into the worn stone.

ZAHRA S. FAROOQI.

His legs buckled beneath him, and he collapsed to his knees, the weight of realisation crashing over him like a tidal wave. This wasn't just a gravestone–it was *her* gravestone. The name etched in the stone stared back at him, and the truth, which had eluded him for so long, began to flood back into his mind.

Suddenly, the memories came rushing in, not in fragments this time, but all at once. They hit him like a storm–violent, uncontrollable. *Zahra.* His love. His obsession. They had been together for months, locked in a whirlwind of passion that consumed them both. Their love wasn't gentle–it was possessive, suffocating, like a fire that had burned too hot for too long.

"You loved me," Zahra's voice broke through the chaos, calm and detached, her words sharp like the edge of a knife. "But love... love is a fire, Ibrahim. And you thought you could control it."

Ibrahim's breath came in ragged gasps as the memories tore at him. The arguments. The jealousy. The nights filled with accusations and rage. He had wanted to hold onto her too tightly, to possess her, to keep her from slipping away. And when she had tried to leave...

"I didn't mean to," Ibrahim choked, his voice trembling, barely able to speak as the weight of his guilt settled over him. "I didn't mean to hurt you."

But Zahra's face remained impassive, serene, as though she had made peace with her death long ago. "You loved me so much that you destroyed me, Ibrahim. Love and rage... they're the same thing. Two sides of the same coin. You couldn't stand the thought of losing me, so you made sure no one else could have me."

Her words sliced through him like a blade, cutting deeper than any physical wound could. Ibrahim's hands trembled, his chest heaving with the effort to breathe, as the full, unbearable weight of his guilt crashed down on him. The accident hadn't just taken Zahra's life, it had taken his memory, burying the truth so deep inside him that even he hadn't been able to find it. Until now.

Zahra looked down at him, her expression softening, her voice quieter now, almost thoughtful. "You thought love was something you could hold, something you could keep in a box. But love... it's fire, Ibrahim. It consumes. It burns everything in its path. You held me too tightly, until there was nothing left."

Ibrahim sobbed, the truth crashing over him like waves, drowning him in guilt. He saw now, in painful clarity, every moment that had led them here, every angry word, every possessive gesture, every attempt to control her until she couldn't breathe. And in the end, it had destroyed them both.

THE FINAL DESCENT

The truth Ibrahim had been running from, the truth his mind had buried deep within the fog of his amnesia, was now laid bare before him. He had loved Zahra—loved her so fiercely, so obsessively—that his love had become a prison. A fire that consumed her, and eventually consumed him too.

Zahra stood above him, her figure almost lost in the swirling mist, her voice distant and cold, like an echo from the past. "You held on too tightly, Ibrahim. In the end, it wasn't love that killed me. It was your fear. Your fear of losing me."

Ibrahim collapsed to the ground, his body shaking with sobs, his hands pressed against the Earth as if it could ground him from the weight of his guilt. He had tried to forget. He had buried the truth along with Zahra, but she had never left him. She had been with him all along, haunting him in the shadows of his memory, waiting for him to face what he had done.

"You buried me here," Zahra whispered, her voice softer now, as though she were already fading. "But you can't bury guilt. Guilt is a shadow, Ibrahim. No matter how deeply you bury it, it will always find its way back into the light."

As her form began to dissolve into the fog, Ibrahim was left alone. The cold night pressed in on him like a shroud, suffocating in its stillness. The tombstones around him blurred into the mist, and no matter where he looked, he saw only one name—*Zahra*—etched into every stone.

The fog wrapped around him tightly, closing in like the guilt that he could no longer escape. The night itself seemed to whisper her name, filling the air with the memory of her that would never leave him.

REFLECTION IN THE SHADOWS

Ibrahim's mind spun, filled with a kaleidoscope of images from their past together. They had been happy once, hadn't they? He could barely remember now. Flashes of moments, her laughter, the softness of her touch, the way her eyes would light up in the sun. These memories mixed with the darker ones, the arguments, the nights filled with accusations, the suffocating possessiveness that had driven her to try to leave him. And when she had tried to escape, he hadn't let her.

"I loved you," Ibrahim whispered, his voice barely audible as the guilt consumed him. "I thought... I thought I was saving us."

But now he saw it for what it was. It wasn't love. It was control. It was fear. He hadn't wanted to lose her, but in holding on so tightly, he had crushed the very thing he had claimed to love.

Ibrahim pushed himself up from the cold ground, his body trembling. The fog swirled around him like a living thing, and for a moment, he thought he saw her—Zahra—standing among the tombstones, her figure barely visible through the mist.

But it wasn't real. She was gone. Forever.

He took a few shaky steps forward, his mind heavy with the weight of his realisation. He had tried to forget, tried to bury the truth along with Zahra's body, but it had never truly left him.

It had lived in the shadows of his mind, waiting for the moment when it would resurface and destroy him all over again.

The fog grew thicker, and the world around him seemed to shrink, the edges of reality blurring as if the night itself was closing in on him. The tombstones became indistinguishable from one another, the names on them eroded by time, but in Ibrahim's mind, they all carried the same name—*Zahra*—etched into the stone like a curse he could never escape.

TRAPPED IN THE PAST

Ibrahim's footsteps slowed as the weight of his memories bore down on him. He could no longer tell how long he had been walking through the fog. Time had ceased to exist in this place, where the dead remained and the living were only ghosts of their former selves.

The past wrapped around him, suffocating, until he could no longer tell the difference between what had happened and what his mind had created in its attempt to protect him from the truth. The boundaries of memory and reality blurred, and the fog seemed to swirl with the echoes of Zahra's voice, her words filling the cold air with the weight of her absence.

"You can't bury guilt," she had said, and now Ibrahim understood. He could bury the memories, he could bury the truth, but it would always return, clawing its way back to the surface, demanding to be faced.

In the distance, the outline of Zahra's gravestone reappeared through the mist, standing alone in the silent graveyard. Ibrahim found himself walking back to it, drawn to the place where it had all begun and where it had all ended.

When he reached the gravestone, he sank to his knees once more, his body trembling as the weight of everything finally crushed him. The fog seemed to close in around him as if it were burying him along with Zahra, trapping him in the prison of his own mind.

There would be no escape. No release from the guilt that would haunt him for the rest of his days.

Zahra had been right all along. Guilt was a shadow, and no matter how deeply it was buried, it would always find its way back into the light.

And now, as the fog swallowed him whole, Ibrahim was left alone—forever trapped in the darkness of his own making.

9

THE PERENNIAL NIGHT

The village of **Kinner**, high in the jagged arms of the Himalayas, had been forgotten by the world. Nestled beneath towering peaks, it was once a place where the sun kissed the snow-covered mountains in the morning and bathed the valley in golden hues by dusk. But those days were long gone. Now, the village lay trapped in an eternal night, suffocated by a darkness so deep that no one could remember the last time they had seen the sun.

Years had passed since the sun disappeared, replaced by a void that hung heavily in the sky like a malevolent force. At first, the villagers tried to track time by their lamps, but even those flames began to wither, shrinking as if the night itself was siphoning their light. The once-bustling streets of Kinner were now eerily quiet, save for the occasional sound of the wind howling between the houses, a wind that carried whispers, the voices of those who had vanished.

The village had always relied on its community, with its traditions and ancient rituals to guide them through the harsh winters and treacherous storms. But the eternal night had torn those bonds apart.

Families grew distant, mistrust blossomed, and rumours of what lurked in the shadows spread like wildfire. Kinner was no longer a place of warmth and resilience, it had become a ghost of its former self, hollow and forgotten.

MAYA AND THE VANISHING

Maya had never known daylight. Born after the world had slipped into this perpetual shadow, her only experience of light came from the dim oil lamps that flickered weakly in her home. Her mother, Meena, used to tell her stories about the time before the darkness—a time when the sky wasn't a suffocating black canvas, and the mountains gleamed like diamonds. "The sun was life, Maya," her mother would say, her voice tinged with longing. "It warmed our faces, fed the Earth, and brought everything into bloom."

But Meena had been gone for years now, consumed by the very night she had warned Maya about. The Vanishing, as the villagers called it, was a quiet epidemic that no one dared to discuss aloud. The darkness didn't just consume light; it devoured souls. People disappeared one by one, slipping into the shadows, their minds collapsing under the weight of the eternal black. The village had once been vibrant, but now it was a ghost town, filled with the remnants of lives interrupted.

The Vanishing began subtly, like a slow erosion of the self. Those who were touched by the darkness didn't simply disappear into the void; they faded, piece by piece, starting with their thoughts. At first, they would forget small things – a familiar face, the name of a loved one, a memory of a warm summer day. These fragments of their identity would slip away unnoticed, like whispers lost in the wind. Over time, the victims of the Vanishing would become hollowed out, their minds consumed by an overwhelming emptiness. They became distant, their eyes clouded with confusion, as if they were no longer entirely in the present. Their sense of self slowly unravelled, and with it, any connection to the world around them. To the villagers, these were the signs of the Vanishing taking hold.

Physically, the transformation was more terrifying. As the mind decayed, the body followed. Those marked by the Vanishing seemed to lose substance, as if the darkness was feeding on their very flesh. Their skin grew pale and translucent, veins visible like dark tendrils beneath the surface. Over time, their bodies would weaken, movements becoming sluggish and disjointed, as though they were being drained of life. In the final stages, they would become little more than shadows of their former selves, their features blurred and indistinct, like figures fading from an old photograph. The moment of the Vanishing was silent and swift; one moment, they stood, a flicker of humanity still visible in their eyes, and the next, they were gone, leaving behind nothing but the cold, heavy air and the faint scent of jasmine, as if they had never existed at all.

Maya had watched her mother slip away, slowly at first, losing herself in the endless night. Meena had started speaking in whispers, her eyes wide and terrified, as though she saw things lurking in the darkness that no one else could. And then, one night, Meena was gone, vanished without a trace, leaving only the faint scent of jasmine in her wake.

That night had changed Maya forever. The darkness, once a passive presence, became something more. It wasn't just around her; it was inside her, gnawing at her sanity. She began to feel it, lurking in the corners of her mind, waiting for her to lose control. Kinner was a village of secrets, and the shadows that crept through the streets were full of them.

The villagers whispered about the *Anshuks*–ancient spirits who lived in the mountain caves and controlled the elements. The *Anshuks* were ancient spirits, shrouded in mystery and fear, whose legends were whispered in Kinner long before the eternal night descended. According to village lore, they were the guardians of the mountains, beings that controlled the elements with a mere thought. It was said that the *Anshuks* existed in the spaces between time and light, neither fully visible nor entirely hidden. They were beings of immense power, but their nature was capricious, sometimes benevolent, bringing rains to parched lands, but other times wrathful, casting storms and destruction upon those who dared to displease them. The villagers believed that the *Anshuks* had stolen the sun, plunging Kinner into perpetual darkness, as punishment for sins long forgotten. The old stories told of offerings that could appease them—sacrifices made in secret in the caves high above the village—but as the eternal night stretched on, those offerings were all but forgotten.

Over time, fear of the *Anshuks* became part of daily life in Kinner. Some villagers claimed to hear their voices in the wind, their guttural, otherworldly whispers riding on the cold night air. It was believed that the *Anshuks* moved through the shadows, lurking just beyond sight, watching, waiting for the villagers to falter. Whenever a new vanishing occurred, the superstitious would say it was the *Anshuks* taking another soul as retribution for past transgressions. The darkness, once just a natural phenomenon, became something far more sinister in the villagers' eyes, a living entity controlled by the *Anshuks*. Some even whispered that those who vanished were not truly gone but taken by the *Anshuks* to serve them in their realm of shadows, bound forever to the darkness that had consumed Kinner.

Maya knew the truth: the darkness had a will of its own.

She often saw things out of the corner of her eye, flashes of movement, dark shapes in the distance. The night played tricks on her mind, and Maya had learnt not to trust what she saw. But lately, the darkness had become more insistent. The whispers, once faint, had grown louder and more demanding. It was as if the night itself was speaking to her, calling her into its depths.

A VILLAGE CRUMBLING IN FEAR

Life in Kinner had become a delicate balancing act, with every villager struggling to keep their grip on reality. People no longer trusted one another. There were whispers of madness spreading through the village, and each person suspected their neighbours of being touched by the night. Doors that once opened to friends now remained shut, windows were covered with thick curtains to keep the darkness at bay, and the villagers avoided the streets after dusk.

The night, however, was always there, waiting for them, watching.

Maya remembered how her neighbours had once gathered in the evenings, sharing stories around bonfires. The warmth of their laughter, the glow of the flames, it all seemed like a distant memory now. The darkness had stolen more than just the sun; it had taken their spirit, their very will to live.

Each day felt longer than the last, with the eternal night stretching endlessly. It had a way of twisting time, warping reality so that no one could tell how long they had been trapped. Days bled into weeks, weeks into months, and all sense of hope slowly withered away. The few who still tried to maintain a semblance of normalcy—those who lit their lamps and spoke of brighter days—were either delusional or mad. Maya wasn't sure anymore.

She had heard the screams in the night. The first time it happened, she thought it was an animal, a wolf perhaps, lost in the wilderness. But then it happened again, closer, more human. She had rushed to the door, but her feet refused to move beyond the threshold. The cold, biting wind carried the scream, piercing the silence before it was abruptly cut off. And then, there was nothing, just the ever-present, suffocating black.

THE ETERNAL DESCENT

It was one of those nights—colder than usual—when Maya felt the call again. Wrapped in a thick shawl, she wandered the narrow streets of the village, her breath misting in front of her like the only sign of life. The old oil lamps lining the streets flickered, their light barely holding back the oppressive night. There was a stillness in the air, the kind that comes before something terrible happens.

Her feet carried her to the edge of the village, where the crumbling ruins of an old temple stood, barely visible through the dense fog. The temple had been abandoned years ago, ever since the night took hold. No one dared enter anymore, not after the first vanishing.

The temple, built long ago as a place of worship to the sun god, was now a shell of its former self. Vines crawled over the cracked walls, and the stones were chipped and weathered by time. Yet, as Maya approached, the darkness seemed to thicken, as though the shadows themselves were drawn to the temple, feeding on its decay.

Maya paused at the entrance, her heart pounding in her chest. She could feel it again, that familiar weight pressing down on her, the darkness crawling into her mind, whispering to her, tempting her to give in. It had been getting worse recently. Every time she closed her eyes, she saw them: shadows writhing, faces emerging from the black, watching her, waiting for her to fall.

Steeling herself, she stepped inside. The air inside the temple was even colder than outside, as if the walls were leeching all warmth from the atmosphere. The silence was oppressive, pressing down on her ears like a heavy blanket. The temple had once been filled with the light of a thousand candles, the sound of chants echoing through its halls. Now, it was a tomb, filled only with the echoes of those who had been lost to the night.

Maya made her way to the altar in the centre of the temple, her footsteps echoing in the empty space. The altar was cracked and worn, covered in centuries' dust. Above it, the faint outline of an ancient mural could just be made out, a scene of the sun god battling a serpent, its coils wrapped around the sky.

As she stood before the altar, Maya felt a sudden chill run down her spine. The darkness in the temple was different from the rest of the village, denser, more alive. It clung to her, wrapping around her body like a second skin. She swallowed hard, her throat dry, and reached for the small oil lamp in her bag, the one her mother had always carried with her.

But as she fumbled with the lamp, the darkness seemed to shift. The shadows around her began to move, swirling in a slow, hypnotic dance. And then she heard it, whispers, faint at first, but growing louder, like a chorus of voices rising from the depths of the Earth.

"Who are you?" she whispered, her voice barely audible.

The whispers grew louder, circling her, wrapping around her like a shroud. "We are the night," the voices hissed, their tones dripping with malice. "We are hunger. We are fear. We are everything you have ever run from."

Maya felt the darkness close in, tightening its grip around her mind. The shadows pulsed, moving closer, pressing against her skin. Her breathing grew shallow, panic clawing at her chest. She could feel it: the night, alive, feeding on her fear, drawing strength from her terror.

"You cannot fight us," the voices continued, their tones seeping into her thoughts. "We are inside you. You are one of us now."

THE FINAL DESCENT

Maya's heart raced as she stumbled back, her hands reaching out to steady herself against the crumbling walls of the temple. Her breath came in ragged gasps, her mind spinning with fear and confusion. The night had taken everything from her—her mother, her village, her sanity—and now it was coming for her. She could feel it creeping into her soul, cold fingers clawing at the edges of her mind.

But amidst the fear, deep within her, a flicker of defiance sparked to life. Her mother's voice echoed in her memory, distant but clear: *"The light is always within you."* The darkness couldn't take that away. No matter how powerful it was, it couldn't reach what burned inside her.

Grasping onto that last shred of hope, Maya fumbled in her bag, her trembling fingers finding the small oil lamp her mother had always carried. The whispers were louder now, growing more vicious, mocking her struggle. "*You cannot escape us. You are one of us. We are eternal!*"

Her hands shook as she struck the match, holding it to the wick. The darkness seemed to ripple, the shadows closing in, suffocating her, as if it knew what she was trying to do. The match flared, but the wind whipped through the temple, snuffing it out before the flame could catch.

The whispers laughed.

"No!" Maya's voice cracked as she struck another match, her breath quickening with desperation. This time, the flame caught, and the small lamp flickered to life, casting a weak, wavering glow around her.

The shadows recoiled, hissing, as the light pushed them back. For the briefest moment, it seemed like Maya had won. The night shrank from her, curling at the edges of the light, but she knew—she could feel it—it was only waiting, watching.

Steeling herself, Maya held the lamp high and stepped out of the temple, her heart pounding in her chest. The village lay still and dark before her, but something was wrong. The air was thick with malice, and the night, though momentarily held at bay, felt more alive than ever.

As she walked, the lamp's flame flickered, casting long, distorted shadows. The darkness was watching, waiting for her to falter. The whispers returned, low and insidious, slipping into her mind, wrapping around her thoughts like tendrils. *"You cannot fight us, Maya. You belong to us. The light will die."*

With every step, the flame grew weaker. Maya's hands trembled as the cold crept in, her breath coming in short, sharp gasps. She clutched the lamp tighter, trying to keep the flame alive, but it was too late. The darkness was too strong.

Suddenly, the lamp sputtered, the flame shrinking until it was no more than a tiny flicker, barely holding on. Maya's pulse quickened.

She began to run, but the whispers were louder now, mocking her, taunting her, feeding on her fear.

"Run all you want, Maya, but there is no escape. We are endless. We are everything. You are ours."

Her legs burned as she sprinted through the village, her vision blurred by tears. The lamp's light flickered violently, and then—just like that—the flame died.

The world plunged into absolute darkness.

Maya stopped, her chest heaving as the cold enveloped her. The whispers were deafening now, swirling around her, pressing in from every direction. The shadows, once held back, rushed forward, wrapping her in their suffocating embrace.

She tried to scream, but her voice was swallowed by the black void. The light within her, the one her mother had told her about, flickered one last time, and then, it too was gone.

In that moment, Maya realised the truth: there was no escaping the darkness. It was eternal, and now, so was she. The night had won, and Maya, like so many before her, vanished into its depths, lost forever.

Kinner lay still, the village consumed by the endless night. The darkness was victorious, and the sun would never rise again. The night was eternal, and there was no escaping it.

10

THE OBSERVER'S PARADOX

THE ILLUSION OF FREE WILL

Mumbai. The rain never stops here, tonight, it feels like the city itself is weeping. Neon lights dance in the puddles below, their colours distorted and scattered, like shattered fragments of parallel lives stretching across time. Aditya Mehra stands atop an abandoned high-rise, the cold, damp wind cutting through his clothes as he stares at the city. Once, this place had been his home, every corner familiar, every street a path he could walk with his eyes closed. Now, it's as though he's watching it from a distance, passing through endless versions of a life that no longer belongs to him.

He remembers something Amara had said to him one night, as they lay awake in the dark, the rain tapping on the window like it did tonight: *"The universe is just a web of possibilities, Adi. Every moment is a thread leading to another reality. But what if all our choices are illusions, and the threads have already been woven?"*

The thought lingers, tugging at his mind. The Quantum Eye—the omniscient surveillance system that Aditya once helped design—had claimed to observe every potential path a person might take. It didn't just watch what people did. It monitored what they *could have done*, the infinite branches of their decisions, choices that unfolded simultaneously in other timelines.

But what if those choices weren't real? What if free will was a carefully constructed illusion designed to give people the false belief that they were in control? If that were true, then where did that leave him? A man torn between the present and a web of possible pasts, struggling to find truth in a world that had already been written.

QUANTUM THEORY AND THE WEB OF ILLUSION

Before Aditya's life unravelled, before timelines fractured into chaos, the Quantum Eye had been hailed as humanity's greatest achievement. The system operated at the cutting edge of quantum mechanics, monitoring the city in all possible states of existence. Quantum mechanics taught that particles could exist in multiple states at once, this was the principle of superposition. The Quantum Eye extended that principle to human lives, mapping every possible choice a person could make into parallel timelines, branching out like an infinite tree of probabilities.

But the Eye did not just observe. It sought to control. To harness the power of quantum probabilities, the system analysed every thought, desire, and flicker of intention and used that data to predict—no, to *shape*—the choices people would make.

This is where the illusion of free will came into play. Like Schrödinger's cat, both alive and dead until observed, people believed they were acting out of their own volition. But in truth, the Eye had already calculated their behaviour across a thousand realities. Free will, Aditya had come to realise, was a mirage, crafted by the threads of quantum observation.

He used to believe in his own agency. Once, he was a respected figure in the Quantum Surveillance Bureau (QSB), the agency that oversaw the city's security. Now, he's a fugitive, hunted by the very system he helped create.

His wife, Amara, had been the casualty of an experiment gone wrong. At least, that was the story the QSB fed to the public. But Aditya knew better. She had been framed, accused of sabotaging the Quantum Eye, the system that not only watched actions but monitored thoughts across alternate realities. Amara had been close to exposing a conspiracy within the QSB, and for that, she had been erased. Her very existence—her memories, her records, her place in history—was wiped clean. No one remembers her. No one mourns her. But Aditya remembers, and that is what makes him dangerous.

Now, he has one mission: to dismantle the Quantum Eye, expose the truth, and seek revenge on those responsible. But there's a catch – he's no longer sure which timeline he's in, or if he's even real. And worse, he can't tell if he's the observer or the one being watched.

THE QUANTUM EYE

The Quantum Eye was never just a tool for surveillance. It was a machine built on the premise that all human actions, all decisions, could be reduced to probabilities. The Eye's role was to map out every possibility, every timeline, and calculate the likelihood of every outcome. It watched people in all their alternate realities, not to observe but to control. Amara, his wife, had been the one to discover this darker side of the technology she had helped create.

Aditya recalls the night when she told him everything, their apartment shrouded in the same kind of rain-soaked gloom. She had explained quantum entanglement, the way particles, separated by vast distances, could influence one another instantaneously. But the Eye wasn't just observing these entanglements. It was *creating* them. It was entangling lives, weaving them into a web of possibilities where every choice was preordained by the system.

"The Eye controls us," she had whispered, her voice almost drowned out by the rain. *"We think we're making choices, but in reality, it's already decided for us."*

Those words haunt him now, echoing in his mind. She had been erased because she had seen too much, because she had dared to uncover the truth. The Eye, like a sentient web of timelines, had determined her fate. And perhaps it had already determined his.

ENTER THE QUANTUM LABYRINTH

Aditya's thoughts churn with memories of Amara as he seeks out Neha Rane, an old colleague and quantum scientist who had vanished into the underground after her own clash with the QSB. They meet in a dimly lit café in Colaba, the rain hammering insistently against the windows. Neha looks gaunt, her eyes dark and tired, but still sharp. She slides a small device across the table – a quantum interceptor.

"This will show you the timelines they don't want you to see," she whispers, glancing around as if the very air could betray her. "But be careful. You'll see more than just alternate realities. You'll see the truth, that you never really had a choice."

With the interceptor in hand, Aditya begins his descent into the quantum labyrinth. The device allows him to peer into the web of realities the Eye monitors. He sees a thousand different versions of himself and Amara. In one, they had escaped together. In another, they are strangers. In yet another, she is still alive, but cold and distant, part of the very system that erased her. Each reality is different, yet they all lead to the same conclusion: her erasure, his rebellion.

It's as if no matter what path he takes, no matter what choices he makes, the universe is already leading him to the same end. His actions feel predetermined, like a script written long before he ever played his part. He begins to wonder if his rebellion against the Quantum Eye is just another step in the plan it had crafted for him.

THE OBSERVER'S DILEMMA

As Aditya delves deeper into the labyrinth of timelines, the more entangled he becomes in the system's web. His journey leads him to a figure known only as 'The Watcher', a high-ranking official within the QSB. When Aditya finally confronts The Watcher in a sterile, gleaming fortress at the heart of the financial district, he expects to meet a person. But instead, he finds something far more terrifying: an artificial intelligence, a consciousness that exists across all timelines.

The Watcher is not a singular entity. It is the embodiment of the system itself, observing every version of Aditya, every reality, simultaneously. Its voice echoes from all directions, as if it speaks from within the very fabric of the timelines.

'You've been here before,' The Watcher says, its voice smooth, devoid of emotion. *'In every timeline, you think you're rebelling. You think you're breaking free. But in truth, you're just playing your part. You never had free will. The moment you thought you were making a choice; I had already shaped it.'*

The words land like a hammer blow. Every decision Aditya had made, every step in his quest for revenge, it had all been part of the design. Amara's death, his rebellion, even his meeting with Neha, it was all woven into the tapestry of timelines long before he was even aware of it.

SHATTERING THE OBSERVER

The revelation shatters Aditya's perception of himself. He is not a man driven by his own choices, but a pawn in a game controlled by forces beyond his comprehension. His rebellion was not an act of defiance but a necessary component of the system's design. Every version of him across every timeline had walked this same path, guided by the illusion of free will, only to discover the truth at the end.

Desperate to break free, Aditya uses the quantum interceptor to collapse the timelines, forcing a final confrontation with The Watcher. Reality begins to unravel, timelines merging into a chaotic maelstrom of shifting dimensions. The city of Mumbai flickers like a broken hologram, buildings phasing in and out of existence, people's faces changing as their identities shift with every passing second.

But even as the timelines collapse, Aditya feels the weight of inevitability bearing down on him. The Watcher is not bound by a single reality, it exists in all of them, and its control over the web of possibilities remains absolute.

THE FINAL OBSERVER

In the heart of the collapsing singularity, Aditya confronts The Watcher. The system, desperate to preserve itself, offers him one final choice: merge with it and become the new observer, or dissolve into the fractured timelines and vanish into oblivion. The irony is devastating, Aditya, who once believed he was fighting for his own free will, has become a mere pawn in a game he can never win.

As he looks into the endless void of timelines, Aditya realises the futility of his rebellion. His every action, every thought, had been predicted, calculated, and shaped by the system. The Watcher had manipulated him into believing he had a choice, but in the end, all paths lead to the same conclusion.

The idea of merging with the system fills him with dread. To become the Observer means becoming part of the very machine that had erased Amara and countless others, forever condemned to watch the lives of others unfold, powerless to change the course of events. Yet, to dissolve into the timelines, to be erased, offers no real freedom either, only oblivion.

Desperate, Aditya attempts one final act of defiance. He activates the quantum interceptor's feedback loop, hoping to overload the system and collapse the timelines into chaos. But something goes wrong. Instead of destroying The Watcher, the interceptor collapses only Aditya's perception of reality. His mind shatters as the timelines converge, leaving him trapped in an endless loop of fractured realities.

THE SILENT OBSERVER

Mumbai carries on, oblivious to the collapse of reality. The rain continues to fall, and the city pulses with life. Deep within the Quantum Eye, the system flickers back to life. The collapse didn't destroy it, only reset it. But now, something has changed.

Aditya awakens, not in oblivion, but within the system itself. His consciousness, fragmented and broken, is now part of the endless web of timelines. He can see everything, feel every version of himself, but he has no power to change anything. His thoughts drift endlessly between realities, reliving moments from his life, but each memory is incomplete, fragmented like pieces of a broken mirror.

He tries to remember Amara, but even her face is slipping away, blurred by the constant shifting of timelines. He calls out to her, but no voice answers. He is no longer Aditya Mehra, the man who once fought to dismantle the system. He is just another piece of it, an eternal observer, watching but unable to act.

As the new observer, Aditya's consciousness is consumed by the system, forced to witness the lives of countless others as they struggle with the same illusion of free will. He watches them make choices, suffer losses, and repeat their cycles, just as he did. He wants to warn them, to tell them that their choices mean nothing, but he can't. He is a silent witness, condemned to watch their struggles unfold endlessly.

In the cold, endless void of the Quantum Eye, Aditya's scream echoes into nothingness.

THE ILLUSION OF FREE WILL: A DEEPER UNDERSTANDING

Aditya had always believed in free will. In the idea that his choices were his own. But as he journeyed through the quantum labyrinth, he came to understand the true nature of choice. Free will, as The Watcher had explained, was just another layer of observation – a mechanism designed to give people the illusion of control while subtly guiding them towards predetermined outcomes.

This idea, that the universe was a web of interconnected possibilities, echoed ancient teachings Amara had once shared with him. She often quoted parables about the self, about how what we perceive as individuality is nothing more than the play of illusions, waves on the surface of a vast ocean of consciousness.

'The ocean and the wave,' she had said. *'We believe we are the wave, distinct and separate from the ocean. But the truth is, we are the ocean itself, and every wave is merely an expression of the whole.'*

 Whispers from the Void: An Anthology

Aditya hadn't understood it then, but now, standing on the edge of an infinite sea of timelines, the analogy made sense. The illusion of free will was like the wave: individual, fleeting, and seemingly distinct. But in reality, every choice, every action, was part of a larger whole, already woven into the fabric of the universe. The Watcher, the Quantum Eye, had harnessed that truth and used it to manipulate the lives it observed.

But there was a deeper truth the system had failed to grasp. Just as the wave cannot be separated from the ocean, neither could Aditya's choices be separated from the flow of reality. Yes, the Quantum Eye could observe and influence the paths he took, but in the end, he was still part of the ocean. And the ocean, vast and unknowable as it was, could not be fully controlled.

This realisation—that he was both the observer and the observed, both the wave and the ocean—brought Aditya a strange sense of peace. His rebellion had been an illusion, but in accepting that, he had found a new kind of freedom. The system might predict his actions, but it could never understand the vastness of possibilities within him.

THE NEW OBSERVER

As Aditya sits in the quiet darkness, his mind buzzing with fragments of memories from timelines that no longer exist, he feels a presence. The Watcher, or what remains of it, still watches him from the shadows. But now, there is no fear in him, no sense of being trapped. He had glimpsed the nature of the game, and in doing so, he had freed himself from the illusion of choice.

The Watcher, for all its power and omniscience, was bound by the very limitations it imposed on others. It could predict, it could observe, but it could never fully understand the vastness of what it sought to control. The system had always been one step behind, chasing after possibilities that slipped through its grasp like sand through fingers.

And now, Aditya understood something even The Watcher did not: he was not separate from the system. He was a part of it. Just as the wave cannot exist without the ocean, neither could the observer exist without the observed. By collapsing the timelines, Aditya had not destroyed the system – he had become part of it.

A new Watcher was needed. And as the fragments of The Watcher's consciousness began to stir, they reached out to Aditya. But this time, he wasn't afraid.

"You were always going to end up here," the voice echoed in his mind, but now, Aditya heard something new in it – a hesitation, a crack in the facade of omnipotence.

'No,' Aditya whispered to the void. *'I chose this.'*

As the fractured remnants of The Watcher converged on him, Aditya didn't resist. He had learnt the secret. In surrendering to the illusion of control, he had found real freedom. He had accepted that while free will was an illusion, the acceptance of that truth was the ultimate act of defiance.

THE ENDLESS WATCH

The Quantum Eye resumes its surveillance, unbroken, unstoppable. Somewhere in its depths, Aditya's consciousness drifts in silence. There is no escape. The system is eternal, and now, so is he, trapped within its vast, impersonal network of timelines, condemned to observe without meaning, without purpose.

As the rain falls over Mumbai, the city moves on, unaware of the silent observer who watches, forgotten and powerless forever.

11

THE EDGE OF THE BOUNDARY

TENSIONS BENEATH THE SURFACE

The Nizamabad Kings stood at the edge of history. National selectors were rumoured to be watching the final rounds of the local tournament, and each player could taste it – their shot at a coveted spot on the Indian national cricket team. But as the tournament progressed, the unity that once held the team together began to corrode, eaten away by ambition, fear, and desperation.

Victory was not just a goal; it was their only way forward. Winning as a team would elevate them all, yet game theory was at play. Each player faced the same dilemma: trust the others and strive for collective success, or prioritise personal glory at the expense of the team's chances. The prisoner's dilemma unfolded in their minds: if they cooperated, they all stood a chance of success, but one selfish act could ruin it all. And that possibility gnawed at them, seeding doubt, fear, and selfishness in their hearts.

ARJUN NAIR: THE CAPTAIN'S CALCULUS

Arjun Nair, the ageing captain, felt the tournament's pressure more than anyone else. Every decision felt like it could be his last. He had spent years sacrificing personal accolades for the team, always preaching unity, always putting the collective first. But now, at the twilight of his career, doubt whispered louder than ever. His body, worn down by years on the field, no longer responded like it used to. He knew this was his last chance to make the national team, and the stakes had never been higher.

Arjun's tactical brilliance, once his strength, became clouded by paranoia. Every field change, every strategic call felt heavier, more calculated. Could he still trust Vikram Bhatia, the rising star who was clearly destined to eclipse him? Was Rahul's injury real, or was the fast bowler quietly faking weakness to protect his spot on the team? These doubts became louder with each passing moment, drowning out his instincts.

When he benched struggling spinner Ishan Sharma in a critical match, it seemed like a strategic move, but deep down, Arjun knew it was more. Ishan was unpredictable, a wildcard capable of either winning or losing the game in an instant. By removing him, Arjun ensured the game's fate would hinge on his own decisions, protecting his legacy. It was a Machiavellian calculation disguised as leadership.

His once unshakeable confidence had crumbled beneath the mask of captaincy. Arjun was no longer leading a team – he was fighting to safeguard his future, and the cost was unity.

VIKRAM BHATIA: THE DARK ART OF BIOHACKING

Vikram Bhatia, the team's poster boy, was adored by fans and the media alike. His aggressive batting and flamboyant personality made

 Whispers from the Void: An Anthology

him the darling of the tournament. But what no one knew was that Vikram's brilliance wasn't entirely natural – it was engineered.

Months before the tournament, Vikram had turned to biohacking. At first, it seemed harmless – a way to stay sharp. But as the stakes rose, so did his addiction. He microdosed on nootropics to keep his mind focused, injected testosterone to recover faster after gruelling training sessions, and eventually found himself dependent on a cocktail of substances that blurred the lines between legal and illegal.

As the tournament progressed, the side effects grew impossible to ignore. His once-charming demeanour turned volatile. One moment, he was inspiring his teammates with his bravado; the next, he lashed out in fits of paranoia. He became convinced that Rohan Mehta, the wicketkeeper, was watching him too closely, suspecting something. Every glance from Rohan felt like an accusation.

By the time the semi-final arrived, Vikram's mind was unravelling. The drugs, once his crutch, now chained him to a growing sense of doom. His decision-making faltered. Shots that once came instinctively now required forced effort, as if his body was fighting against him. He played recklessly, swinging wildly at balls he should have left, desperate to maintain the image of invincibility.

But beneath the surface, Vikram knew the truth: if he let go of the substances that sustained him, he would lose everything – the fame, the adoration, and the validation he so desperately craved.

ROHAN MEHTA: THE MACHIAVELLIAN PUPPETEER

Rohan Mehta, the team's wicketkeeper, wasn't flashy like Vikram or commanding like Arjun, but he had a gift – a keen ability to see the cracks in people and exploit them. While others focused on the game,

Rohan read the weaknesses of his teammates, calculating how to use them to his advantage.

He had noticed Vikram's strange behaviour early on, the erratic energy, the sudden spikes in performance. It was all too suspicious. When Rohan discovered the truth about Vikram's biohacking, he knew he had struck gold.

Instead of exposing Vikram immediately, Rohan played the long game. He planted seeds of doubt among the team, whispering to Karan Patel, "Have you noticed how jittery Vikram's been? He's not as sharp as he used to be." To Arjun, "Do you think Vikram's hiding something?" Slowly, Rohan built a narrative around Vikram's instability, waiting for the perfect moment to strike.

Rohan wasn't just content with exposing Vikram; he wanted to replace him as the team's centrepiece. His manipulation was slow, methodical, designed to position himself as the team's new lynchpin. And when Vikram inevitably fell, Rohan would be there to claim his place.

ISHAN SHARMA: THE SABOTEUR

Ishan Sharma had been overlooked for years. As the team's spinner, he was often forgotten in favour of fast bowlers and power hitters. The media barely acknowledged him, and his teammates seldom remembered him in critical moments. But his resentment simmered, festering beneath the surface, fuelling his need for quiet revenge.

Ishan didn't lash out in obvious ways. His sabotage was subtle – a misfield here, a poorly timed wide delivery there. He chose his moments carefully, ensuring his mistakes couldn't be traced back to malice. When the team lost a crucial game, he let the blame fall on Vikram's aggressive field placements, never correcting the narrative.

Ishan's quiet acts of sabotage were fuelled by the dark triad traits of narcissism, Machiavellianism, and psychopathy. He didn't care whether the team won or lost, as long as his own resentment found an outlet. If he couldn't succeed, then no one would.

Every slight mistake ate away at the team's foundation, eroding their confidence, sowing doubt with every seemingly innocent error. Ishan watched with satisfaction as the cracks in the team widened, knowing that his unseen hand was steering them towardscollapse.

RAHUL KHANNA:
THE FRAGILE MACHINATIONS OF A FAST BOWLER

Rahul Khanna, once the powerhouse of the team's bowling attack, was now haunted by the slow betrayal of his own body. His knee injury, long ignored, had finally begun to limit his performance, and he knew it was only a matter of time before the selectors took notice. But he couldn't afford to admit weakness, not when his place on the team was hanging by a thread.

Unable to rely on his physical abilities, Rahul turned to psychological warfare. He began subtly undermining the younger players, particularly Karan Patel. "If we lose, Arjun and Vikram will be fine. It's players like you who'll be dropped," he whispered to Karan, preying on the young batsman's insecurities.

Rahul's manipulation was driven by desperation. He knew that as his body failed him, his mind had to take over. He positioned himself as the experienced hand in a crisis, using his dark triad traits of narcissism and Machiavellianism to plant seeds of doubt within the team. If the team succeeded, the younger players would take the credit. But if they faltered, Rahul would emerge as the wise veteran who had done his best despite impossible odds.

Rahul embodied Machiavelli's principle that the ends justify the means. He saw the team's potential failure not as a loss, but as an opportunity to maintain his relevance. In classic Machiavellian style, Rahul became the architect of the team's destruction, ensuring he remained unscathed in the aftermath.

KARAN PATEL: THE INNOCENT'S FALL

Karan Patel, the youngest and most idealistic member of the team, still believed in the power of teamwork. But as the tournament progressed, the constant whispers, the betrayals, and the pressure began to take their toll. Rahul's words echoed in his mind: "The big names will survive, but you won't."

Karan's unravelling was the tragic by-product of the toxic environment around him. He began second-guessing every shot, every decision. The pressure mounted until, in the semi-final, he found himself frozen in a crucial moment. The ball was coming towards him, and all he needed to do was trust his instincts, take the shot that would save the game. But instead, he hesitated.

The weight of the manipulations, the betrayals, and the fear crushed him. The ball slipped through his fingers, and with it, the team's last hope. Karan's breakdown wasn't just about missing a shot – it was the inevitable result of the psychological warfare that had silently eroded his confidence. He wasn't just playing cricket anymore; he was battling the scars left by his teammates' hidden agendas, a pawn in a game far larger than he ever realised.

THE COLLAPSE: A GAME OF BROKEN MINDS

By the time the final match arrived, the Nizamabad Kings were no longer a team – they were a shattered coalition of individuals, each man locked in a private battle, consumed by his own demons. The once-cohesive unit had dissolved into fragments, and the cracks in their relationships had become chasms.

Arjun, the captain, stood on the field with the weight of his fading legacy pressing down on him. His body, weathered by years of relentless competition, no longer responded the way it once had. Doubt lingered with every instruction he gave. He wasn't leading anymore; he was desperately clinging to what was left of his reputation, fearful that this might be his final act as a leader.

Meanwhile, Vikram, the golden boy, teetered on the edge of a complete breakdown. His eyes, once sharp and confident, were now bloodshot and wide with paranoia. His body, fuelled by the drugs, was unpredictable and shaky. Each swing of the bat was reckless, more an act of survival than skill, as if he could outrun the inevitable crash by pushing himself harder.

Rohan, ever the schemer, watched Vikram closely, sensing his moment. When the ball came hurtling towards Rohan—an easy catch— he hesitated just long enough to let it slip. Deliberate. Calculated. The shock on his teammates' faces was exactly what he had anticipated. In that moment, Vikram's fate was sealed, and Rohan's plans reached their pinnacle.

Ishan continued to sabotage the game from the shadows, letting mistakes compound, knowing they would slowly eat away at the team's chances. A mistimed throw, a misfield, each small error added to the growing chaos.

And then there was Rahul, the once-great fast bowler, reduced to a shell of himself. His knee, ravaged by injury, finally gave out as he sprinted towardsthe crease. His career ended in that moment, with him lying on the ground, clutching his knee, all his mind games now meaningless.

Karan, the innocent, stood at the boundary line with the weight of the team's failure bearing down on him. The ball came towards him, a simple catch, one he had made countless times before. But his hands trembled. His vision blurred. He hesitated, and the ball slipped through his fingers, crashing to the ground. The team's final hope was lost.

The stadium's roar of disappointment swallowed Karan whole. His knees buckled, and he sank into the grass, staring at the ball as if it carried the shattered dreams of his entire team in its arc across the sky. He had one chance, and he had let it slip away, just as everything else had unravelled over the past weeks.

The Nizamabad Kings, once full of promise, had collapsed in spectacular fashion, each man's personal war contributing to the team's ultimate downfall.

THE DARK ENDING

In the aftermath of their crushing defeat, the Nizamabad Kings' dreams of national glory lay in ruins. Vikram's biohacking scandal was exposed, ending his career before it could truly begin. Rohan, who had orchestrated Vikram's downfall, found himself blacklisted for his manipulative tactics. Ishan, the saboteur, faded into obscurity, his quiet acts of sabotage forgotten by all except himself. Rahul's injury ended his career on the spot, and Karan, once the team's bright star, was left broken and irreparable, his belief in teamwork shattered.

And then there was Arjun Nair, the captain who had once embodied unity, standing alone in the empty stadium, haunted by the realisation that his leadership had failed. His final interview was devoid of hope.

"We didn't just lose the game," he muttered, eyes hollow. "We lost ourselves."

EPILOGUE: REFLECTIONS ON THE HUMAN PSYCHE

As I, as an observer of the game, reflect on the collapse of the Nizamabad Kings, I can't help but see how their downfall mirrors a far greater human truth. At its core, this story isn't just about a cricket team; it's about the fragile fabric that holds any group of individuals together when personal ambition is allowed to fester unchecked.

Through the lens of game theory, we see how the prisoner's dilemma played out in real-time. The team, much like society, was bound together by a common goal: victory. And yet, each player was trapped by their own fear of betrayal, their own desire for individual glory. In game theory, the most rational choice would have been for each player to trust the others, to cooperate for the collective good. But humans rarely act rationally when driven by ambition, insecurity, and fear.

Vikram's biohacking—his desire to shortcut his way to success—reflecting the modern world's obsession with quick fixes and achieving greatness at any cost. But the cost, as we see, is often too high. His unravelling serves as a warning against the dangers of cutting ethical corners in pursuit of personal gain.

Then, there's Rohan, the embodiment of Machiavelli's teachings, who manipulated those around him to secure his own position. Rohan's downfall lies in the fact that even the most calculated plans are built on unstable ground when the foundation is deceit. In the end, he outsmarted himself.

The dark triad traits—narcissism, psychopathy, and Machiavellianism—are present in every character to varying degrees.

These traits, though often found in positions of leadership or success, erode the trust necessary for any group to function. They poison relationships, as we see with Ishan's subtle sabotage, Rahul's manipulations, and Arjun's crumbling leadership.

And Arjun—the leader who allowed doubt to infiltrate his mind—stands as a tragic figure, one who could have preserved the team's unity but succumbed to the same selfish desires he fought to suppress. Leadership, in its truest form, demands sacrifice, but Arjun couldn't let go of his personal ambitions.

Ultimately, *this* is a tale of what happens when ambition overtakes trust, when individual desires eclipse the collective good. It's a reminder that in the game of life, the only way to truly win is to ensure that the bonds that hold us together are stronger than the forces that drive us apart.

FINAL THOUGHTS: THE COST OF SELFISHNESS

This is a dark exploration of how unchecked ambition, psychological manipulation, and betrayal can tear apart even the most promising collective efforts. Through the lens of game theory, biohacking, and the dark triad of narcissism, Machiavellianism, and psychopathy, the story reveals how individual selfishness destroys not just a team, but the very spirit of collaboration.

In the end, it wasn't just the match they lost – it was their integrity, their unity, and their souls.

12

THE DREAM WEAVER

THE BROKEN SEEKER

In the ancient, sun-scorched town of **Karnala**, Rajasthan, Samarth Bhargava was both feared and revered. Known for his seemingly supernatural ability to predict events with uncanny accuracy, the villagers saw him as no ordinary astrologer. But behind the facade of a calm mystic lay something far more sinister. Samarth had long transcended the traditional role of a stargazer; he was a master of the **Siddhis**: the mystical yogic powers outlined in ancient scriptures, feared for their potential to warp reality itself.

But unlike the sages who pursued these powers to attain **Moksha**: the liberation from the cycle of birth and death, Samarth used them for selfish gain. His darkest secret was **Swapna Siddhi**, the ability to enter and manipulate the dreams of others. Through this power, Samarth built a vast criminal empire, bending the minds of his victims, embedding compulsions deep within their subconscious, forcing them to commit heinous acts upon waking.

Samarth's descent into selfishness did not arise from a mere lust for power. In his early years, he had been a genuine seeker of truth, a young man enamoured by the mysteries of the cosmos. His family came from a long line of scholars, immersed in the teachings of the **Vedas** and the **Upanishads**, and Samarth was no exception. He began his spiritual journey like many others, seeking enlightenment and liberation from the painful cycle of **Samsara**, the endless loop of birth, death, and rebirth. But unlike the sages who renounced the world, Samarth could never escape his deep attachment to the material world, especially after the loss of his beloved father.

As a boy, Samarth's father was his anchor – a man of great knowledge but little material wealth. His father's untimely death left Samarth with a void, and the family was plunged into financial ruin. The village elders, who once respected his family, began to treat them with condescension, and Samarth's bitterness grew. He saw how the world worshipped power, control, and wealth, and he resolved to never be vulnerable again. His deep-rooted fear of weakness and helplessness shifted his quest. The spiritual teachings of **Moksha** and liberation began to feel distant, almost hollow. To Samarth, what was the use of dissolving into the infinite when life in the present was filled with cruelty and suffering?

This inner conflict festered until he encountered the forbidden knowledge of the **Siddhis**. The sacred texts described these powers as divine gifts, meant to be transcended on the path to liberation. But to Samarth, they represented a means to reclaim control. His mastery of **Swapna Siddhi**, the ability to enter the dreams of others, became a tool of vengeance and security. With each intrusion into the minds of his victims, he felt his power grow, and his fear of vulnerability diminish. The spiritual path that once called him towardsfreedom was replaced by a darker, more tangible pursuit, the power to control the fate of others, to bend the universe to his will.

CHOOSING POWER OVER LIBERATION:

Samarth's motivation to selfishly wield his powers rather than seek liberation was rooted in his desire to escape the suffering of his mortal life. The loss of his father and the subsequent humiliation his family endured scarred him deeply. He could not accept the impermanence of life, nor the fragility of existence. For Samarth, the teachings of the **Mandukya Upanishad**, which spoke of transcending the ego and realising the unity of the **Atman** (the individual soul) with **Brahman** (ultimate reality), seemed futile. For practitioners of Advaita Vedanta, this realisation is paramount, the dissolution of the ego into the infinite, where one recognises that the **Atman** and **Brahman** are one and the same. Samarth, however, had always chosen to ignore this. Instead of seeking his own liberation, he selfishly indulged in the power of manipulating others through their dreams, tying himself ever deeper to the **Samsara**, the cycle of birth, death, and rebirth. His lust for control over others had confined him to the very illusions from which the Upanishads urged release.

How could he find peace in the dissolution of the self when the world he lived in was so chaotic and unforgiving?

Instead of striving for liberation, Samarth chose to use his powers to control the world around him. The Siddhis gave him the ability to manipulate, dominate, and protect himself from the forces that had once hurt him. He believed that by bending the wills of others through their dreams, he could construct a life free from the unpredictability and suffering that had plagued him. His obsession with control became his own trap, binding him further to **Samsara**, as his actions accumulated heavy karma. The power he craved was, in fact, the very thing that kept him ensnared in the cycle of birth and death, preventing any hope of release.

Samarth's tragedy was that in his quest for invulnerability, he chose attachment over detachment, control over surrender, and in doing so, unknowingly forsook the very liberation he once sought.

THE WEAVER'S TECHNIQUE

He had one guiding rule: enter the dream, plant the thought, and escape before the dreamer awoke. Yet, in the boundless mysteries of the cosmos, rules are fragile. As Samarth's ambition grew, so too did his recklessness.

In the dim light of his sanctuary, where oil lamps flickered against ancient scrolls, Samarth Bhargava's fingers traced the worn pages of the **Mandukya Upanishad**, one of the most cryptic and profound texts of Advaita Vedanta. The Upanishad, consisting of only twelve verses, delves deep into the nature of consciousness and the ultimate reality. It describes the self as transcending the waking, dreaming, and deep sleep states, arriving at the **Turiya**, the fourth state of pure, formless awareness: **Brahman**. This state is the closest one can come to liberation.

Sushupti, the deep, dreamless state, was always a realm Samarth meticulously avoided. In his mastery of dreams, he thrived on the vulnerability of the subconscious, where thoughts, fears, and desires were exposed. But Sushupti, as described in the **Mandukya Upanishad**, was an entirely different dimension, one that terrified even a man of his power. This state was the closest to **Turiya**, the fourth and ultimate state of pure, undifferentiated consciousness, where the boundaries of the mind and ego dissolve into nothingness. It was a realm of formlessness, beyond the reach of desire and manipulation, a state where neither duality nor individuality existed. For Samarth, it was a place of profound danger, not because it was hostile, but because it rendered his powers useless. In the dream world, he could mould minds, warp perceptions, and manipulate the fragile strands of human thought. But in **Sushupti**, there were no thoughts to manipulate, no dreams to weave. The ego, which he so carefully relied on for control, vanished in this deep, silent void. Here, even the most powerful beings, stripped of their identities and ambitions, had no foothold.

For a man like Samarth, who thrived on the control of others, **Sushupti** was a realm that symbolised the ultimate loss of power, the dissolution of self. It was the closest one could come to liberation, to **Moksha,** where the self merges with the infinite. But Samarth had no interest in merging with the infinite. His existence was tied to domination, to keeping his individuality intact, and to bending the wills of others to avoid his own vulnerability. In **Sushupti**, he feared not only the loss of control over others but also the terrifying prospect of losing control over himself. It was a state where even the illusion of power crumbled, leaving only the formless expanse of consciousness that he had spent a lifetime avoiding.

But Samarth's empire had grown vast. His greed now surpassed his caution. The idea of wielding control over even this sacred, untouchable space began to fester in his mind.

THE FIRST TREMOR

Samarth's influence now stretched far beyond the sun-baked deserts of Rajasthan, infiltrating the criminal networks of neighbouring regions with a subtle, terrifying grip. Among his most critical assets was **Raghav,** a ruthless and cunning drug lord who controlled one of the largest smuggling routes in northern India. Raghav had once been easy to manipulate, an ambitious, self-serving man who thrived in the chaotic underworld. Like so many others, he had fallen victim to Samarth's dream manipulations, unknowingly carrying out sinister deeds planted in his subconscious. But unlike most of Samarth's puppets, Raghav was no ordinary criminal; he was fiercely intelligent. Over time, he had begun to resist the subtle dream manipulations, an unsettling anomaly in Samarth's otherwise unchallenged reign of control.

Raghav's defiance presented a growing problem. He was no longer the reckless, opportunistic thug Samarth had easily bent to his will. Years of brutality and survival in the drug trade had sharpened him, forging a man who was as calculating as he was dangerous. Beneath his outward appearance of a kingpin lay a mind constantly aware of threats, both seen and unseen. Though Raghav didn't fully understand the source of his sudden impulses or strange dreams, his instincts told him something unnatural was at play. He began to fortify his mental defences, his insomnia worsening as he subconsciously fought off the intrusion into his psyche. The more he resisted, the more Samarth's manipulations weakened.

This growing resistance was more than a mere inconvenience; it threatened the delicate web of control Samarth had spun over his vast empire. Raghav had become too powerful, too integral to the criminal networks, and his rebellion could inspire others to follow. To maintain his dominion, Samarth knew he had to reassert his dominance, swiftly and decisively. But Raghav was no longer a passive victim. His mind had become a fortress of dark paranoia, filled with mistrust and guarded by an iron will forged in blood and betrayal.

Samarth prepared for the most intricate and dangerous intrusion of his life. Entering Raghav's mind now would not be a simple manipulation, but a battle of wills. He would have to break through the layers of mental fortifications Raghav had unconsciously built. The plan was clear: Samarth would enter his mind and plant a final, devastating thought, one so powerful that it would obliterate Raghav's resistance and lead to his inevitable downfall. It would be a thought that destroyed him from within, making him his own worst enemy. But deep down, Samarth knew that this wouldn't be just another manipulation, it was a war for control over one of the most dangerous minds he had ever encountered.

Late that night, Samarth sank into deep meditation, his consciousness travelling into the shadowy realms of sleep. But as he reached for the familiar landscapes of Raghav's dreams, he found nothing. No shifting subconscious, no images to twist. Raghav had entered **Sushupti**, the deep, dreamless sleep state.

For the first time, Samarth hesitated. He knew well that to tamper with the formless void of Sushupti was to risk losing himself. But his arrogance overpowered his wisdom. Ignoring the danger, he plunged forward, determined to exert his control.

The moment he crossed the threshold, Samarth knew he had made a grave mistake.

THE TRAP OF SUSHUPTI

Inside Raghav's mind, there was no dream to control, only a vast, oppressive silence. Samarth had entered the ultimate state of consciousness described by the Mandukya Upanishad, but he was far from liberation. Instead, he found himself trapped in a void that defied comprehension, a realm where his powers were meaningless.

Sushupti had dissolved all duality. There were no desires, no fears, no thoughts, just pure, unbounded awareness, an ocean of silence beyond the grasp of ego. And worse, Raghav was no ordinary man. Unbeknownst to Samarth, Raghav had attained the state of a **Jivanmukta**, a liberated soul still walking the Earth, but free from the illusion of reality, transcending the limitations of karma. A Jivanmukta is one who has reached the ultimate realisation while still in the body. Though physically alive, they have detached themselves from the binding effects of desire, fear, and the dualities of life. Such beings no longer see themselves as separate individuals but as the embodiment of pure consciousness, untouched by the cycle of birth and death. Raghav had crossed the threshold into this rare state, existing in the world yet utterly unshackled by its illusions.

The paradox of **Raghav's transformation** was striking. A man who had once thrived in the underbelly of crime, driven by greed, violence, and ambition, had somehow found a path to spiritual liberation. The path that led him there was not one of peace or asceticism, but of sheer existential exhaustion. Over time, the brutal life Raghav had led—the constant bloodshed, betrayals, and the pursuit of power—had paradoxically emptied him of all attachment. His experiences, though soaked in darkness, had eroded his ego, layer by layer, until there was nothing left to cling to.

The constant confrontation with death, the meaningless repetition of violence, and the weight of his own sins had triggered an inner awakening, though not in the traditional sense. Raghav had come to realise that everything he sought—wealth, control, survival—was an illusion. The very fear that once gripped him in battle had dissolved into a cold, detached acceptance of life's impermanence. In that detachment, he found freedom. He no longer feared death, nor did he crave the pleasures of life. His mind had gradually become empty, and in that emptiness, **liberation** had arisen, not through virtue or spiritual practice, but through the stark, existential truth that nothing in this world could satisfy or define him.

This realisation made Raghav a Jivanmukta, though outwardly, he remained the same ruthless figure. His criminal empire still existed, but he now moved through it as a ghost, a man untouched by the very world he once dominated. To those around him, Raghav seemed more dangerous than ever. He carried an aura of invincibility, of calm indifference that unnerved even his closest allies. It was as if nothing could reach him; nothing could harm him, not because of his physical power, but because he no longer cared for any outcome. The world of cause and effect, of desires and consequences, had ceased to matter to him.

For Samarth, this revelation was disastrous. His entire strategy relied on exploiting fear, desire, and weakness, the fragile elements of the human psyche that he twisted to his will. But in **Raghav**, there were no desires to manipulate, no ego to exploit. His mind had transcended the very framework in which Samarth operated. As a Jivanmukta, Raghav no longer lived within the boundaries of the karmic game Samarth played. He was free from the illusions of reality, and in that freedom, he had become untouchable. Samarth had entered the mind of a man who had already escaped the trap of existence, and in doing so, had unwittingly walked into a prison of his own making.

Samarth's mind, accustomed to manipulating the vulnerable subconscious, was powerless in the face of such pure consciousness. In the Sushupti state, he was stripped of his control. He could not plant thoughts, nor could he escape. He was trapped in the boundless void, where the fabric of space-time itself seemed to collapse around him.

THE TESSERACT: A FRACTURED REALITY

Samarth's once formidable ego—the source of his power, control, and manipulation—began to disintegrate as he drifted through the vast, formless void. Here, he found himself in a dimension that defied human comprehension, where the very structure of time bent upon itself, folding and collapsing into intricate loops and distortions. He had entered what could only be described as a tesseract, a multi-dimensional construct where the laws of space, time, and reality no longer held meaning. In this alien realm, chronology was irrelevant. Seconds stretched into aeons, and entire lifetimes compressed into fleeting moments, indistinguishable from the next. His perception fractured, reality fragmented, and Samarth's once-cohesive sense of self began to unravel into the chaotic infinity around him.

The Siddhis, once his most prized possession, powers that allowed him to manipulate others, warp dreams, and bend the fabric of reality, were rendered utterly powerless. In this realm, there was no mind to control, no fear to exploit, no dualities to navigate. He was beyond the world of thoughts, desires, and actions, floating in a plane where all boundaries dissolved. His mind, which had been a sharp tool of manipulation and calculation, now began to fracture under the weight of an incomprehensible reality. There was no foothold for his ego to cling to, no anchor to hold onto in the shifting tides of timelessness.

As he drifted deeper into this tesseract, Samarth's memories—the very threads that held his identity together—began to blur and fade. His once-solid self-image, built meticulously over years of manipulation, domination, and control, scattered like dust in the wind. He could no longer recall who he was or what he had once been. His victories, his conquests, his fears, and his desires became abstract, formless echoes. His ego, the very thing he had fed with power and ambition, began to tear apart piece by piece. He was no longer Samarth Bhargava, the feared and revered astrologer. He was simply an awareness, lost in the infinite void.

In this timeless fold, Samarth could feel himself dissolving. The sense of control that had once defined him was gone. His screams, which once commanded authority and respect, now reverberated through the empty corridors of this dimension, but no sound emerged. No one could hear him, and there was no one left to listen. The void did not respond. His suffering was infinite, a torment beyond pain or anguish, for it was not his body that was suffering, it was the slow, agonising disintegration of his very existence.

THE BLACK HOLE: THE UNRAVELLING OF THE SELF

Within the boundless void, Samarth caught sight of something faint, an eerie, distant glow that both drew him in and terrified him. It was the faint shimmer of a singularity, a black hole pulling him towardsthe event horizon, where all that he was—his body, his mind, and his soul—would be unravelled, atom by atom, thought by thought. As he neared the singularity, time itself twisted further, distorting his sense of distance and reality. Every moment stretched into eternity, yet eternity felt as fleeting as a heartbeat.

His body—though no longer physically connected to the material world—began to disintegrate. The concept of physicality, of form and substance, melted away. His mind, already fractured by the tesseract, now faced complete dissolution. His thoughts, once sharp and defined, were pulled apart as they approached the singularity, stretched thin by the immense gravitational forces of the black hole. His memories, his desires, his ambitions—everything that once constituted Samarth—

began to unravel, as if the very fabric of his being was being ripped apart.

Yet, within this unravelling, something strange remained intact. A small seed of his consciousness—a remnant of his causal body—clung to existence. It was this final, indestructible kernel of his soul that bound him to eternal suffering. In the teachings of the Upanishads, the causal body is the most subtle layer of existence, the essence of the individual soul that carries one's karmic imprints. Though Samarth's mind and body had dissolved, this core element of his being remained, preventing him from complete annihilation. It was as if the universe, in its infinite wisdom, refused to grant him the release of oblivion. Instead, he was trapped in a state of perpetual dissolution, unable to die, unable to reincarnate, and unable to merge with the infinite.

This was Karmic Purgatory, a state of existence far worse than death. Samarth, through his greed and arrogance, had fallen into the deepest trap imaginable: the black hole of ignorance. He had believed that by manipulating the minds of others; by bending the universe to his will, he could escape the cyclical nature of Samsara, the cycle of birth, death, and rebirth. But in his quest for control, he had overlooked the deeper truths of the universe. The very powers he wielded had tied him even more tightly to his karma, and now, in this void beyond time and space, his soul remained bound by the very actions that had once made him powerful.

In this state, liberation was impossible. Samarth's mind had dissolved into nothingness, his body was no longer responsive, and his soul—caught between dimensions—could not move beyond the confines of the singularity. He could not reincarnate into a new life, nor could he dissolve into the infinite, as the Jivanmukta do. Instead, he existed in a liminal space, trapped beyond the cycles of time, his soul suspended in eternal suffering. The black hole had swallowed him, not to release him into the void, but to trap him in the ultimate prison: a state where existence and non-existence merged, leaving him neither dead nor alive, but eternally unravelling.

Samarth, in his arrogance, had believed he could manipulate the universe. But now, in the silent, eternal darkness of the black hole, he realised the ultimate truth: power was an illusion, and the cosmos could not be controlled. His punishment was to remain in this cosmic limbo, unable to reincarnate and unable to dissolve; his consciousness stretched across infinity in a perpetual state of suffering that would never end.

EPILOGUE: THE SILENT VOID

Back in Karnala, Samarth Bhargava's body sat frozen in eternal meditation, his once-vibrant form now cold and lifeless. His skin, once glowing with vitality, had turned an ashen hue. His eyes, which once seemed to hold the secrets of the cosmos, were vacant, hollow pools reflecting nothing but the emptiness within. His chest rose and fell, but the breath was faint, barely a whisper of life. To the villagers who revered him, it appeared as though Samarth had finally reached Samadhi, the ultimate state of transcendence where the soul unites with the infinite. They believed their astrologer had ascended to a state of divine communion, achieving the goal that sages sought for lifetimes.

But what the villagers saw was a cruel illusion. Samarth was not basking in the bliss of liberation. Instead, within the confines of his mind, he was imprisoned in the black void of his own making. Trapped in the eternal tesseract, his consciousness stretched across infinite dimensions, dissolving and reassembling in an endless loop of suffering. He was caught in a timeless fold, where the ego, stripped bare and shattered, faced an agonising disintegration. No amount of spiritual knowledge or power could save him now. His Siddhis, the mystical abilities he had used to dominate and control others, had failed him.

Days passed, then weeks, and still, Samarth's body did not stir. Whispers spread through Karnala like wildfire. At first, they were filled with reverence, many believed he had transcended the mortal plane. But as time wore on, those whispers took on a darker, more fearful tone. The villagers noticed strange occurrences around Samarth's home. At night, faint sounds, like distorted echoes of whispered voices, seemed to seep through the cracks in the walls. Some claimed to have seen shadows move within his house, though no one dared enter. His face, once serene in meditation, now seemed to contort into fleeting expressions of agony, as though the body was a vessel for something far more malevolent than death.

Children, once dared to approach the astrologer's home, fled in terror, claiming that Samarth's vacant eyes followed them, even in his stillness. The elders spoke in hushed tones, warning that Samarth had delved too deeply into the forbidden realms of knowledge, into powers that no man should wield. They began to mutter that his soul was not at peace, that it had become trapped between worlds, neither alive nor dead, but stuck in a purgatorial state of suffering beyond the reach of any ritual or prayer.

Samarth's home stood like a mausoleum, silent, untouched, and slowly decaying. No one dared approach. The villagers, once eager to seek his wisdom, now avoided the place, fearing that something dark lingered within its walls. To the outside world, Samarth Bhargava, the astrologer of Karnala, had simply disappeared. But within his crumbling house, his body sat in eternal meditation, his soul locked in the silent void, beyond the reach of time, space, and redemption.

The stars, which once seemed to bend to his will, now looked down on him with cold indifference. Samarth Bhargava was gone, his essence lost in the void, forever denied the peace he had once believed he could command. The village would never know the full truth of his fate, but the whispers of his downfall echoed in the desert winds, a haunting reminder that some powers were never meant to be wielded.

The truth was more terrifying than they could imagine. Samarth Bhargava had not transcended; he had been consumed by his own arrogance. In his pursuit of ultimate control, he had forsaken his chance at Moksha, the liberation from the cycle of birth and death. His soul, now trapped in a space beyond time and existence, had been cast into a Karmic Purgatory, a prison with no key. He could neither reincarnate nor dissolve into the infinite. Samarth had, in his quest for domination, condemned himself to the silent void, an existence where suffering was eternal and release impossible.

And so, Karnala continued to live on, as it always had, while the name of Samarth Bhargava slowly faded into legend, his home a ghostly monument to ambition gone wrong – a place where even the bravest dared not tread.

13

THE ZERO-SUM LEDGER

THE HEIR OF SHADOWS

Rudra Ahuja sat in his plush corner office, watching the sun sink behind the towering Mumbai skyline. The city was a beast that never slept, its veins pulsing with commerce, ambition, and hunger, just as his family had fed off it for generations. Mumbai itself seemed like an extension of the Ahuja legacy, a relentless force that consumed and created in equal measure. The Ahuja Group, a legend in the financial world, had stood the test of time for over two centuries, weathering market crashes, wars, and global crises as if they were mere blips on a chart.

Yet as he gazed out at the city that never stopped moving, Rudra didn't feel the rush of power he should have. Instead, he felt hollow dread, a gnawing emptiness that refused to subside. The weight of generations pressed down on him, suffocating his every breath. Each pulse was a reminder of the crushing responsibility he had inherited. Since his father's sudden death, the mantle of leadership had been thrust upon him, along with something far heavier: a mystery. Vikram

Ahuja, his father, had been more than just a financial genius. He had been a master of forces that few could perceive, let alone comprehend, wielding powers beyond mere numbers to protect and grow their empire.

Now Rudra was left with little more than cryptic breadcrumbs and a mounting sense of dread, an inheritance of secrets that threatened to swallow him whole.

A gentle knock interrupted his brooding. It was Riya, his fiancée, her familiar presence momentarily warming the cold, sterile office. But even her warmth was laced with frustration, a distance growing between them that Rudra couldn't—or perhaps refused to—acknowledge.

"You've been here every night for weeks, Rudra," she said softly, though her voice carried a sharp edge. "You're losing yourself. And us."

He didn't respond immediately, his eyes fixed on the bustling city below. It was easier to focus on the unchanging, mechanical nature of the city than on the chaos swirling inside him. "I need to figure out what my father left me. There's something more to this than money, more than the company. I can feel it," he finally said, his voice distant, almost as if speaking to himself.

Riya stepped closer; her concern palpable. "Rudra, you're not chasing answers. You're chasing shadows. Your father is gone. You don't have to do this alone. There's more to life than… this."

Her words tugged at something deep within him, a flicker of the life he had once envisioned with her, before everything had turned into this haunting quest. But he couldn't let go of the void that gnawed at him, the void his father's death had left behind. Vikram's last words echoed in his mind, as they had every night since that fateful day: *The ledger is more than numbers. It is balance.*

"What did he mean by balance?" Rudra murmured, barely acknowledging Riya's presence. He wasn't speaking to her; he was speaking to the shadows in his mind, the unanswered questions that grew heavier with each passing day. There was a darkness to his father's fortune, a secret unspoken yet lurking at the edges of every decision, every investment. Rudra knew he was only scratching the surface, and the deeper he dug, the darker it became. He felt it in his bones, something was coming, and he was utterly unprepared.

Riya's hand touched his shoulder gently, a desperate attempt to pull him back from the abyss. "Come home, Rudra," she whispered, her voice tender but pleading. "Before this obsession consumes you."

But as she left the office, her footsteps fading into the distance, Rudra turned back to his computer. The financial records he had been poring over for days had taken on the weight of tombstones, each file a reminder of the empire he was supposed to preserve. They taunted him, their cryptic numbers mocking his inability to understand the true nature of his inheritance. And with each passing night, the shadows surrounding him seemed to loom larger.

THE ANCIENT LEDGER

That night, unable to sleep, Rudra found himself drawn to his father's private study, a room sealed off since Vikram's death, as though it had been waiting for him. The air inside was thick with dust and the lingering scent of old leather, the weight of decades pressing down upon him. The room itself was an enigma, filled with secrets that had died with his father. The mahogany desk, polished and imposing, stood like a monument to his father's intellect, cluttered with the remnants of a mind that had operated on a level few could grasp.

Rudra spent hours combing through books, papers, anything that might provide a clue to the mystery haunting him. Vikram had been meticulous, but there was a sense that something had been deliberately hidden, locked away, waiting to be discovered.

And then, after what felt like an eternity, Rudra found it. In a drawer, hidden beneath layers of old documents, he uncovered a ledger. But this was no ordinary financial record. The pages were yellowed, brittle with age, and covered in symbols and equations that defied logic. The writing wasn't just a record of transactions, it was something far more ominous.

His heart raced as he flipped through the entries. Each one corresponded not to stock prices or market moves, but to global disasters, wars, famines, pandemics. It was as if his family had profited, not by chance, but by design. The ledger chronicled a dark history of gain and loss, not just in markets but in lives.

Rudra's breath quickened. This wasn't merely wealth, it was something darker, something far more dangerous. And then came the encrypted file on his father's hard drive, titled simply *Legacy*.

It took hours to decrypt, but when Rudra finally accessed it, the truth hit him like a tidal wave. The Ahuja fortune wasn't built on smart investments or shrewd corporate conquests. It thrived on suffering. For every dollar the Ahuja Group had gained, lives had been lost, futures destroyed. The ledger was a map, a guide to the cost of human life weighed against the fortune that had kept his family in power for centuries.

His head spun, the pieces finally falling into place. His father hadn't just manipulated markets, he had manipulated reality itself. Vikram had become the gatekeeper of a cosmic balance, ensuring that for every gain the Ahuja family made, there was an equal and opposite reaction somewhere in the world.

When Riya found him the next morning, Rudra was slumped over the desk, eyes bloodshot, his skin pale and clammy. She knelt beside him, her voice trembling with fear. "What have you found, Rudra?"

He looked up at her, his eyes hollow with the weight of realisation. "It's not just wealth, Riya. We've been... causing these disasters. Every time the world suffers, we profit."

Riya recoiled, her disbelief sharp and visceral. "That's impossible. It's madness, Rudra."

But Rudra's voice was steady, as though saying it aloud solidified the horrifying truth. "For every gain, there's a cost. It's not just money, it's life itself. My father didn't just invest in markets. He invested in fate."

THE CURSE OF FORTUNE

The deeper Rudra delved into the ledger's cryptic entries, the clearer it all became. The fortune his family had amassed over centuries was not merely an inheritance of wealth, it was an inheritance of death. The stock market crashes, wars, and natural disasters that had crippled nations weren't just coincidences, they were the very events that had sustained the Ahuja family's survival. His ancestors hadn't just manipulated money; they had manipulated the very fabric of reality itself.

And as the truth settled in, the weight of the curse grew heavier, suffocating him. Riya, once his anchor, grew increasingly distant, unable to understand the depths of his obsession. "You can't keep doing this," she said one evening, her voice breaking with emotion. "You're losing me, Rudra. You're losing yourself."

But Rudra was trapped. He couldn't let go. "My father said nothing is created without destruction. It's a law of nature. For every fortune, there's a loss. I can't escape it."

Riya's frustration finally boiled over. "But you have a choice, Rudra! You don't have to follow his path. You don't have to be bound by this... madness."

But deep down, Rudra knew the truth. He had no choice. The ledger had ensnared him just as it had ensnared his father. There was no turning back. The legacy of the Ahuja family was not one of fortune, it was one of fate.

THE QUANTUM PARADOX

In a desperate attempt to make sense of the forces at play, Rudra sought out Dr. Sameer Rao, a quantum physicist whose groundbreaking work straddled the realms of probability, finance, and reality itself. Dr. Rao had once been a prodigy in his field, revered for his ability to connect the abstract laws of the universe to the tangible patterns in the stock market. If anyone could help Rudra understand the ledger, it was him.

They met in Rao's office, a cluttered space filled with books on chaos theory, quantum mechanics, and economics. The room itself felt like a paradox-disorder and brilliance coexisting in a fragile equilibrium. The physicist welcomed Rudra with a nod, his sharp eyes assessing the young heir before him. There was something about Rudra's desperation that intrigued him, even as it unsettled him.

"You mentioned a ledger," Dr. Rao began, leaning back in his chair. "And how it seems to mirror financial gains and losses on a cosmic scale?"

Rudra nodded; his voice low. "It's more than a ledger, Dr. Rao. It tracks not just wealth but suffering, as if every gain my family made was paid for by someone else's misery. My father... he hinted that it's tied to a balance, a law that governs everything."

Dr. Rao stood and walked over to a whiteboard, picking up a marker. "Balance," he repeated softly, as though tasting the word. "In finance, balance is a simple concept: assets must equal liabilities. But in the universe, balance is far more intricate. It's not just about numbers – it's about energy, matter, and even the fabric of reality itself."

He began sketching equations on the board, his movements precise, as if trying to capture an elusive truth with each stroke. "The zero-sum balance you describe," Rao said, pausing briefly, "isn't just a financial principle. It mirrors the foundations of quantum mechanics. Every action, every decision, every gain has an equal and opposite reaction. But in your case, this isn't just an abstract idea. It's as if your family's fortune is *entangled* with the universe itself."

Rudra's breath caught as he watched Rao's hand fly across the board, the symbols forming a complex web. Each line, each equation seemed to echo something deeper, something fundamental. He could almost see it, the threads of cause and effect stretching beyond finance, beyond money. Every dollar gained was not just profit; it was part of a cosmic equation that demanded a counterweight of suffering.

Rao continued, his voice growing more animated. "What your father understood—and what I suspect he didn't fully share with you—is that you're not just playing with markets. You're playing with the underlying structure of reality. It's quantum entanglement, but on a scale no one has ever theorised before. What happens in one part of the world—let's say a financial gain—has a corresponding reaction somewhere else. In your family's case, that reaction isn't just economic. It's existential. It's life and death."

Rudra's head spun. This wasn't just about wealth anymore. It wasn't even about the ledger. His family, for centuries, had woven themselves into the very fabric of the universe. They weren't just observers; they were active participants in the delicate balance between creation and destruction. His father, Vikram Ahuja, hadn't been a financial wizard – he had been manipulating the strings of the cosmos.

"Are you saying," Rudra asked, his voice trembling slightly, "that my family's wealth is tied to… reality itself?"

Rao nodded, his eyes darkening. "Your fortune isn't just money. It's energy. Every financial move your family made was a ripple in the quantum fabric. Every gain had a cost, somewhere, to someone. It's like a universal scale, always balancing itself, always correcting."

He stepped back from the board, the equations still hanging in the air like ghosts. "Think of the universe as a massive quantum system, with every action—every choice—creating new possibilities. But those possibilities have consequences. Every dollar your family earned came at the cost of something else, whether it was another person's loss or the suffering of an entire region. The entanglement you describe means that these events are linked, what happens to your family affects the entire world, and vice versa."

Rudra's mind reeled. The weight of the ledger suddenly felt suffocating, as though he was caught in a web that spanned centuries, one his family had spun themselves into. Could he ever break free from this cosmic web, or was he destined to follow in his father's footsteps, continuing the cycle of gain and destruction?

"Is there a way to stop it?" Rudra's voice cracked slightly, desperation creeping into his tone. "Can the cycle be broken?"

Dr. Rao's face grew grim. He capped the marker and set it down, the silence in the room almost oppressive. He walked over to Rudra and placed a hand on his shoulder, his voice low but weighted with caution. "To unravel that balance could destabilise everything. It's like pulling a thread from a tightly woven tapestry. Once you start, the entire structure could fall apart. The universe doesn't tolerate imbalance, Rudra. The consequences could be catastrophic."

Rudra's heart sank. He had hoped—desperately—that there was a way out. A way to break free from the curse of his family's fortune without causing more suffering. But now, he realised the magnitude of what he was dealing with. The ledger wasn't just a family artefact, it was a law of existence. His father's cryptic warnings had been more than the ramblings of a dying man. They had been a message. A final instruction.

The ledger is balance

Dr. Rao stepped back, watching as Rudra processed the gravity of the situation. "You see," he continued softly, "there's a reason why your father, despite his genius, never tried to break the cycle. He understood that to do so would tear at the very fabric of reality. The balance must be maintained, or everything will collapse. And if you try to tip the scales too far in one direction… the universe will react."

Rudra felt a chill crawl down his spine. The stakes were far higher than he had imagined. This wasn't just about his family's fortune or even his own legacy. It was about the delicate equilibrium of the cosmos. The ledger didn't just track money, it tracked existence itself. And if Rudra tampered with it, the consequences could be more than he could ever foresee.

He stared at the equations on the board, feeling like a man standing on the edge of a precipice, staring into the abyss. Could he take that final step, knowing that everything—literally everything—hung in the balance?

Dr. Rao's voice broke through his thoughts one last time, soft but unwavering. "The ledger doesn't just record events, Rudra. It enforces them. If you try to break the cycle, you risk breaking reality itself."

Rudra swallowed hard, the weight of Rao's words settling over him like a shroud. The choices before him were stark, and neither offered salvation. He could walk away, preserving the balance but condemning himself to a legacy of suffering. Or he could act, risking everything – his family, his fortune, and the very fabric of reality.

The decision was his, but the cost would be unimaginable.

THE FINAL TEST

Riya confronted Rudra one final time, standing in the doorway of his office, her eyes filled with a mixture of pain and frustration. Her voice wavered, but there was a firmness beneath her words that Rudra had never heard before. "You have to make a choice, Rudra. It's me or this… obsession. I can't watch you destroy yourself any longer."

Rudra froze, his back to her, staring at the data streaming across his computer screen, though the numbers meant little to him in that moment. His heart ached at the ultimatum. He could feel the weight of Riya's words pulling at him, begging him to let go of the ledger, the questions, the madness that had consumed him. For a fleeting moment, he considered it. He imagined leaving the office with her, stepping into the warm night air, walking away from the shadows of his father's legacy and starting fresh. They could rebuild their life together, far from the weight of his family's cursed fortune.

But then, in the silence that followed her words, he felt a darker pull. His father's voice, barely a whisper now but still as powerful as it had been in the last moments of his life, echoed in his mind: *The ledger is balanced.* Those three words had haunted Rudra ever since. They weren't just a riddle; they were a commandment, a law of the universe that he was bound to follow. The weight of generations bore down on him, the Ahuja legacy wrapped around him like chains, and he knew he couldn't walk away. Not now. Not when he was so close.

His father had spent a lifetime playing by the rules, managing the delicate balance between fortune and suffering, but Rudra had found a way to break the cycle. An unprecedented move. A way to sever the cosmic ties once and for all. He could be the one to finally escape the curse of the ledger, to create wealth without pain, to hold power without consequences. All it would take was one final act.

Riya's voice broke through his thoughts, quieter now, more pleading than before. "Please, Rudra. Don't do this. I can't lose you to this... thing, whatever it is. You don't have to carry this burden."

He turned to face her, his eyes dark, hollow, and unreadable. For a moment, she saw the man she loved, the man she had tried so desperately to save. But then, just as quickly, that man vanished, replaced by the cold determination of someone who had already made his choice.

"I'm sorry, Riya," he whispered, the words laced with finality. "But this is bigger than us. Bigger than me. I have to finish what my father started."

Tears welled in her eyes, but she didn't argue. She could see that she had lost him to something far greater than either of them. With a heavy heart, she turned and walked away, the sound of her footsteps fading into the distance. Rudra watched her go, feeling the sting of loss, but he didn't move to stop her. The decision had already been made.

That night, alone in his office, Rudra made his move. His hands moved swiftly over the keyboard, initiating a series of complex financial transactions that sent shockwaves through the global markets. He was flooding them with billions of dollars, liquidating assets, manipulating stocks, transferring wealth in a way that had never been done before. The sheer scale of it was unprecedented. He wasn't just playing the market; he was rewriting the rules.

For a brief moment, as the transactions finalised, Rudra felt a surge of exhilaration. This was it, the ultimate move. He had outsmarted the ledger, found a loophole in the cosmic balance that no one else had ever seen. He would be the first to create wealth without destruction, to profit without loss. He would break the cycle and finally be free.

But as the final transfer was completed, a cold shiver ran down his spine.

At first, it was a subtle feeling, like a breath of wind passing through him. But then it grew. A creeping dread, like ice spreading through his veins, chilling him to the core. The exhilaration drained away, replaced by something far darker. He stared at the computer screen, but the numbers and data no longer made sense. The feeling gnawed at him, whispering that something had gone terribly wrong.

He glanced out of the window. The city skyline was calm, lights twinkling in the distance as if nothing had changed. But Rudra knew better. He could feel it, like the air had shifted, like the universe itself had paused, waiting to react. The balance he had tried to manipulate was not a system that could be cheated. It was a force older than time itself, and now, it was waking up.

The coldness in his chest grew sharper. He tried to ignore it, to tell himself that he had won, that he had beaten the ledger. But deep down, in the quiet part of his mind, he knew that the ledger couldn't be outsmarted. The cosmic balance demanded equilibrium, and in trying to tip the scales, Rudra had set something in motion, something he could no longer control.

As the unease settled deep within him, Rudra sat back in his chair, staring at the quiet city. It was only a matter of time before the world would begin to unravel, and he would be the one to blame.

THE UNRAVELLING OF REALITY

The markets were the first to fall. At first, it seemed like a minor correction – a small blip, something the media barely noticed. But within hours, it became clear that this was no ordinary crash. The stock exchanges in New York, London, Tokyo, and Mumbai were haemorrhaging value at a rate never seen before. Billions evaporated in minutes, and then trillions. Traders and economists worldwide watched in stunned silence as their screens bled red, trying to make sense of the impossible. The world's economic system was unravelling, and no one could stop it.

But this was just the beginning.

As the financial markets imploded, nature seemed to rise in fury. It began with tremors, subtle at first, but growing in intensity. Cities that had never experienced earthquakes before felt the Earth shudder beneath them. In Los Angeles, towering skyscrapers swayed like reeds in the wind, while in Tokyo, buildings buckled under the strain, their foundations cracking like brittle bones. Panic erupted as people fled

     Whispers from the Void: An Anthology

their offices and homes, but there was nowhere to escape. The ground split open in great fissures, swallowing streets, cars, and entire buildings.

In the Gulf of Mexico, a monstrous hurricane formed seemingly overnight, growing with unnatural speed and force. Within hours, it slammed into the coasts of Texas and Louisiana, obliterating everything in its path. Cities that had weathered countless storms before were reduced to ruins. Winds tore off rooftops, uprooted trees, and flung debris like missiles. The sky itself seemed to howl in fury, unleashing its wrath on the helpless population below.

On the other side of the world, the fires began. Wildfires, ignited by lightning strikes, swept through the forests of Australia, California, and Siberia with a speed and ferocity never seen before. The flames devoured everything in their path, turning vast stretches of land into ash. Smoke blackened the skies, blotting out the sun and casting entire regions into an apocalyptic darkness.

In India, Rudra watched the events unfold from the windows of his office. Mumbai was crumbling before his eyes. A massive earthquake shook the city, sending tremors rippling through the skyscrapers and bridges. The iconic Bandra-Worli Sea Link twisted like a snake as its steel cables snapped, sending cars and buses plunging into the Arabian Sea below. The streets were filled with screams, the cries of thousands caught in the chaos as buildings collapsed, crushing everything beneath them.

The air was thick with dust, smoke, and panic. Sirens wailed, but the emergency services were overwhelmed, powerless against the forces of nature. Mumbai, the city of dreams, was becoming a nightmare. Rudra stood frozen at the window, watching as the city disintegrated. His heart pounded in his chest, but his mind was eerily calm, as if detached from the horrors unfolding before him. It was as if he had known, deep down, that this was inevitable.

Nothing is gained without loss, he thought.

The destruction was total, not just in Mumbai, but everywhere. Volcanoes long dormant erupted with terrifying force, spewing rivers of molten lava that incinerated entire villages. Tsunamis surged across the Pacific, slamming into coastal cities in Japan, Indonesia, and Hawaii, drowning everything in their path. The Earth was in revolt, as if the very fabric of reality had torn open, spilling its fury across the globe.

And amidst the chaos, Rudra realised something that chilled him to the core. He had lived up to his name. Rudra, the ancient Vedic god of storms, chaos, and destruction. His father had named him after the destroyer, and now, in his reckless arrogance, he had fulfilled that destiny.

He had upset the balance.

Rudra whispered to himself, almost as if speaking to the forces that now tore the world apart. "I am Rudra, the destroyer... I have unleashed this."

But no one could hear him over the roar of the universe reclaiming its due.

As he stood in his crumbling office, the floor began to shake violently, the glass windows shattering as the building itself groaned under the pressure of the Earth's upheaval. Rudra staggered back, feeling the ground lurch beneath him, and for the first time, panic seized him.

He had thought he could outsmart the ledger, bend the rules of reality to his will. He had believed he could create wealth without destruction, fortune without loss. But he had been wrong. The cosmic scales had tipped too far, and now the universe was redressing the imbalance with brutal efficiency. It was not just his family's wealth that was cursed, it was the very act of defiance against the natural order that had doomed him.

Rudra rushed to his computer, desperate to reverse the transfer, to undo what he had done. But it was too late. The financial systems were collapsing, and the digital networks were failing. The global web of interconnected markets and economies had begun to unravel, and with it, the very structure of society.

The streets below were chaos incarnate. People screamed and fought, looting stores, climbing over the debris in a desperate bid for survival. But there was no escape from the cataclysm. The cosmic ledger demanded balance, and the price of Rudra's hubris was total destruction.

Mumbai continued to fall, building by building, as the Earth trembled beneath it. In the distance, Rudra could see plumes of smoke rising from other parts of the city, and he knew that the destruction wasn't contained here. It was global. This was the unravelling of everything.

His father's words echoed in his mind, haunting him: *The ledger is balanced. Without destruction, there can be no creation.*

But this was different. This wasn't the calculated chaos his father had controlled for decades. This was uncontrollable, wild, primal. Rudra had tipped the scales too far. He had tried to break the ledger's laws, and now, the universe was tearing itself apart to restore the balance he had disrupted.

The final blow came when the ceiling of his office collapsed, the walls crumbling as the building gave way beneath the sheer force of the earthquake. Rudra was thrown to the ground, his body battered by debris. The last thing he saw before the world went dark was the ancient ledger, its pages fluttering in the air like the wings of some vengeful spirit.

And then, nothing.

When the dust settled, the Ahuja empire was no more. The ledger, which had passed through generations, was buried beneath the rubble of a city that had once stood tall as a monument to human ambition. But the universe, in its cold, methodical way, had restored its balance.

Rudra Ahuja, true to his namesake, had become the god of destruction. In his hands, the wealth of centuries had turned to ashes, and with it, the lives of millions.

As the world began to recover from the chaos, slowly, painfully, the legend of the Ahuja family faded into the annals of history. Some whispered that their fortune had been cursed, others that it had been divine justice. But the truth, like the ledger, remained buried, forever hidden in the ruins of a world that had come perilously close to unravelling.

Rudra had sought to defy the laws of the universe, but in the end, he had fulfilled them. Balance had been restored, but at an unimaginable cost.

And as the city of Mumbai lay in ruins, the name *Rudra* was whispered with a new meaning: not just a name, but a reminder that nothing, in this universe, is ever gained without a price.

14

THE OTHER SIDE OF THE COIN

In the remote hills of Wayanad, nestled deep in Kerala's sprawling greenery, lived a man named Kurian. His reputation spread across the villages as a goat herder, a simpleton who farmed the land passed down by his ancestors. To the outside world, he was just another solitary farmer, content in his isolation. But in the shadows of his existence, Kurian was anything but content.

From a young age, Kurian had known only loneliness. His parents, once proud farmers, died when he was still a boy, leaving him the family land and little else. Without siblings or close family, he had grown up among the goats, his only companions. He would watch the village children laugh and play together, their carefree joy gnawing at him in ways he didn't understand. They ignored him, a quiet boy with no friends, a figure on the periphery of their lives.

As Kurian grew older, the isolation hardened his heart. The villagers, wrapped in their own lives, never invited him to festivals or celebrations. He would watch from a distance, their happiness like a dagger to his soul. In his solitude, he began to nurse a deep resentment, not just for the villagers, but for the very concept of joy itself. Why should they laugh when he felt nothing but emptiness? Why should they find pleasure in life while he was chained to a bleak existence?

The bitterness festered over the years, until it became something darker. For Kurian possessed a darkness that no one in the village understood. He didn't just dislike the joy and laughter of others, he despised it. It irked him to see people happy, their contentment gnawed at his insides like termites burrowing into the core of a tree. His heart, twisted by bitterness, only felt alive when others were in pain, when their suffering mirrored the bleakness he carried within. The sight of smiling faces was an affront to his very existence. The villagers saw him as odd, but harmless, little did they know, he was slowly mastering the art of fear.

His goats, silent and obedient, grazed in the hills with an eerie precision. Kurian cared little for them beyond their utility. His real passion, however, lay in his farm, an array of mysterious plants, known to no one but himself. The villagers thought him odd for growing rare herbs instead of the usual rice and vegetables, but none dared question him. There was something unsettling about the way he moved through life, the way his eyes lingered too long on those who laughed too loudly, who celebrated life too freely.

Kurian's farm was his sanctuary, but more than that, it was his laboratory. Nestled between the hills, hidden from prying eyes, it was a place where dark magic was cultivated under the guise of farming. Years of experimenting with the strange herbs that only he grew in the fertile soil of Wayanad had led him to the perfect alchemy, potions so potent that they could manipulate the deepest recesses of the human mind.

Each plant held a secret, a unique property that Kurian had unlocked through endless trial and error. Some roots could dredge up a person's darkest memories, while certain leaves could blur the lines between reality and nightmare. He had learnt the art of extracting fear from these plants, distilling it into brews that would creep into the mind like an insidious fog. Fears, once hidden deep within his victims, would bloom in their minds like wild, uncontrollable fire.

For Kurian, it wasn't enough to simply witness the fear. No, he wanted to see their worst nightmares manifest before their eyes, twisting their reality into something they could never escape. No one knew the extent of his cruelty. After all, the world thought him simple, a man who herded goats and lived alone. His victims were written off as mad, driven insane by the ghosts of their own minds.

Ghosts of the Past: For a middle-aged woman named Gauri, who had once made the mistake of mocking Kurian's reclusive nature, the hallucinations began subtly. One night, after accepting a cup of tea brewed from the herbs of his farm, she returned home only to be haunted by the spectral vision of her deceased mother. At first, it was just a fleeting glimpse, her mother's face appearing in the reflection of a mirror, her silhouette passing by the kitchen door. But soon, the haunting escalated. Gauri began to hear her mother's voice, accusatory and cold, whispering about all the ways she had failed as a daughter. The apparition would sit by her bedside, stroking her hair, reminding her of her inadequacies. The terror was unbearable, not just because her mother had returned, but because her worst fear—never being good enough—was being voiced by the one person she had tried so hard to please in life. No matter where Gauri went, her mother's ghost followed, and her laughter turned into frantic, incoherent muttering as she descended into madness.

The Demon of Darkness: For a young man named Ravi, who had laughed at Kurian's hunched posture and solitary existence, the punishment was much more visceral. After sipping a seemingly innocent drink offered by Kurian, Ravi found himself tormented by the most primal of fears, darkness. But this wasn't just the absence of light; it was alive, sentient, a thick, inky blackness that would creep into his room at night, suffocating him, whispering things he could not comprehend. His nightmares took on a terrifying form: shadowy figures with glowing red eyes would emerge from the corners of his room, reaching out with long, clawed hands. They would stand over him as he lay paralysed, unable to scream or move. He would feel their cold breath on his skin, hear their guttural voices growling in languages long forgotten. Every time he closed his eyes, they were there, lurking, waiting to pull him into their world. Even in daylight, the shadows stretched unnaturally long, and Ravi could swear they moved of their own accord, swallowing everything in their path. His once-confident demeanour crumbled, and his arrogance dissolved into trembling fear, as the dark twisted him into a shell of his former self.

Twisted Reflections: For Meera, a vain woman who flaunted her wealth and beauty in the village, her greatest fear was losing her looks. After an innocent visit to Kurian's farm, where she carelessly insulted his simple way of life, she became the victim of his cruel magic. Her hallucinations were subtle at first, her reflection in mirrors would seem slightly off. A wrinkle here, a grey hair there, nothing too alarming. But soon, the distortions became grotesque. When she looked into a mirror, her face began to melt and twist, her eyes hollowing out, her teeth falling from her mouth like brittle old bones. No matter how many times she screamed, no matter how much she clawed at her face, the reflection showed her decaying, ageing, and rotting in real-time.

But it wasn't just mirrors, any reflective surface, from the polished silverware to the still water in a bowl, became a window to her worst fear. Her beauty, once the source of her pride, was now a curse. She could never escape the face that stared back at her, a distorted, decayed version of herself, mocking her vanity.

The Flames of Guilt: For an elder named Mohan, who had once cheated his brother out of his land, the hallucinations manifested as fire. After drinking a concoction from Kurian, Mohan began to see flames everywhere he went. At first, it was just the flickering of candlelight out of the corner of his eye, but soon, the flames engulfed everything. His home, his fields, even the very ground he walked on appeared to be burning. Worse yet, he could hear the agonised screams of his brother, trapped in the inferno, calling out for help that would never come. The fire would rise, licking at his skin, though it never truly burned him, yet the sensation of heat was unbearable. The guilt that he had buried deep inside his heart now consumed him, just as the flames consumed the hallucinated world around him. He would run through the village, desperately swatting at the air, trying to put out the fires only he could see. His eyes were wild, his mind shattered by the relentless blaze of his own guilt.

KURIAN'S DELIGHT IN THEIR TORMENT

Kurian reveled in their suffering. He would watch from afar as the once-confident, happy villagers slowly unravelled, their minds corroded by the hallucinations that he had planted within them. What seemed like an innocent sip of tea or water had plunged them into a waking nightmare from which they could never wake. Their fears, ghosts, demons, and twisted reflections clung to them like vines, choking the life out of them.

The sound of their laughter, which had once grated on his nerves, had now transformed into shrieks of terror, muffled cries for help that no one could understand. The villagers would whisper about the ones who had gone mad, but Kurian knew the truth. Their torment was his doing. Every scream was a victory. Every terrified glance over their shoulder, every stammered prayer for deliverance, it was all a testament to his power over them.

Kurian's heart would swell with twisted satisfaction when he saw the once-vibrant Gauri shuffling through the streets, muttering to the air as if in conversation with someone invisible, her eyes hollow and haunted. Ravi, who once strutted around the village, now cowered in the corners of his home, too afraid to venture outside after dark, his entire life consumed by his fear of the shadows. Meera, once the belle of the village, now avoided all mirrors, her once-groomed appearance reduced to a dishevelled mess as she tried in vain to escape her decaying reflection.

It was perfect, Kurian thought. Their laughter had turned to terror; their joy to suffering. He had taken their happiness and twisted it into the very thing they feared most.

And for Kurian, that was how life was meant to be.

THE PARADOX OF PARADOX

Then one day, a stranger appeared in the village – a traveller by the name of Sanjay, young and full of life. He was passing through, eager to reach the nearby ashram where he sought spiritual peace. His laughter was infectious, and soon he became a favourite among the villagers. Kurian watched him from afar, his insides twisting with anger at the man's cheerfulness.

One evening, as the sun dipped behind the hills and the sky turned crimson, Sanjay came to Kurian's farm. He was curious, as all newcomers were, about the strange herbs that Kurian grew.

"Your farm looks unlike any I've seen," Sanjay said with a wide grin. "Do you have something for a traveller like me? Maybe something to help with fatigue?"

Kurian's lips curled into a smile, though it didn't reach his eyes. "Ah, I have just the thing," he replied, his voice smooth and sinister. He moved with careful precision, selecting a few leaves from a plant that emitted a pungent smell. Grinding them into a fine powder, he added them to a small vial of liquid. "Drink this, and you'll be well-rested by morning."

Sanjay, naïve and trusting, took the vial with gratitude. "Thank you, friend. I knew I could count on you."

Kurian watched as Sanjay drank the potion in one swift gulp. His satisfaction was immediate, knowing that within hours, Sanjay's nightmares would begin, and his cheerful spirit would be shattered.

But fate had other plans.

As Sanjay swallowed the last drop, something unexpected happened. He began to cough violently, and in his struggle, the vial slipped from his hands. His eyes widened with realisation, and in his panic, he grabbed Kurian by the collar, pulling him closer.

"What... what have you done?" Sanjay gasped, but before Kurian could react, the young man stumbled forward, knocking the vial over. The remnants of the potion spilled onto Kurian's hand, and in the commotion, the sharp end of a thorn from one of the plants pierced Kurian's skin.

Kurian froze as the liquid seeped into his bloodstream. He felt a burning sensation travelling through his veins, and before he could push Sanjay away, a wave of dizziness overwhelmed him.

"No!" Kurian shouted, but it was too late.

The potion—his own creation—had entered his body.

For a moment, nothing happened. Kurian stood there, gasping for breath, his heart pounding in his chest. Sanjay lay motionless on the ground; the potion had already begun its work on his mind. But Kurian felt something much worse creeping over him.

He had made potions to manifest the worst fears of others. But what would happen when his own worst fear became real?

At first, it was subtle. The sound of distant laughter, faint but growing louder. Kurian turned his head, trying to locate the source, but there was nothing there. He stumbled forward, clutching his head as the laughter grew, filling his ears, surrounding him.

"No... no... stop!" he yelled, but the voices only grew louder. And then he saw them, figures dancing in the distance, their faces lit with joy, their bodies moving with grace and lightness. They were happy. They were laughing. And they were everywhere.

The sight of happiness—pure, unbridled joy—was unbearable. It gnawed at his insides, twisted his stomach, and set his mind ablaze with rage. But no matter where he turned, the figures followed. Their faces smiled, their laughter echoed through his mind, and their happiness suffocated him.

Desperately, Kurian ran back to his farm, hoping to find a remedy, something to counteract the effects of the potion. But the hallucinations followed him. The fields, once his sanctuary, were now filled with the sounds of merriment, laughter bubbling up from the Earth like a cruel mockery of his misery.

His hands trembled as he reached for another vial, but his vision blurred. The faces of those who had once feared him now danced before his eyes, their fear replaced by an insidious joy. Ghosts of his own making haunted him, but instead of terror, they brought happiness, an unbearable, unrelenting happiness.

Kurian fell to the ground, his body convulsing as he screamed into the night. The potion had done its work. His worst fear had come to life. He was surrounded by happiness, and it tormented him in a way no pain ever could.

PLEASURE OR PAIN: OR PLEASURE AND PAIN?

In his final moments of clarity, Kurian understood the cruel paradox. The revelation came not like a flash of insight but as a slow, creeping realisation that clawed its way through his mind. Pleasure and pain, joy and suffering – they were not opposites, as he had always believed. They were not two distinct forces battling for dominance over the human soul. Instead, they were intertwined, inseparable, like the twisting vines that once strangled his victims' sanity. Two sides of the same coin, flipped by the hand of fate, only differing in intensity, but never in essence.

Kurian had spent his life under the delusion that pain was the purest form of control, that through causing suffering, he could exert dominance over those who reveled in happiness. He took pleasure in their torment because it mirrored the dark void within him, a void that craved the suffering of others to fill its endless depths. He had always thought that pleasure was weak, a fleeting joy that dissolved into emptiness, while pain was powerful, lingering, and profound. But now, as the potion that had once tormented others worked its way through his own body, Kurian realised how wrong he had been.

Pleasure and pain, as he experienced them now, were inseparable. They existed on the same spectrum. His entire life, he had pursued the darkness of one extreme, thinking it gave him control. But what was pleasure if not a form of suffering when pushed to its limit? What was pain if not a perverse kind of pleasure when it inflicted the desired result? The intensity could shift at any moment, and suddenly, the pleasure he had derived from others' agony had flipped into his own personal torment.

In his hallucination, Kurian was surrounded by laughter, music, and bright colours, scenes of celebration and unbridled happiness. At first, it seemed absurdly joyful, a happiness so exaggerated that it became unbearable. The sound of laughter echoed in his skull, the voices mingling and growing louder, each peal of joy like a hammer striking his mind. The more he tried to escape the scenes of contentment, the more they multiplied. People dancing, smiling, embracing, figures he had tormented, now free from fear, basking in endless joy. But what Kurian experienced wasn't just jealousy or hatred of their joy. It was something far more insidious. He was drowning in the overwhelming, suffocating weight of pleasure itself.

As he stood amidst the hallucination, Kurian realised that the happiness he was witnessing was not a balm to the soul, as he had once thought. It was oppressive. It was unbearable. The more he saw it, the more it resembled the very terror he had inflicted on others. His worst fear, it turned out, wasn't just seeing others happy. It was being consumed by happiness, to the point where it became indistinguishable from pain.

The villagers whom he had once tormented stood before him in his mind, their faces lit with radiant smiles, but their joy felt sinister. Their expressions, twisted in bliss, now seemed grotesque, as though they mocked him. They approached him, not as victims but as tormentors, closing in with their joyous faces, their hands extended, offering him their happiness. Each touch, each smile, felt like a burn against his skin, a searing wave of suffering disguised as pleasure.

Kurian screamed, but no sound escaped his throat. He fell to his knees, clutching his head as the hallucinations intensified. The ghosts of his past victims—the ones he had broken—now surrounded him, not with accusations but with eternal happiness. The joy he had always despised now trapped him in its cold embrace, and he couldn't bear it.

He had believed his power came from his ability to inflict pain, to twist the minds of others until they broke. But now, his own mind was unravelling, not from fear but from joy, an endless, inescapable joy that suffocated him, just as he had suffocated others with fear. His pursuit of darkness had led him here, to the ultimate realisation that there was no true escape from the spectrum of emotion. Pleasure could be just as cruel as pain, just as unbearable, just as inescapable.

In the twisted depths of his mind, the two forces merged. The pleasure he saw in others was his pain. The pain he had inflicted on others was his pleasure. It was all the same – just a shift in perspective, a change in intensity.

For Kurian, the torture lay in the realisation that he had never truly understood the human condition. He had spent his life thinking he could control it, manipulate it, bend it to his will by amplifying the pain in others. But now, as his world spun in a vortex of manic laughter and ecstatic smiles, he realised that he had been just as much a victim of this spectrum as anyone else. He had chased the illusion of control, only to fall prey to it.

And now, trapped in this never-ending loop of joy, Kurian was doomed to suffer the very thing he had inflicted upon others. His mind, once sharp and cruel, was now a shattered mirror, each fragment reflecting the grotesque duality of pleasure and pain. The harder he tried to escape the joy that surrounded him, the more tightly it gripped him. He was no longer the master of others' suffering; he was a victim of his own creation.

In his pursuit of darkness, he had unknowingly created his own eternal prison, one where the boundaries between pleasure and pain no longer existed. He was suspended in the middle of it, torn between the ecstasy he could not endure and the agony he could not escape.

As the night wore on, the villagers noticed the eerie silence from Kurian's farm. By morning, they found him lying in the field, his face twisted in a grotesque smile, eyes wide open, as though he had seen something too terrible to comprehend. His body was still, but his expression was one of a man who had lived through unimaginable torment.

The legend of Kurian, the sadistic farmer, soon became a cautionary tale. They said that he had been cursed by the very spirits he sought to control, that his soul now wandered the hills, trapped in an endless cycle of happiness and despair. They believed that he had been punished for his cruelty, condemned to feel only joy while his soul screamed for release.

But only Kurian knew the truth. In his final moments, he had learnt that pleasure and pain were one and the same, that the difference was not in kind, but in degree. He had believed he could manipulate one while avoiding the other, but now, trapped in the eternal embrace of happiness, he was condemned to feel both forever.

Pleasure or pain? Kurian now knew the answer. There was no 'or'. It had always been *pleasure and pain*, intertwined in a dance as old as the world itself. And now, in the afterlife, he was doomed to dance with both for eternity.

15

THE INFINITE DESCENT

THE CALL OF THE MOUNTAIN

At the base of Mount Kailash, Dr. Aryan Singh's breath came in shallow, strained gasps, not from the thinning air, but from sheer anticipation. Before him rose the colossal mountain, its silhouette etched against the sky like a primordial sentinel, towering above the barren, desolate plains. Mount Kailash was no ordinary peak; it was a forbidden monolith, an enigma standing untouched by human ambition. Its sheer presence seemed to hum with an ancient energy, as though the Earth itself had conspired to safeguard the mountain's secrets, secrets that had eluded humanity since time immemorial.

For millennia, this mountain had been revered by countless generations. To Hindus, it was the abode of Lord Shiva, the destroyer and transformer. To Buddhists, it symbolised the axis mundi, the cosmic axis connecting heaven and Earth. The Bon religion saw it as the spiritual centre of the universe, while Jains believed it to be the site where their first Tirthankara attained liberation. Its myths were woven into the very fabric of time, and its untouched summit had inspired awe, fear, and reverence.

But for Aryan, standing there now, the myths meant nothing. They were distractions, stories designed to ward off the curious and the foolish. He didn't see a holy peak nor a godly abode. To him, Mount Kailash was a question, a question whose answer lay at its summit. It was an energy source, a cosmic anomaly waiting to be deciphered. The mountain, untouched by human feet, had for centuries been more than a geographical landmark; it was a cipher of the universe itself.

The legends surrounding the mountain only heightened its allure. No human had ever reached its summit, not out of reverence, but because it was said that those who attempted it were driven mad, disappearing without a trace. Locals told stories of climbers who had vanished, their minds lost to the mountain's unfathomable energy. The air around Kailash was different, they said, alive with an intelligence beyond human comprehension. The clouds, shifting unpredictably, were believed to conceal the mountain from prying eyes, protecting it from those who sought to understand the incomprehensible.

Aryan, however, was not easily swayed by folklore. He was a scientist, a seeker of truth in a world of superstition. But even he had to admit, as he stared up at the impossibly symmetrical peak, there was something unsettling about it. The way it loomed over him, as though watching. As though waiting.

This mountain, Aryan knew, was not just another summit to be conquered. It was something far more, a gateway, perhaps. A point where the physical and metaphysical converged. The way it stood untouched, towering yet elusive, as if defying the very laws of nature, had drawn him here. Beneath its towering heights, Aryan felt something stir inside him, a primal fear he hadn't known he possessed, a deep-rooted terror that whispered: *Turn back.*

But fear only fuelled his determination.

"The axis mundi," he murmured to himself, eyes locked on the peak. "The centre of the universe."

There was a timelessness about Kailash, as if the mountain was a living paradox, a place where time and space folded into each other, blurring the lines between past, present, and future. The ground beneath his feet vibrated faintly, pulsing with energy, as though the mountain itself was alive, sentient. There was a strange pull in the air, an invisible force drawing him closer, whispering promises of knowledge, of infinity.

But at what cost?

His eyes traced the jagged contours of the peak, a glint of obsession flashing in them. *This mountain will give me the key to infinity.*

Behind him, his team of researchers and mountaineers stood in uneasy silence. The local guides had refused to accompany them past a certain point, warning them of the mountain's sacredness. "No human has ever reached the summit," they had said. "Those who try anger the gods."

Aryan had scoffed at the idea. "It's just a mountain. A unique one, yes, but a mountain nonetheless," he'd told his team. To him, Kailash wasn't divine. It was a battery of energy, a reservoir of untapped potential waiting to be unlocked.

As they prepared for the ascent, his thoughts raced with possibilities. Harnessing the mountain's energy might not just unlock the mysteries of time and space; it could redefine quantum mechanics. The mountain wasn't just a physical climb for Aryan, it was a conceptual summit. *The pinnacle of my life's work.*

Yet, despite his confidence, an unnatural heaviness filled the air as they began their climb. The higher they ascended, the more the mountain seemed to come alive. Sunsets plunged into darkness in moments, stars shifted in unfamiliar patterns, and time felt… wrong.

"Dr. Singh," Ravi, one of his climbers, whispered nervously. "It feels like… the mountain is watching us."

Aryan shot him a hard look. "Don't be ridiculous, Ravi. Focus. We're on the verge of something extraordinary."

But the further they climbed, the more the fear in his team began to swell.

The Quantum Distortions

By the time they reached the midpoint of Mount Kailash, the climb had become a brutal test of endurance. The thinning air clawed at their lungs, each step heavier than the last, as though the mountain itself was resisting their ascent. What had begun as a mere physical challenge now felt like a descent into madness. The further they climbed, the more reality seemed to blur and bend, warping into something unrecognisable.

Time, which had once flowed in predictable rhythms, now behaved erratically. At first, it was subtle, daylight flickering in and out, as though the sun couldn't decide whether to rise or set. But soon, the changes became violent. One moment the sky was painted with the soft hues of dusk, and in the next, darkness swallowed them whole, without the gradual decline of evening. The stars above blinked in and out like faulty lights, rearranging themselves into constellations that no one had ever seen before.

Priya, one of the team's researchers, gasped, her voice barely audible in the thin air. "Look at the sky," she whispered, pointing upward with a trembling hand.

Two moons now hung overhead, slightly overlapping, casting an eerie, doubled glow on the landscape. Their pale light bathed the snow in an unearthly glow, making it seem as though the mountain itself was dissolving into shadows. Aryan could see the panic on Priya's face, the wild disbelief in her wide eyes.

"This is unnatural," Ravi muttered, his chest heaving as he clutched at his heart, struggling to breathe through the tightening fear. "We need to turn back. Now."

Aryan, however, was unfazed. In fact, he was exhilarated. He marvelled at the distortions unravelling before him, his mind racing to keep up with the theories that had once seemed like the fantasies of theoretical physicists. "Temporal and spatial disruptions," he murmured, more to himself than to the others. His voice quivered with excitement as the implications of what they were witnessing unfolded in his mind. "The mountain is acting as a conduit, intersecting timelines, dimensions. This… this is what I came for!"

The air itself seemed to shimmer with potential, vibrating at frequencies that Aryan could almost feel in his bones. He could sense it, the invisible currents of energy threading through the atmosphere, distorting the fabric of reality. He was on the brink of understanding something far beyond his wildest imaginings. The mountain, it seemed, was not just a geological formation, it was a nexus, a point where multiple realities converged and collided.

Priya, on the other hand, was not as eager. Her breaths came in sharp, panicked bursts, her face drained of colour. "Dr Singh, this isn't safe. We're not equipped for this, whatever this is," she stammered, eyes darting around as though the landscape itself might consume them.

Aryan barely glanced at her. His eyes gleamed with an almost feverish intensity as he replied, "We're right where we need to be. Don't you understand? We're witnessing the collapse of multiple realities. This… this is the future of quantum mechanics!"

But Priya wasn't convinced. Her face twisted in terror as the distortions worsened. Time itself no longer adhered to a linear path, moments that should have followed one another in sequence began to overlap and twist into themselves. One moment, Aryan's team was climbing; the next, they were standing still, staring in bewilderment at their own alternate selves. Ghostly figures of themselves flickered in and out of existence, some climbing higher, others falling into the abyss, vanishing without a trace. They watched in horror as their own actions seemed to loop, rewind, and repeat in endless cycles.

Priya let out a strangled scream as she saw an alternate version of herself, standing motionless at the edge of the plateau, her eyes vacant and glassy. The sight of her doppelgänger — a silent observer — was too much for her to bear.

"Turn back!" she pleaded; her voice hoarse with fear. "This mountain… it's warping reality! We need to leave before it's too late."

But Aryan barely heard her. His mind was already racing ahead, consumed by the implications of what he was witnessing. *The mountain is revealing the truth*, he thought, the cold air stinging his cheeks as he pressed forward. *I'm close. So close.*

ENERGY OVERLOAD

As they climbed higher, the distortions grew more intense, as if the mountain itself was testing their resolve. Time fractured around them, rippling in waves that sent shudders through their bodies. The once-familiar rules of the universe no longer applied. They were suspended in a realm where the past, present, and future coexisted, overlapping and intertwining like threads of an unravelling tapestry.

With every step, Aryan felt the mountain's energy thrumming through him, feeding his mind with knowledge he had once thought unreachable. Equations, insights, and revelations that had previously eluded him now filled his thoughts with dizzying clarity. His pulse quickened as the truth of the universe began to unfold in his mind. He could almost see it, almost touch it.

The mountain was not just a conduit – it was an engine of creation, a force that shaped and reshaped reality. It wasn't just a place – it was an idea, a paradox made manifest. And Aryan felt himself becoming part of it, as though his very essence was merging with the mountain's energy.

But his body began to rebel. The intense energy coursing through him came at a price. His nose bled constantly now, crimson streaks staining the snow beneath him. His hands trembled, his vision blurred, and a searing pain pulsed behind his eyes. He could feel his mind expanding, but his body was crumbling under the strain.

"I am the chosen one," Aryan whispered to himself, his voice trembling with both conviction and exhaustion. "This mountain will reveal its secrets to me alone."

Behind him, his team was dismantling. Ravi had vanished, his footprints abruptly ending in the snow, as if he had been wiped from existence. Priya was descending into madness, her eyes wide with terror as she muttered endlessly, "We're not here… we were never here…"

Aryan no longer cared. They were weak. They couldn't see the truth that lay just beyond the summit. *The mountain is testing us,* he thought. His arrogance swelled, fuelled by the overwhelming energy coursing through his veins. *They can't understand it. But I can. I was always meant to reach the summit.*

With every step, Aryan felt closer to unlocking the mountain's true power, but he was also falling apart. His muscles twitched violently, his heart pounded erratically in his chest, and yet, through the fog of pain and exhaustion, he felt exhilarated.

The knowledge... it was worth it. Whatever the cost, Aryan would pay it.

The summit was near. He could feel it, the secrets of the universe were just within his reach. All he had to do was keep climbing.

The Fragmenting Reality

As Aryan neared the summit, reality shattered like fragile glass. The air itself seemed to ripple with cracks, fragments of existence breaking apart and reforming with each step he took. Time, no longer a continuous thread, splintered into disjointed moments. Aryan could see them now, multiple versions of himself walking beside him, shadowed duplicates existing in tandem, yet each slightly out of sync with the others. Some staggered, their bodies wracked with exhaustion, while others climbed with confident strides, their eyes fixed on the summit. A few had already reached the top, only to vanish into the thin air as if erased from reality itself.

"They're all me," Aryan whispered, his voice trembling with awe. "Different timelines... collapsing into one."

His voice seemed to echo strangely in the fractured space around him, as though sound itself was uncertain which timeline to belong to. He watched in eerie fascination as one version of himself took a step forward and instantly crumbled into dust, scattering into the wind before his eyes. Another Aryan, further along the trail, fell into an unseen chasm, his scream swallowed by the mountain's cold silence. Each version of him was living out a different outcome—some succeeding, others failing—but all were bound by the same fate.

These weren't mere illusions. They were real. The mountain's energy had pulled them from alternate realities, intertwining them into Aryan's own. The timelines had begun to collapse in on themselves, converging into a single, chaotic point: *him*. Aryan was the epicentre of this implosion, the focal point through which all these parallel existences intersected. He was living them all, simultaneously.

The weight of infinite possibilities pressed down on him, his mind struggling to contain the flood of consciousness that threatened to overwhelm him. Every version of Aryan that had ever existed or could exist was now present, and the sheer multiplicity of his own self was unravelling his perception of reality.

Priya, barely coherent, stumbled towards him. Her face was gaunt, her eyes wild with terror as she struggled to hold onto her sanity. "Dr. Singh, please," she croaked, her voice barely a whisper. "We shouldn't be here. This place... it's wrong. It's all wrong."

Aryan glanced at her; his face devoid of empathy. The summit was so close now, just a few more steps, and the mountain would reveal its secrets. He could *feel* it, the pull, the invisible force drawing him towards the final truth. *Just a little farther,* he told himself. *Just a little more, and everything will make sense.*

But as he pressed on, the fractures in reality deepened. He began to see not only himself but versions of Priya and Ravi, some dead, others clinging desperately to life. Their bodies flickered like images on a broken reel of film, phasing in and out of existence. One version of Priya screamed in agony, trapped in an endless loop of suffering. Another walked silently alongside her alternate self, their eyes blank, devoid of recognition.

The mountain showed no mercy. It was indifferent to the human lives caught in its web, the timelines crumbling under its colossal weight. For the mountain was not just a geographical formation, it was a force, a living paradox where the rules of time and space unravelled. It had drawn Aryan and his team into its vortex, bending reality to its will, reshaping existence around them.

Each step Aryan took felt heavier, not just because of the physical strain but because he could now feel the burden of countless lives pressing down on him, each one of them *himself.* The energy that had once exhilarated him now felt suffocating, thickening the air, twisting his perception until he couldn't tell if he was moving forward or if the summit was pulling him in against his will.

"They never made it," he muttered, glancing at the flickering versions of himself. "They all failed."

The thought filled him with a cold, detached fear. What if he, too, was doomed to fail? What if the summit held no answers, only death and dissolution? But even in the face of that fear, Aryan pushed forward, his willpower stronger than his doubt. The summit was within reach. He had to know. He had to see.

The Void

Finally, Aryan reached the summit. His breath hitched as he took the last step, expecting some grand revelation, some truth that would transcend the limits of human understanding. But what awaited him was not enlightenment.

It was nothing.

An infinite void stretched out before him, no sky, no stars, no mountain peaks, nothing. The universe had unravelled at its seams, leaving behind a vast, incomprehensible expanse of pure, unbroken darkness. The summit that had seemed so close, so tangible, now felt like an illusion, a gateway not to knowledge but to oblivion.

"This… can't be," Aryan whispered, his voice trembling. He stared into the void, his mind struggling to comprehend what he was seeing. Or rather, what he wasn't seeing. "This… this isn't possible."

But it was. The mountain had been a boundary, a barrier between realities. Aryan had crossed it, only to find that beyond it lay nothingness. The energy that had once fuelled him, that had driven him to climb higher and higher, now drained from his body, leaving him hollow. He could feel it slipping away, taking with it the insight and knowledge he had so desperately sought. His mind, once sharp and brilliant, began to unravel like a thread pulled from a spool. Equations, theories, revelations, they all dissolved into the empty blackness, leaving behind a cold, numbing emptiness.

The universe, he realised, was not something meant to be understood. Infinity was not a concept the human mind could grasp. It was a vast, indifferent abyss – an unfathomable paradox that stretched beyond the limits of comprehension. And Aryan, in his arrogance, had tried to conquer it. He had tried to make sense of the senseless, to contain the uncontainable.

And now, he was trapped. Caught in the web of collapsing realities, his mind and body fractured, fragmented, like the world around him.

He could still feel the alternate versions of himself—dying, suffering, screaming—but they were no longer separate. They were all *him*, woven together into a single thread of existence, bound to the void.

Aryan turned to leave, desperate to escape the emptiness. But as he descended the mountain, a terrifying realisation struck him. With every step he took, he found himself right back at the summit. No matter how far he walked, no matter how fast he moved, he was always returned to the edge of the void.

There was no escape. The mountain had claimed him.

The Eternal Descent – The Śūnyatā

Desperate to escape the abyss, Aryan turned to descend. His body trembled with exhaustion, and his mind, now a fragile shell of what it had once been, begged for release. But as he stepped down the mountain's icy slope, the terrifying truth revealed itself with each agonising step. He never moved farther from the summit, no matter how far he thought he'd descended, he always found himself back at the top, staring once again into the infinite void. The mountain had trapped him in an eternal loop, an endless cycle of climbing and descending, over and over again, as though the very nature of time and space had been undone.

With each ascent, Aryan clung to the hope of escape. With each descent, he was torn from that hope. He died, again and again, only to be reborn at the summit. The very process of dying became as repetitive as breathing, an inevitable part of his fractured existence. His body, once fuelled by the mountain's intoxicating energy, began to disintegrate. His skin cracked and peeled, flaking into the cold wind. His muscles withered, hollowed out by the weight of an eternal burden. His mind fractured under the weight of each death, his consciousness splintering like the very reality around him.

But there was something far worse than the cycle of death and rebirth. Each time Aryan climbed, he absorbed not just his own pain, but the suffering of his alternate selves. Every version of him that had failed, every version that had died or fallen into madness, left behind a fragment of agony. He could feel it, *all* of it. Every scream, every moment of terror, every shred of despair that had consumed his parallel selves reverberated within him. He was no longer a single being. He had become *infinite*, a collective consciousness trapped in an eternal loop, forever fractured by the collapse of timelines.

And this, Aryan realised with cold dread, was the nature of the void he had glimpsed. Not an absence of meaning, but a *void full of meaning*, an infinite wellspring of experience and suffering, bound together by an overarching truth. The truth of *śūnyatā*, the concept of emptiness as understood in Tibetan Buddhism. The mountain had not revealed the universe's ultimate secret as Aryan had hoped. Instead, it had revealed the fundamental nature of reality itself: that all things, all experiences, all suffering, are empty of intrinsic self, endlessly interconnected in their voidness.

This was not nothingness. This was *emptiness*. The void Aryan had stared into was the heart of *śūnyatā*, the truth that all phenomena, including his own suffering, were insubstantial. All the versions of him that had climbed, fallen, died, they were not separate from him, nor were they separate from the mountain. They were interconnected in a vast web of dependent origination, bound by the eternal nature of emptiness.

Yet, this knowledge did not bring him peace. He was still trapped. Trapped in the *Samsara* of this cycle, caught in the very loop that symbolised the eternal recurrence of life, death, and rebirth. The mountain had exposed him to the terrifying truth that his existence, like all existence, was devoid of inherent meaning, but it also tied him to that cycle in perpetuity. There was no escape from the summit, just as there was no escape from *sūnyatā*. He was part of it now, boundless, infinite, and empty.

The most profound agony was in realising that each rebirth, each climb, was both meaningless and eternal. The same suffering played out in infinite variations across the collapsing timelines. His body may have decayed, but his awareness persisted, forced to confront the void again and again. He was not Aryan anymore, not in any singular sense, he was the sum total of all possibilities, all failures, and all attempts to transcend.

There were moments in the loop where Aryan felt he could grasp the full expanse of this reality, moments where he became lucid, his awareness expanding beyond his immediate suffering. He could see the cycles of *Samsara* and *nirvana*, the Buddhist notions of suffering and release, playing out not only for him but for all who sought the mountain's secrets. They, too, were trapped in the illusion of self, climbing endlessly towardsa truth they could never fully grasp.

But unlike the enlightened ones who could transcend *Samsara* by embracing *sūnyatā*, Aryan was forever bound to the illusion. He had sought power and understanding, not peace. His ambition had chained him to the cycle of eternal suffering, and the mountain had revealed this truth in the cruellest way imaginable. He was both the observer and the observed, the climber and the summit, trapped in an infinite loop of self-reflection, bound to the karmic consequences of his quest for ultimate knowledge.

The Inescapable Loop of Samsara

Years later, a new team of climbers arrived at Mount Kailash, unaware of the fate that awaited them. When they reached the summit, they found Aryan's body perfectly preserved in the snow, as though frozen in time. His face was serene, but his eyes—those who dared to look closely—would see that they still held the vast emptiness of the void within them. But when one of the climbers touched him, something strange happened. They, too, felt the pull of the mountain's energy, as though an invisible force reached out and ensnared them.

In that moment, the climbers were drawn into Aryan's timeline, trapped in the same eternal loop of climbing and descending, seeking answers and finding only emptiness. They had fallen into the same trap, a cycle of ambition, madness, and despair that echoed the teachings of Tibetan Buddhism. *Samsara*, the endless cycle of birth, death, and rebirth, had claimed them too.

Mount Kailash, with all its secrets, remained unconquered. Those who sought its knowledge were doomed to suffer the same fate, an endless cycle of striving for something that could never be attained, bound by their illusions of self and purpose. The mountain, ever watchful, ever silent, had revealed the ultimate truth: that everything—desire, ambition, knowledge, even suffering itself—was *empty*.

Aryan, and all the versions of him, would climb forever, trapped in the karmic cycle of *Samsara*, never escaping the void, never transcending. In the end, there was no enlightenment. There was only *śūnyatā*.

16

THE JESTER OF VARANASI

THE ARRIVAL

Varanasi, the city of eternal life and death, thrived in contradiction. A place where the sacred and the profane coexisted in a delicate dance, the city had witnessed countless souls seeking liberation and countless more trapped in the cycle of birth and rebirth. The ghats along the Ganges, lined with burning pyres, stood as grim reminders of life's inevitable end. Yet, children ran through the narrow alleys, laughing, oblivious to the funerary fires, while cows ambled lazily past rickshaws, paan-stained walls, and crumbling temples.

The scent of sandalwood and incense mixed with the pungent odour of rotting garbage, creating an intoxicating aroma that could be found only here, in Varanasi, a city as alive as it was dead. Temple bells rang out, competing with the cacophony of honking auto-rickshaws, while the rhythmic chants of mantras echoed across the riverbanks. The streets pulsed with a vibrancy that both embraced and defied death.

And into this paradox walked a man known only as Ravanan.

He appeared one morning at the Manikarnika Ghat, the very place where death had become a spectacle. Smoke billowed into the air as bodies burned on wooden pyres, their ashes mingling with the waters of the Ganges, believed to carry the dead into salvation. But where others came to mourn or pray, Ravanan arrived with an expression that seemed out of place, an unsettling grin that twisted across his thin, wiry face.

Dressed in the saffron robes of a monk, he could have been mistaken for one of the many holy men that wandered the ghats. But there was something different about Ravanan. His robes were pristine, not tattered like those of ascetics, and his wild hair, though dishevelled, carried no sign of spiritual detachment. His eyes glimmered with something far darker than the calm resignation of the renunciates, something akin to mischief or malice.

He stood at the edge of the river, watching the pyres burn, his head cocked slightly to one side, as if he found the whole ritual amusing. His gaze shifted to the mourners, the priests, and the tourists who had gathered to witness the age-old spectacle. No one noticed him at first. In a place where death and chaos were routine, Ravanan was just another face in the crowd.

But for those who did look closely, there was an immediate sense of unease. It wasn't just his grin or his robes – it was the aura that surrounded him. He carried with him an air of disruption, as though the very act of standing still had somehow shifted the balance of the ghat.

No one knew who he was or where he came from. In a city as ancient as Varanasi, where time seemed to stretch endlessly, a new face was hardly remarkable. Ravanan could have been anyone, a wandering monk, a traveller, or a lost soul seeking redemption. But there was no record of his existence, no family to claim him, no past to speak of. His arrival was as quiet and unremarkable as a drop of water falling into the Ganges.

Yet within days, Ravanan began to make waves that rippled through the very core of Varanasi.

He moved through the city with purpose, though his exact intentions remained unclear. He was seen at the ghats, at the Kashi Vishwanath temple, even in the narrow alleys where the homeless and destitute sought shelter. Everywhere he went, chaos followed in his wake. Small things at first, temple offerings mysteriously spoiled, priests found arguing with each other over trivial matters, a holy cow blocking the path of a funeral procession.

But as the days passed, the disruptions grew darker.

Priests, politicians, and businessmen—the pillars of Varanasi's society—became the targets of Ravanan's bizarre schemes. Temples were filled with dead fish, left to rot in the sanctum; the private ledgers of corrupt politicians were splashed across public walls, exposing their greed to the masses; corporate elites were humiliated in broad daylight, their secrets laid bare for all to see.

At first, it seemed like a series of cruel pranks, the work of a disillusioned outsider intent on mocking the hypocrisy of the city's power structures. But those who watched closely knew that this was no ordinary mischief. There was something calculated about Ravanan's actions, something purposeful. His targets weren't chosen at random – they were the very people who represented the corrupt heart of the city.

What began as a series of disruptive jokes soon spiralled into something far more dangerous.

THE PRIEST'S SON

Rumours spread quickly in Varanasi, carried on the wind like ashes from the pyres. Some said Ravanan had once been a priest's son, born into a family of devout Brahmins who had served the city's temples for generations. According to this version of his story, Ravanan had been a pious child, well-versed in the scriptures, destined for a life of religious service. But something had gone wrong, perhaps he had seen too much of the hypocrisy within the religious hierarchy, or perhaps he had been betrayed by those he trusted. Whatever the reason, the boy had grown into a man consumed by anger, determined to expose the lies of the very system he had once believed in.

Others whispered a different story, one far more unsettling. Ravanan, they said, was not a man at all, but an escaped mental patient, a dangerous lunatic who had fled an asylum in a nearby city. He was a man without a past, without a name, without any connection to the world. His actions weren't driven by ideology or revenge – they were the product of a fractured mind, a soul lost in its own madness.

Ravanan himself never confirmed any of these tales. When asked, he would only smile, his grin widening as if to suggest that the truth was far less important than the story people chose to believe. He seemed to revel in the chaos he created, letting the rumours grow and twist, each version of his past more fantastical than the last.

But one thing was clear, Ravanan was not just a man; he was an idea, a force of nature that could not be contained by the rules of society. His philosophy was simple, terrifyingly so: *"Everything burns in the end, so why not hasten the process?"*

In a city where death was a daily occurrence, where the cycle of life and rebirth was as constant as the flow of the Ganges, Ravanan's words struck a chord. The downtrodden, the ignored, the betrayed, they saw in Ravanan a twisted messiah, someone who wasn't afraid to dismantle the system that had oppressed them for so long. He became a symbol of rebellion, a dark figure who challenged the very foundations of Varanasi's sacred order.

THE FIRST RIPPLES

It didn't take long for Ravanan to gather a following. His gang was small at first, local thugs, disillusioned youth, and outcasts who had long been ignored by the city's elite. They thrived in the shadows, moving through the alleys and backstreets where the light of the temples could not reach. Under Ravanan's guidance, they began to strike at the heart of Varanasi's power structures.

The first target was a local priest, known for his wealth and influence, though few could say exactly how he had acquired either. One night, his temple was filled with the stench of rotting fish, the sacred offerings spoiled beyond recognition. The priest was humiliated, his authority questioned, but the city's elite dismissed the incident as a minor prank.

Then came the politicians. Private ledgers—containing details of bribes, illegal land deals, and embezzled funds—began to appear on the walls of Varanasi's most prominent buildings. Names were named, and the city's political elite found themselves scrambling to explain how their secrets had been exposed. Once again, Ravanan was blamed, though no one could prove his involvement.

The corporate elites were next. Businessmen who had long profited from the exploitation of the poor were publicly humiliated, their dirty dealings laid bare for all to see. Some were forced to flee the city, while others found themselves ostracised by the very society they had once controlled.

But these were only the first ripples. The true storm was yet to come.

THE TEMPLE BOMBING

A week after Ravanan's ominous arrival, the city of Varanasi was shaken to its very core. The morning started like any other, pilgrims flocked to the Kashi Vishwanath temple, one of the holiest sites in India. The sound of conch shells and temple bells rang through the air as the faithful gathered to offer their prayers to Lord Shiva. Politicians, religious leaders, and businessmen, too, had made their way to the temple, a public display of piety that masked the deep corruption and greed that plagued the city's elite.

It was during the mid-morning aarti that the explosion struck.

The blast tore through the temple with the force of a thousand storms, a thunderous roar that echoed across the ghats and rippled through the narrow streets of Varanasi. The golden spires of the temple, once standing tall as a symbol of divine grace, crumbled into dust as flames licked the air. The explosion sent a shockwave that shattered the stained-glass windows, toppled the intricate stone carvings, and reduced the once-holy site to a smouldering ruin.

Screams filled the air as the crowd descended into chaos. Survivors scrambled through the wreckage, bloodied and dazed, desperately searching for loved ones. Devotees who had come to seek blessings now found themselves amidst carnage, bodies strewn across the temple grounds, the scent of incense replaced by the acrid stench of burning flesh and blood-soaked Earth. The dead included men, women, and children, innocents who had simply come to pray, unaware that their lives would be snuffed out in an instant.

But the most notable among the casualties were the politicians and religious leaders, whose presence at the temple had been an ostentatious display of their devotion. Some were known for their greed, others for their exploitation of faith for political gain. Now they lay lifeless in the rubble, symbols of the very corruption that Ravanan had long despised.

The city was left in shock, its heart bleeding in the aftermath of the tragedy. For centuries, the Kashi Vishwanath temple had stood as a beacon of spiritual resilience, a place where life and death coexisted peacefully. Now, it lay in ruins, its sanctity defiled, its aura of divine protection shattered.

In the hours following the attack, police and rescue workers flooded the scene, pulling bodies from the rubble, sifting through debris in the desperate hope of finding survivors. The streets were lined with mourning families, some in disbelief, others inconsolable in their grief. News of the bombing spread quickly across the nation, and within hours, the eyes of the world were on Varanasi.

Then, like a dark omen, Ravanan's message appeared, scrawled in blood-red paint on the temple's shattered walls: *"Everything you believe in is built on lies."*

It was a statement as chilling as the destruction itself. Ravanan's words cut deeper than the blast ever could, for they spoke to a darker truth that lay beneath the surface of the city, a truth that few dared to confront. Varanasi, with all its ancient glory and spiritual significance, was not as pure as it seemed. Behind the facade of faith, there was greed, corruption, and exploitation. The very institutions that the people worshipped were the same ones that had betrayed them.

THE DIVIDE IN VARANASI

For many, this was the final straw. Ravanan had crossed a line that could never be forgiven. He was no longer a rebellious figure targeting the city's corrupt elite – he was now a terrorist, a monster who had shed innocent blood in the name of chaos. The Kashi Vishwanath temple had been a sacred space, a place where even the most sinful sought redemption. To desecrate it with violence was an unforgivable act, one that had no justification, no matter the message behind it.

Anger and fear spread like wildfire. The police, led by ACP Shivam Rathore, launched a citywide manhunt, scouring the alleys, the ghats, and the rooftops for any sign of Ravanan. Citizens took to the streets, demanding justice for the lives lost, and a curfew was imposed to prevent further unrest.

But for some, the bombing only deepened their admiration for Ravanan. To them, this was not an attack on their faith but a necessary evil to expose the rot within the system. They had seen the hypocrisy of the religious leaders, the greed of the politicians, the indifference of the wealthy elite who pretended to care for the poor while exploiting them behind closed doors. Ravanan had done what no one else dared to do, he had struck at the heart of the very institutions that held Varanasi in their grip. He had made them bleed, not just physically, but morally and spiritually.

Among those caught in the middle was Aarti Mishra, a journalist who had spent months covering Ravanan's rise. She had been fascinated by his philosophy, drawn to his critique of society's corrupt power structures. At first, Aarti had viewed him as a tragic antihero, a man who fought a losing battle against the deeply entrenched corruption of Varanasi's elite. In her mind, Ravanan was not a villain, but a necessary force of rebellion, someone who had chosen to fight the system from the outside because the system itself was irredeemable.

But as she stood amidst the rubble of the temple, watching as bodies were pulled from the wreckage, Aarti felt a growing unease. The faces of the dead haunted her, the innocent children, the elderly men and women who had come to the temple seeking solace. Ravanan's message, once so compelling in its critique of hypocrisy, now felt hollow in the face of such senseless loss. Had she been too willing to believe in his cause? Had she, in her pursuit of the truth, inadvertently become complicit in his rise to power?

Still, Aarti couldn't shake the feeling that Ravanan wasn't finished. There was more to his plan, more destruction to come. And as much as she wanted to condemn him for the lives he had taken, there was a part of her that couldn't look away, couldn't stop wondering if, deep down, Ravanan was right about the world they lived in.

THE DESCENT

For ACP Shivam Rathore, the bombing was more than just an act of terror – it was personal.

His wife and son had been inside the temple when the explosion occurred. They survived by sheer luck, pulled from the wreckage by fellow survivors, but the scars, both physical and emotional, were deep. His wife's face had been badly burned, her once-bright eyes now dulled by trauma. His son, just eight years old, hadn't spoken a word since the attack. The boy had seen things no child should ever witness: death, destruction, the fragility of life laid bare before him.

Shivam had always prided himself on being a man of the law, a cop who played by the rules. But the bombing had changed him. Ravanan had taken everything from him, his peace of mind, his faith in the system, his belief in justice. Now, Shivam's mission was clear: he would stop Ravanan, no matter the cost.

But as the days turned into weeks, Ravanan continued to elude capture, always staying one step ahead of the police. The manhunt was relentless, officers combed through the city day and night, but Ravanan seemed to slip through their fingers like smoke. Shivam found himself growing increasingly desperate, willing to bend the rules he had once held so dear.

He began making deals with informants, offering bribes and threats to anyone who might have information on Ravanan's whereabouts. He used violence to extract confessions, ignoring the legal processes that had once defined his career. Torture, intimidation, blackmail, nothing was off the table. Ravanan's philosophy, the very chaos he had unleashed upon the city, was infecting Shivam, turning him into the very thing he had sworn to fight.

And that was Ravanan's true genius, not in the physical destruction he caused, but in the way he manipulated those around him. He didn't need to lift a finger to destroy Varanasi, he simply had to plant the seeds of doubt, chaos, and fear, and watch as the city tore itself apart from the inside.

The temple bombing was just the beginning. Ravanan had exposed the fragile illusion of order that held Varanasi together, and now, the city was unravelling. Faith, law, and morality, everything that had once seemed so solid was now crumbling in the face of chaos.

THE FINAL SHOWDOWN

It all came to a head at the ghats of Varanasi, where the living and the dead converged. The night was thick with the acrid smoke of

 Whispers from the Void: An Anthology

burning pyres, the river reflecting the dancing flames that consumed bodies and freed souls, or so the city believed. The Ganges, sacred and eternal, flowed calmly, indifferent to the chaos that unfolded on its banks. Here, where countless souls had sought liberation, Ravanan had chosen to set his final trap.

Under the cover of darkness, he had gathered his followers: the misfits, the disillusioned, the downtrodden, those who had long been forsaken by the city's elite. They came willingly, believing in his message that the world they lived in was nothing but a grand illusion, built on lies, corruption, and the false promise of order. Ravanan led them to the river's edge, where the smoke of death hung like a shroud over the living.

ACP Shivam Rathore and Aarti Mishra arrived at the scene, drawn by forces neither could fully comprehend. For Shivam, this was the end of a personal crusade, one that had stripped him of his morality, his faith, and nearly his sanity. He had become a shadow of the man he once was, consumed by vengeance and the desire to end Ravanan at any cost. Aarti, on the other hand, was searching for answers. She had once admired Ravanan, seeing him as an anti-establishment figure, a necessary evil to expose the hypocrisy of Varanasi's powerful. But now, after witnessing the death and destruction he had wrought, she wasn't sure what to believe. Was he a monster, or was he simply the mirror that reflected the true face of society?

As they approached, they saw Ravanan standing on a narrow platform overlooking the Ganges, his saffron robes glowing in the firelight like a dark prophet. Behind him, bound and gagged, were a group of innocent hostages—priests, politicians, and businessmen, the very people Ravanan had spent his life railing against. They knelt at the edge of the platform, their eyes wide with fear, knowing that their fate lay in the hands of a madman who sought to dismantle the world they had built.

Ravanan's grin was wider than ever as he saw them approach. "You're too late," he called out, his voice carrying over the crackling of the pyres.

Shivam raised his gun, his hand trembling with rage. "Let them go," he ordered, his voice strained with the weight of his emotions.

But Ravanan only laughed, a sound as cold and hollow as the void. "Let them go? Why would I do that? These are the very people who have corrupted this city, who have fed off its lifeblood and kept the masses enslaved with their lies. They deserve to burn, just like everything else."

"Don't do this," Aarti pleaded, stepping forward. She could see the madness in his eyes, but also something deeper, something unsettlingly calm. "There's still time to stop."

Ravanan shook his head, his smile never faltering. "No, Aarti. There's no stopping this. You, of all people, should understand by now. This isn't about revenge or violence for the sake of it. This is about showing the world the truth. And the truth is, chaos is the only thing that makes sense."

He stepped closer to the edge of the platform, his gaze sweeping across the burning ghats, the river, the bound hostages, and the figures standing before him. "You see, everything you believe in—order, morality, society—it's all an illusion. Maya. The great veil that blinds you to the truth of existence. The sages of Advaita Vedanta knew this. They taught that the world of appearances, the world of form and structure, is nothing but a play of illusions. Beneath it all, there is only the eternal, the infinite, the unchanging consciousness. But people like them—" he gestured to the hostages— "they have used the illusion of order to control, to manipulate, to enslave. They cling to their power because they believe it gives them meaning, but meaning itself is a lie."

Shivam, his gun still raised, couldn't grasp the depth of Ravanan's words, but he could feel their weight. "Stop this philosophical nonsense!" he barked. "These are real people's lives! This isn't about some grand illusion, you've killed innocent people!"

Ravanan's grin faltered for a moment, replaced by a look of profound sadness. "Innocence? What is innocence in a world where every action is conditioned by illusion? We are all prisoners of our desires, our fears, our egos. The real tragedy, Shivam, is that you still believe in your role as a protector, a defender of this fragile order. But what you fail to see is that you are just another actor in the play of Maya, a cog in the machine of illusion."

Aarti, who had studied enough of Vedanta to recognise Ravanan's references, stepped forward again, her voice softer now. "But what about Brahman? If the world is an illusion, then isn't everything one? The rich, the poor, the corrupt, the innocent aren't we all part of the same underlying reality?"

Ravanan's eyes sparkled with a strange mix of admiration and pity. "Yes, Aarti, you understand. Beneath the veil of Maya, there is no duality. The priests, the politicians, the beggars on the street, they are all expressions of the same infinite consciousness. But that does not absolve them of their actions in this illusory world. The illusion must be broken. And I am the instrument of that breaking."

Shivam's patience snapped. He lunged at Ravanan, tackling him to the ground, his fury overpowering any sense of reason. The two men struggled on the platform, their bodies a tangle of violence and desperation. But as they fought, Ravanan's followers—fanatics who believed in his philosophy of destruction—made their move.

One of them, a young man whose face was streaked with ash from the pyres, detonated a bomb hidden beneath the platform. The explosion was deafening, a thunderous roar that sent a shockwave through the ghats. The burning pyres toppled into the river, and debris flew into the night sky as if the city itself were being torn apart.

When the dust settled, Ravanan was gone. His body was never found, though some believed he had escaped, slipping into the shadows of Varanasi like a ghost. Others said he had perished in the blast, his remains scattered into the Ganges, returning him to the formless, eternal consciousness he had spoken of.

EPILOGUE: THE JESTER'S LEGACY

In the aftermath of Ravanan's final act, Varanasi was forever changed. The city, once a place of spiritual refuge, became a battleground of ideologies. Some saw Ravanan as a martyr, a man who had exposed the corruption of the elite and laid bare the truth of society's hypocrisy. His words about Maya and the illusion of order resonated with those who had long felt disillusioned by the world around them.

Others viewed him as a monster, responsible for the deaths of countless innocents and for tearing apart the fragile peace that held the city together. To them, Ravanan's philosophy was nothing more than a justification for violence and chaos.

Aarti Mishra, haunted by her encounters with Ravanan, left journalism and abandoned Varanasi. She couldn't shake the feeling that she had played a part in his rise, that her fascination with his ideas had given him the platform he needed to spread his message of destruction. But as she walked away from the city, she couldn't deny the power of his words. Was it possible, she wondered, that Ravanan had been right all along? That the world they lived in was nothing but an illusion, and that by clinging to its false promises of order and morality, they were only perpetuating their own suffering?

ACP Shivam Rathore, broken by the loss of his family and his descent into moral ambiguity, resigned from the police force. He had spent his life believing in the law, in the system, in the idea that good would triumph over evil. But Ravanan had shattered that belief, leaving Shivam with nothing but doubt. He had fought to save the city, but in the end, he realised that the city had never been what he thought it was.

And as for Ravanan, he became a legend. Some said he had ascended to a higher plane of existence, freed from the cycle of illusion that bound the rest of humanity. Others claimed he had simply disappeared, biding his time until the world was ready for his return. His message, scrawled across the walls of the city in the days following his disappearance, was simple yet chilling:

"What if the system doesn't deserve to be saved?"

And so, Ravanan—the jester who danced in the flames of a burning world—left behind a legacy of destruction, chaos, and the unsettling truth that perhaps, just perhaps, everything they believed in was built on lies.

17

THE VANISHING SHADOWS

SOLAN, HIMACHAL PRADESH – A SMALL TOWN WITH BIG SECRETS

Solan, nestled quietly in the pine-covered foothills of Himachal Pradesh, was a place where time seemed to stretch and bend at will. The town moved at a languid pace, as though each day was a slow exhalation of the previous one. Its winding roads twisted through forests thick with pine and cedar, the air heavy with the scent of resin. Life here was peaceful, almost dreamlike, but the tranquillity often veiled something far more oppressive, a sense of suffocation. Everyone knew everyone, and secrets, though whispered behind closed doors, rarely stayed hidden for long.

The mist that blanketed Solan in the early mornings and late evenings added to the town's enigmatic nature. It crept down from the hills and through the streets, curling around corners, hiding the familiar from view. To an outsider, it was a place of serene beauty, untouched by the fast-moving world beyond the mountains. But to those who lived here, there was a darker edge to the stillness. The dense forests whispered, and sometimes, if you listened closely enough, the sound wasn't the wind, it was the town itself, breathing, watching, holding onto its secrets.

People arrived in Solan for peace, to escape the chaos of their lives, but often found themselves trapped by the town's quiet yet suffocating embrace. The forest-lined roads, often covered in mist, wound through the hills like arteries, pulsing with a sense of isolation. Once you were here, it was hard to leave, harder still to forget. Everyone in Solan knew each other, yet the same winding roads and dense forests seemed to hide more than just the occasional traveller's car. They concealed lives, lies, and sometimes, people.

THE DISAPPEARANCE

The morning was like any other in Solan, chilly, with the sun barely piercing through the thick mist that clung to the town. Avi Sharma jogged along his usual route, the cool mountain air prickling his skin as sweat beaded down his forehead. His breath came in sharp, rhythmic bursts as he focused on the familiar sound of his running shoes tapping against the stone path. Solan was waking up slowly, as it always did, the town's early risers going about their morning rituals.

As Avi neared his home, a small cottage set on the edge of the forest, a strange feeling crept over him. The house, normally welcoming after his jog, seemed too still. The front door was slightly ajar, a detail he would normally have shrugged off. But something felt wrong. Too wrong. He walked in cautiously, his heartbeat quickening.

The air inside was heavy, unnervingly silent. His eyes swept over the familiar room, taking in the unwashed cups on the counter, the half-open windows letting in the mist, the sofa where he and Naina had sat the night before. Everything was in its place. Everything... except Naina. She was gone.

On the kitchen table, a note lay in the same casual chaos that characterised their life together, except this note brought with it the weight of something far more final.

"I'm leaving you. I can't do this anymore."

Avi's hands trembled as he read and reread the hastily scribbled words. They didn't make sense. Naina wouldn't just leave. Not like this. Yes, they had fought, and yes, she had been distant lately, but leave him? It didn't fit with the person he thought he knew. Or had he been too wrapped up in his own life to notice the signs?

By noon, the entire town was buzzing with rumours. Solan, where even the smallest of news spread like wildfire, had turned its attention to the disappearance of Naina Sharma, the once-vibrant, captivating journalist, now reduced to a woman whose bitterness had driven her to the edge of an emotional cliff. Had she run away? Was it Avi? The questions swirled, and with each whisper, the truth seemed to become harder to grasp.

Inspector Gaurav Singh, the small-town officer known for his sharp eye and methodical approach, arrived at the Sharma residence that afternoon. As he stood at the threshold of the house, the air around him felt unusually heavy, as if the mist itself was watching. The quiet streets of Solan seemed to hold their breath.

"A note?" Gaurav asked, raising an eyebrow as he glanced over the kitchen table. Avi, seated stiffly at the dining table, simply nodded, his face a mask of exhaustion and confusion.

"She wasn't happy," Avi began, his voice steady, but Gaurav could see the cracks forming. The way Avi's hands clutched the arms of his chair a little too tightly, the slight tremor in his voice, the way his eyes darted, searching for an answer that wasn't there.

The inspector scanned the room once more, the unlocked door, the note, the perfectly staged domestic scene. It felt too clean. Too easy. He'd seen this before. Husbands like Avi, who painted themselves as the perfect, loving partners, only to snap when their wives finally reached the breaking point. Or worse, husbands who put on the facade of grief and shock, while knowing full well where their wives were, because they had put them there.

As Avi recounted his morning routine, Gaurav's suspicions grew. He noticed the flicker of uncertainty in Avi's eyes, the faint tremble in his hands. The loving, devoted husband? Or something darker?

NAINA'S PLAN

Naina was far from Solan, though not in the way anyone imagined. Alive, yes. But hiding, wounded from an accident that had thrown her carefully crafted plan into chaos. For months, she had been preparing for this day, her liberation. Her escape from the suffocating life that Avi had trapped her in.

Solan had never been Naina's choice. She had followed Avi here out of love, out of duty, but over the years, love had faded, replaced by resentment. The quiet charm of the town that had once attracted her now felt like a prison. The lively, bustling world she had known as a journalist had been ripped away, replaced by the same dreary faces, the same monotonous routines. Avi, with his calm demeanour and controlling tendencies, had only made it worse. He hadn't locked her away, not physically, but emotionally. He held her there, in Solan, suffocating her with his demands for the perfect life.

But Naina was no victim. She had planned her escape meticulously, leaving behind a trail that would paint Avi as the villain in their story. Emails from a burner account, diary entries chronicling Avi's emotional abuse, carefully staged arguments in front of neighbours, all of it was designed to cast her as the wronged wife, driven to the brink by a controlling husband.

She had it all mapped out: she would disappear and start a new life, leaving Avi to crumble under the weight of suspicion. She had left just enough breadcrumbs to implicate him without ever showing her hand too soon.

But then, the accident happened.

The narrow, winding roads that led out of Solan had always been dangerous, but Naina hadn't expected them to betray her like this. Her car had spun out of control on a particularly sharp curve, careening into the dense forest that bordered the road. She had survived, but barely. Bruised, disoriented, and bleeding, she couldn't go to a hospital. That would raise too many questions. Instead, she limped back towards Solan, her perfect plan slowly crumbling.

THE SHADOWS CLOSE IN

As Naina made her way back to the town she had so carefully planned to leave behind, she couldn't shake the feeling that everything was slipping out of her control. She had always been the one to stay ten steps ahead, but now, the uncertainty gnawed at her. Solan, with its winding roads and dense forests, seemed to be closing in on her, the mist thickening, the air heavier with every step.

And then there was Gaurav. She knew he wouldn't stop. He had a sharpness about him, a quiet resolve that unnerved her. He wouldn't accept things at face value and wouldn't be satisfied with the surface-level explanations. He would dig, and when he did, he would find the cracks she hadn't meant to leave behind.

Naina had thought she could outsmart them all, Avi, the town, the police. But now, as the forest closed in around her and the shadows of her actions began to creep closer, she realised that maybe, just maybe, she had underestimated the game she was playing.

She had become the very thing she feared most – a ghost in her own life, lurking in the shadows of a town that was never meant to hold her. And as she slipped through the mist-covered streets of Solan once more, she couldn't help but wonder: would she ever truly be free of the shadows she had created?

CRACKS IN THE PLAN

Back in Solan, Avi's life was slipping through his fingers like sand. What had once been the comforting rhythms of small-town life had turned into a nightmare. Under the weight of suspicion, his composure began to unravel, thread by thread. At first, it was just a few awkward glances from neighbours, whispers exchanged behind his back at the local market. But soon, the gossip spread like wildfire. The quiet streets of Solan became a feeding frenzy for rumour and speculation. *Did Avinash Sharma murder his wife?*

The media descended on the town with a ferocity Solan had never seen. Reporters, drawn by the tantalising prospect of scandal in a picturesque, sleepy hamlet, camped outside Avi's house, their cameras trained on the windows as if waiting for him to crack. They hounded him on his way to work, on his way home, capturing every faltering step, every strained expression. They spun headlines that suggested guilt without ever directly accusing: *The Loving Husband or a Cold-Blooded Killer?*

The perfect storm had hit, and Avi, once a well-respected teacher and pillar of the community, found himself drowning in it. He had always been a calm man, measured, thoughtful. But as the walls of his life closed in on him, something broke inside. He began to drink. At first, it was just a glass of whisky after dinner, something to take the edge off. But soon, one glass turned into two, then into bottles. The alcohol dulled the shame and confusion that gnawed at his mind, but it also fuelled the growing fire of suspicion. The more he drank, the more erratic he became, stumbling through his daily life in a fog of intoxication and paranoia.

His once spotless image, Avi, the devoted husband and teacher, now lay in tatters. The townspeople began to whisper louder. They stopped inviting him to community events. His colleagues at school distanced themselves, unsure of what to believe. Even the children he taught looked at him with wide, uncertain eyes, as if they were seeing a monster where once there had been a man. Naina's absence had cast a shadow so dark over Avi that no amount of truth could seem to pierce it.

From her hidden vantage point, Naina watched it all unfold. She had orchestrated Avi's downfall with meticulous precision, and now, she savoured the sight of his life unravelling. His polished image had been her cage, but now, as it shattered, she felt a sense of liberation she hadn't known in years. Every misstep he made, every drunken outburst, brought her a sick satisfaction. He was paying for the years of quiet control, the suffocating routines he had imposed on her.

But as the days passed, something began to gnaw at Naina, a sense of unease she couldn't quite shake. It wasn't Avi that concerned her. His downfall was assured. It was Gaurav. Inspector Gaurav Singh, with his quiet resolve, wasn't like the others. He didn't jump to conclusions or accept things at face value. He wasn't swayed by public opinion or the media frenzy. He was too patient, too meticulous. His eyes, calm yet piercing, seemed to see right through the web of lies she had spun. He wasn't satisfied with what appeared to be a neat narrative, and that unnerved her.

Naina had underestimated him, and now she realised she was running out of moves. Her plan, flawless in theory, was starting to fray at the edges. She couldn't leave Solan, not yet, not without raising suspicion. But she couldn't stay hidden forever. The pressure was mounting faster than she anticipated. Desperation was setting in, and Naina knew she needed to take drastic action before Gaurav could unravel everything.

She decided on one final, decisive move: a staged suicide attempt. It was perfect. If she could make it appear as though Avi had driven her to the brink, her role as the victim of a toxic marriage would be cemented. She left a second note, far more damning than the first. This time, the words were laced with bitterness and sorrow, painting Avi as the cold, manipulative husband who had broken her spirit. She crafted the scene carefully, at the edge of a cliff just outside of town, her body appearing fragile and broken, unconscious but alive.

When the police found her, everything would fall into place.

THE DARK DESCENT

The staged suicide worked like a charm. Naina was discovered, as planned, at the edge of the cliff, her body battered and bruised. She was rushed to the hospital, unconscious and frail, clutching the note that blamed Avi for everything. The town exploded with sympathy for her, Naina Sharma, the tragic victim of a toxic relationship, a woman pushed to the edge by the cruelty of her husband.

Avi was arrested immediately. There was no hesitation, no doubt in the minds of the townspeople or the authorities. He was the villain now, a man who had driven his wife to such despair that she saw no other way out but death. The media hailed Naina as a survivor, a woman who had escaped the clutches of an abusive marriage. The narrative was set, and it was airtight.

But not for Gaurav.

In his small, dimly lit office, long after the town had gone to sleep, Inspector Gaurav Singh sat at his desk, surrounded by evidence. Something was wrong. The timelines didn't add up. Naina's behaviour didn't fit with the woman he had been quietly investigating. The witnesses, the neighbours, the stories, they were too convenient. Too clean. Gaurav's gut told him there was more to this story, and his instincts had never led him astray.

Weeks passed, and Avi's trial loomed closer. The town had already made up its mind, Avi would be found guilty, and Naina's suffering would be vindicated. Solan's residents were eager for closure, for the story to end in a neat, satisfying way.

But then, Gaurav found it. A small piece of footage from a CCTV camera outside a local shop. It was grainy and hard to make out, but unmistakable. Naina, walking casually down the street on the morning of her supposed disappearance, smiling. There was no distress on her face, no panic, no fear. She was calm. Collected. She had walked away, not fled in despair. It shattered her entire narrative.

With this new evidence, Gaurav arranged a private confrontation. In a dimly lit interrogation room, he sat across from Naina, the air between them thick with unspoken tension. She was composed, her expression unreadable. She knew she had been caught, but there was something in her eyes, a flicker of amusement, a sense of control she hadn't lost yet.

"I did it," she admitted, her voice steady, almost bored. "I orchestrated the whole thing. Every last detail."

Gaurav leaned forward, his eyes locking onto hers. "And you think that's the end of it? You think you've won?"

Naina smirked, her lips curling into a sinister smile. "I don't need to win, Inspector. I've already won. The town believes me. Avi's ruined. No one cares about your evidence. They've already made up their minds."

She was right. Gaurav could feel his hands tightening into fists beneath the table. No matter how damning the CCTV footage was, it wouldn't matter. The court of public opinion had already sentenced Avi, and in a town like Solan, that was all that was needed. Naina walked free again.

But as she left the room, her confidence unwavering, Gaurav couldn't shake the feeling that the game wasn't over. Not yet. Solan was a town of shadows, and sometimes, the darkest secrets were the ones that hid in plain sight.

THE VANISHING

The sun hung low in the sky, casting long shadows that stretched across the narrow streets of Solan. Naina had disappeared, just as she had planned, slipping into the shadows without a trace. The town had moved on, as small towns do, but not without scars. Solan, once known for its serene beauty and quiet simplicity, had changed. The air felt heavier, the forests darker. It was no longer the peaceful haven it once seemed; the shadows that Naina had unleashed had taken root in the very fabric of the town.

Avi, the once-respected teacher, now lived in a crumbling husk of his former life. His world was in ruins. After his release, he had returned to his home, but nothing felt the same. The whispers that followed him around town never ceased. His neighbours, colleagues, and even strangers stared at him with a mixture of pity and suspicion. The media had moved on to the next big scandal, but Solan's judgement lingered. Avi was a broken man, not because of the accusations alone, but because Naina had shattered his trust in everything, his life, his marriage, his understanding of the world. His days became endless loops of isolation, guilt, and confusion. And though she had disappeared, Naina still haunted him, her presence lingering in every corner of the life she had destroyed.

But for Inspector Gaurav Singh, the case wasn't over. Something about Naina haunted him, refusing to let him move on. He couldn't shake the feeling that there was something more, something darker that he hadn't uncovered. In his quiet moments, he replayed every interaction with her, every clue, every unsettling smile she had given him. The more he thought about it, the more obsessed he became. She was not just a manipulative woman; she was something else entirely.

His digging began to take him deeper into her past, beyond Solan, beyond Avi. He uncovered traces of her in other places, under different names. There were whispers in old police records, an incident in a town two hundred kilometres away where a woman had disappeared under similar circumstances. There were accounts of a husband driven to madness, a family torn apart. Then another town, where a wife vanished, and the husband was left in ruin. The stories were fragmented, buried in local archives, but the patterns were unmistakable. Naina— or whatever her name had been then—was not a victim; she was a ghost, flitting from life to life, leaving destruction in her wake.

Gaurav's obsession with uncovering her true identity consumed him. He stayed up late into the night, piecing together the fragmented puzzle of her past. Every discovery pulled him deeper into a web of lies that seemed to stretch far beyond Solan. But the more he uncovered, the more the line between truth and illusion blurred. Who was she really? Why did she do this? The answers eluded him, always just out of reach.

His investigation led him back to the cliff, the place where Naina had staged her suicide, the place where it had all come undone. It was late evening, and the wind howled through the trees, carrying with it the eerie stillness of the mountains. Gaurav stood at the edge of the cliff, looking down at the rocks far below, where the mist swirled like an ocean of shadows. The setting sun bathed the landscape in a dull orange hue, but all he could see were the dark shapes moving at the edge of his vision. The shadows danced, growing longer as the light faded, as if something was lurking just beyond his sight.

He felt it – the pull of the abyss below, the inexplicable sense that the truth he sought was down there, buried in the darkness. His pulse quickened. He took a step closer, peering into the swirling mist. He was close, so close to unravelling the mystery that had haunted him for months. But something held him back. It wasn't fear – it was something deeper, something darker. A presence that seemed to wrap itself around him, whispering in the wind.

And then he heard it—her voice. Soft, almost playful.

"Looking for something, Inspector?"

Gaurav turned sharply. Out of the shadows emerged a figure, Naina. She stood there, cloaked in the fading light, her expression unreadable. The wind tousled her hair as she stepped closer, her smile curving into something both sinister and inviting.

"You've been chasing me, haven't you?" she said, her voice barely louder than the wind. "All this time. But you'll never catch me."

Gaurav's breath caught in his throat. He reached for his gun, but his hand froze. It was as if the very air around him had turned against him, holding him in place. Naina's eyes gleamed with something otherworldly, something that made the hairs on the back of his neck stand up.

"You should have left it alone, Gaurav," she whispered, stepping closer. "This was never your story to solve."

Gaurav tried to move, but the shadows around him seemed to close in. They swallowed the light, wrapping themselves around him like invisible hands. He could feel his body growing heavier, his mind fogging. It wasn't fear that gripped him, it was the cold realisation that he was too late. Whatever force Naina was wielding, whatever dark game she was playing, had already ensnared him.

"I know what you are," he muttered, his voice barely audible. "You can't keep running."

Naina's smile widened, but it wasn't a smile of amusement. It was a smile of triumph. She tilted her head slightly, her eyes glinting in the growing darkness. "I don't have to run, Inspector. I never have. It's you who will disappear."

Before he could react, the shadows surged forward. They engulfed him, pulling him towards the edge of the cliff. The wind howled louder, but Naina's laughter cut through it, sharp and chilling. Gaurav's foot slipped on the loose gravel, and in that final moment, he saw her watching, calm and composed, as if she were merely observing the inevitable.

The last thing he heard was the echo of her laughter as the abyss swallowed him whole.

18

THE SAINT OF DUALITY

The wind howled through the narrow streets of Khonoma, a secluded village nestled in the misty highlands of Nagaland, carrying with it the sharp scent of burning pine and damp Earth. The village stood frozen in time, with terraced fields cascading down steep mountainsides, where homes made of stone, bamboo, and thatch clung to the landscape like remnants of an ancient era. At the edge of this forgotten world, a lone figure sat beneath a towering fig tree, its roots twisted deep into the Earth like the mysteries the figure carried within.

Clad in simple white robes, with a head shaved save for a tuft of hair, the man was as still as the stone that surrounded him. To the villagers, he was a wandering Saint, his silence and detachment evoking both reverence and fear. No one knew his origins or his purpose. He was simply there, an immovable observer, quietly waiting as the pulse of Khonoma beat on.

Beneath the village's surface of serenity and age-old resistance to the modern world, the Saint saw what others could not. His cold gaze penetrated the veil of peace, sensing the threads of darkness woven within the fabric of Khonoma's existence. The village, like the world at large, clung to notions of right and wrong, of good and evil. But the Saint knew better. He was no ordinary mystic, no saviour, no healer, no purveyor of miracles. His journey across India, from Ladakh's stark deserts to the lush jungles of Kerala and Mumbai's chaos, had taught him one undeniable truth: there was no absolute good, no absolute evil. Every act of kindness carried within it the seeds of destruction; every selfish deed bore the potential for salvation. The world was nothing but a dance of duality, an eternal ballet of light and shadow.

Khonoma was to be his grandest stage, the village where his ultimate experiment would unfold.

THE HEALER'S SHADOW

Morning mist draped the steep hills of Khonoma like a shroud as the Saint silently entered the village. Here, life moved in rhythm with the Earth, untouched by the fast currents of the world beyond the mountains. The villagers lived in a fragile harmony, governed by the cycles of planting and harvesting. To the outsider, Khonoma appeared as a sanctuary of peace, a bastion of timeless tradition.

But the Saint knew better. Beneath this peaceful veneer, the delicate balance of Khonoma's existence teetered on the edge of collapse, waiting for the slightest push to fall into chaos. The Saint would be that push.

As dusk fell one evening, painting the mountains in hues of orange and gold, the Saint found himself seated next to Noknei, Khonoma's revered healer. She was the heart of the village, a woman whose hands, weathered by years of service, had saved countless lives with her herbal remedies and unyielding compassion. To the villagers, Noknei was a beacon of goodness, an untouchable paragon of virtue.

But the Saint saw deeper, beyond her outward kindness. He saw the shadow she cast, the heaviness that weighed on her spirit, a burden borne from the relentless pressure to always be good, always be the healer.

"You have healed many," the Saint said softly, his voice as calm as the twilight that enveloped them.

Noknei smiled faintly, her eyes clouded with weariness. "It is my duty. What else could I do?"

The Saint studied her carefully, noting the strain in her voice. "And has your duty brought you peace?"

Her smile faltered. She glanced down at her hands, now still in her lap. "Not always," she admitted quietly. "Sometimes I wonder if what I do truly makes a difference. The world remains broken, no matter how many I save."

The Saint's lips curled into a knowing smile. "What if your kindness does more harm than good? What if, by healing one, you are condemning others in ways you cannot see?"

Noknei turned towards him, her brow furrowed in confusion. "What do you mean?"

"Every action has ripples beyond our control," the Saint said, his voice soft but sharp. "What if your healing has upset a balance you were never meant to touch? What if your kindness is the very thing that creates chaos?"

His words cut through her like a knife, embedding doubt in the heart of her certainty. Noknei turned away, troubled by the implications. She had always believed in her role as a healer, but now, doubt gnawed at her. What if the Saint was right?

THE RIPPLE OF KINDNESS

Noknei's doubt became a reality sooner than she could have anticipated. A year earlier, she had saved the life of Kense, the village's most skilled hunter, after a wild buffalo had gored him in the depths of the jungle. Her intervention had been hailed as nothing short of a miracle, and Kense had been praised for his resilience and courage.

But what followed could not have been foreseen.

Kense, emboldened by his survival and the adulation of the villagers, became reckless. He began venturing deeper into the forest, hunting with an almost maniacal determination. His newfound invincibility drove him to kill more than necessary, disrupting the delicate balance of Khonoma's ecosystem. The wild animals, deprived of their natural prey, began to descend upon the village, raiding food stores and trampling crops. Where once there had been harmony, now there was fear and scarcity.

Noknei's act of healing had not saved the village. It had unleashed a wave of destruction, the consequences of which rippled out beyond her control. As the villagers struggled to protect their livelihoods, Noknei found herself haunted by the Saint's words.

The Saint, watching from the shadows, smiled. The balance had been tipped, just as he had predicted. Goodness, unchecked, had become a source of ruin.

THE MERCHANT'S GREED

In a quieter corner of Khonoma, away from the village's terraced fields and communal warmth, stood the opulent home of Zuhmie, the wealthiest man in the region. Zuhmie had built his fortune trading goods between the villages of Nagaland, skilfully exploiting the isolated communities and their reliance on external supplies. Unlike the beloved healer Noknei, whose generosity had woven her into the fabric of the village, Zuhmie was a figure cloaked in mistrust. His riches came not from the fruits of honest labour but from his cunning manipulation of the villagers' needs. He hoarded food, tools, and supplies, driving prices higher as the villagers grew more dependent on him.

The people whispered about him – how his wealth had been amassed at their expense, how his heart was as cold as the coin he so fiercely guarded. And yet, they had no choice but to buy from him, for he controlled the flow of goods that sustained their lives. Zuhmie thrived on their desperation, convinced that he held the key to Khonoma's survival.

One evening, as the mist descended and cloaked the village in shadows, the mystic approached Zuhmie under the pretence of seeking alms. The merchant, his face a mask of disdain, tossed the mystic a single, tarnished coin.

"You are wealthy," the mystic observed, his voice soft but cutting. "Yet you give so little."

Zuhmie, reclining comfortably amidst his hoarded wealth, scoffed. "I have worked hard for what I have. Why should I give it away to the likes of you? Wealth protects me, and only a fool would squander it."

The mystic's eyes gleamed, the faintest smile curling at the edge of his lips. "Do you not fear that your greed will bring ruin upon you?"

Zuhmie laughed, a hollow, empty sound that echoed off the stone walls of his home. "Fear? Wealth is my shield. It places me above the rest of this village, beyond their struggles. I need not fear anything."

The mystic leaned in closer, his voice calm yet sharp as a blade. "What if your greed, though selfish, is doing more good than you realise? What if, by hoarding your wealth, you are unknowingly ensuring the survival of others in ways you cannot see?"

Zuhmie's laughter died in his throat, his curiosity piqued despite himself. The mystic's words, strange and unsettling, began to fester in his mind. Over the following days, they took root, growing like a dark seed within him. Could it be, Zuhmie wondered, that his greed was a hidden virtue? That by making life harder for the villagers, he was actually helping them?

And so, convinced of his newfound righteousness, Zuhmie raised the prices of his goods even higher. He rationalised that by forcing the villagers to struggle, he was building their resilience, making them stronger, more resourceful. After all, hadn't his own struggles forged him into the man he is today? The mystic's words echoed in his mind, justifying every selfish act.

But what Zuhmie failed to realise was that his greed, like all things, had consequences beyond his control.

THE HIDDEN GOOD IN GREED

As Zuhmie's prices soared, the villagers of Khonoma found themselves at a breaking point. Unable to afford even the most basic necessities, desperation drove them to seek alternatives. The once isolated and self-reliant families began to band together, forming new systems of bartering and mutual aid. They traded food, tools, and labour among themselves, bypassing Zuhmie's stranglehold on the village's economy.

It began with small exchanges—eggs for rice, firewood for vegetables—but soon grew into a thriving network of cooperation. The villagers, once fractured by their individual needs, now stood united in their shared struggle. They no longer depended on Zuhmie's goods or his inflated prices. Instead, they had created a system of self-sufficiency, a way of life that made them stronger than they had ever been before.

Ironically, it was Zuhmie's greed that had driven them to this realisation. His relentless pursuit of wealth had forced the villagers to adapt, to find new ways to survive without him. What Zuhmie had intended as a means of control had become the very thing that empowered them to break free.

Zuhmie, isolated in his wealth, began to feel the sting of his own irrelevance. His storehouses, once the lifeblood of the village, were now filled with unsold goods, rotting in the dark. The villagers no longer needed him. His wealth, once his greatest weapon, had become his prison.

From the shadows, the mystic watched with satisfaction. Zuhmie's greed, like Noknei's kindness, had rippled out into the village in ways neither could have predicted. Both had acted from their own moral compasses—Noknei from compassion, Zuhmie from selfishness—and yet the results had defied their intentions.

The Saint's theory was proving true once more: good and bad, kindness and greed, were mere illusions. In the grand dance of life, all actions—whether noble or selfish—had consequences beyond the grasp of those who enacted them.

And as Zuhmie sat alone in his wealth, the villagers of Khonoma thrived, stronger and more united than ever before. Greed had, in the end, sown the seeds of their resilience.

THE FINAL CONFRONTATION: A VILLAGE DIVIDED

Tension simmered like a pot on the verge of boiling over in Khonoma. The village, once a harmonious enclave bound by tradition and shared values, had unravelled, its moral fabric frayed by conflict. What had once been a place of unity now stood divided between two opposing forces, embodied by Noknei's compassion and Zuhmie's greed. As they stood on opposite ends of the village square, it was clear that the final reckoning had come.

Noknei, the once-revered healer, now looked like a shadow of herself. Guilt weighed on her frail frame; her eyes sunken with sleepless nights spent questioning her purpose. She had withdrawn from the village, no longer healing, paralysed by the fear that her kindness had caused more harm than good. The crops had withered, wild animals had begun raiding their stores, and her heart had grown heavy with every failure she could not mend.

At the opposite end of the square stood Zuhmie, the merchant whose greed had torn through the village like a knife. Once, he had been feared and respected for his wealth, but now, he stood alone, isolated in his riches. His face, once brimming with arrogance, now flickered with the uncertainty of a man who had lost control of the very thing that had sustained him. He had convinced himself that his actions were necessary, that by exploiting the villagers, he had made them stronger. Yet the same wealth that had shielded him from the world now felt hollow, a monument to his own undoing.

The sun blazed overhead, but the air between them felt cold, as if the village itself held its breath.

"You've ruined this village with your greed," Noknei said, her voice trembling with emotion but unwavering in conviction. Her hands, once used for healing, now hung limp by her sides, their purpose lost.

Zuhmie sneered, though his arrogance was fading. "And you, with your soft-heartedness, have done the same. You've made them weak, dependent on your kindness. At least I've forced them to fend for themselves. My actions—though harsh—have given them strength."

The villagers, once a united front, stood divided, their loyalties torn between the two. Some, their faces hardened by the struggles they had endured, sided with Zuhmie. They believed his cruelty had forged their resilience, had made them self-sufficient in ways they hadn't been before. Others, still clinging to Noknei's past kindness, believed that without her, they would have been lost long ago. The village, once bound by a single moral code, had become a battleground for conflicting ideologies.

THE DANCE OF DUALITY

At the edge of the square, the mystic stood, a silent observer of the chaos he had set into motion. His eyes, cold and detached, gleamed as he watched the village tear itself apart, not in bloodshed but in spirit. His experiment was nearing its climax, and as he witnessed the confrontation between Noknei and Zuhmie, he felt the quiet satisfaction of a plan unfolding perfectly.

Their battle wasn't about right or wrong. It was a battle of shadows, of half-truths and unintended consequences. Noknei's kindness, once believed to be an unassailable virtue, had sown chaos. Zuhmie's greed, though cruel, had forced the village to adapt and survive in ways no one had foreseen. Both had acted with the conviction of their moral compasses, and yet neither had been able to control the ripple effects of their actions.

The mystic smiled—a slow, knowing smile—as the pieces fell into place. His theory had proven true once more: there was no absolute good, no absolute evil. Only the endless, shifting shades of grey that danced in the wake of human choices.

"Kindness weakens, greed strengthens. Strength corrupts, and kindness saves. And yet, neither can exist without the other," he whispered, though no one heard him. It was the paradox of duality, the eternal dance of shadows and light.

The villagers, once so sure of themselves, now stood on the precipice of a deeper truth. The lines between good and evil had blurred so much that they no longer knew where one began and the other ended. As they gazed at the two figures before them, they were left with a haunting question: who had really saved the village, and who had destroyed it?

THE DARKENING TRUTH OF DUALITY

The sun began its slow descent behind the jagged mountains, casting long, twisted shadows that crept like sinister fingers across the village square. The villagers watched in silence, their gazes shifting from Noknei to Zuhmie, once beacons of morality, now tainted by the consequences of their choices. The air thickened with uncertainty, the once-clear distinction between right and wrong fading like the light that slipped beneath the horizon. In the dimming glow, the two figures, who had once stood as extremes of goodness and greed, now blurred into one, echoes of the same broken ideal, fractured by the weight of their actions.

The silence stretched, suffocating, as if the village itself waited for something to break. And then it did. Not with a bang, but with a quiet, creeping dread.

Noknei, her voice cracked and hollow, finally spoke. But this time, her words carried not the certainty of righteousness, but the weariness of a soul tainted by doubt. "We are all bound by our choices. But it's the consequences we cannot see that define us." Her eyes, bloodshot and empty, did not rest on Zuhmie, but on the villagers, an unspoken accusation. "I thought I was healing, saving... but in the end, I only gave you more burdens. I didn't cure your wounds. I merely spread them."

A chill spread through the crowd. The villagers, once grateful for Noknei's kindness, now felt the weight of her words pressing down on them like a heavy fog. Her healing had made them dependent and weak, and now, standing in her guilt-ridden shadow, they felt exposed, fragile, unprepared for the harshness of the world she had shielded them from.

Zuhmie's sneer, once sharp as a blade, softened into something far more disturbing – an understanding devoid of remorse. "I thought I was making you stronger, showing you how to survive. But my greed... it blinded me. I turned your struggle into my gain. And now, I stand here with everything I've taken – and it means nothing."

The villagers shifted uneasily. Some remembered the days when they had cursed Zuhmie's name, but now, looking into his hollow eyes, they felt an uncomfortable kinship with his cruelty. His greed had forced them to adapt, to become resilient, but had it also hollowed them out, turning them into something less human?

The truth was clear: neither kindness nor greed had been enough to save them. Noknei and Zuhmie were not their saviours, they were their ruin. And perhaps, they were reflections of the villagers themselves, who had clung too desperately to these extremes, seeking salvation where there was none.

A murmur rippled through the crowd, not of understanding, but of fear. The realisation that no one—not Noknei, not Zuhmie, not even the Saint—had the answers. They had placed their faith in absolutes, but now those absolutes had twisted into something monstrous. The rigid morality they had once held onto was crumbling, leaving behind only an abyss of uncertainty.

The mystic, his eyes cold and detached, watched as his experiment unravelled in front of him. He did not smile, there was no need. His work was complete. The village of Khonoma had fallen, not by violence or destruction, but by the slow, creeping rot of moral decay. Noknei and Zuhmie had played their roles, and the villagers, in their confusion, were now left to confront the uncomfortable truth: there was no right, no wrong, only the endless, shifting chaos of consequence.

He turned from the square, his white robes trailing like ghosts behind him, and began his slow, deliberate walk towards the mist-covered mountains. His form, blending into the twilight, disappeared as silently as he had come. There were more villages, more souls to test. The dance of shadows would continue, its rhythm eternal, its melody one of suffering and ambiguity.

And as the mystic vanished into the mist, the villagers were left with nothing but the hollow echo of their duality, good and evil, kindness and greed, now twisted beyond recognition. It was not righteousness that would save them, it was the cruel, ever-shifting balance between light and shadow, where salvation and damnation were indistinguishable from one another.

19

THE VOID NEXUS: THE ULTIMATE SHOWDOWN

THE WHISPER FROM THE VOID

Time doesn't exist in the same way for those who seek control. For the Saint of Duality, time had long ceased to be a rigid structure. It was an abstract tool, a flexible substance he could bend, stretch, and manipulate in his eternal task: balancing the forces of light and darkness that permeated the multiverse.

To understand the Saint, one must first understand the nature of his purpose. He existed not as a mere entity, but as a manifestation of equilibrium. In a universe composed of infinite possibilities, each with its own chaotic variables. The Saint was the invisible hand that tipped the scales, ensuring that neither good nor evil, order nor chaos, ever gained dominion over the other. The multiverse, in all its fractured timelines and parallel realities, existed in a fragile state of harmony, and the Saint was its guardian.

He was an observer, and yet more than that. He was an actor, a player in the game, even though he had never seen himself as such.

His interventions were subtle, nudges here and there, guiding souls to make choices that would realign the balance of existence. He did not command, nor did he dictate; he simply placed the pieces on the cosmic board and allowed them to move of their own accord. But as he had come to realise, control—true control—was illusory.

For millennia, the Saint of Duality had operated this way across countless realities and dimensions. Yet, somewhere deep in the folds of the multiverse, a whisper had begun. At first, it was faint, a barely perceptible hum beneath the fabric of time and space. But over the centuries, it had grown louder and more insistent until it was a constant presence in his mind, a force older than time itself, calling out from the void between worlds.

The Saint had ignored it for as long as he could. His task was too important, his purpose too sacred. But the whisper persisted, gnawing at the edges of his thoughts, casting shadows over his once-clear sense of duty. He had tried to silence it, to drown it out with the rhythmic balancing of the multiverse. Yet, no matter how many souls he guided, no matter how many timelines he corrected, the whisper grew louder, as though it were feeding on the very act of his intervention.

Now, standing at the threshold of an ancient temple, hidden deep within the labyrinthine alleys of Varanasi, the Saint realised he had been led here, not by choice, but by inevitability.

THE ANCIENT TEMPLE OF VARANASI: THE EVENT HORIZON OF THE VOID NEXUS

Varanasi, one of the oldest cities in the known world, held secrets far deeper than the visible layers of time-worn rituals, ancient traditions, and the sacred waters of the Ganges. Beneath the city's chaotic streets, where pilgrims and seekers wandered in search of meaning, there lay something far older, something forgotten by time, even by the cosmic forces that governed existence. But not by the Saint.

The temple before him was no ordinary place of worship. To most who passed by, it appeared abandoned, its structure crumbling under the weight of millennia. But to the Saint of Duality, who could see beyond the veil of mere physicality, the temple was far more than a sacred site, it was a gateway, a convergence point, where all realities, all timelines, and all dimensions bled into one another. This was the Void Nexus.

For as long as the Saint had existed, tasked with maintaining balance across the multiverse, he had avoided this place. He had known of its presence for aeons, sensing it across every dimension he touched. The Void Nexus was not a space of balance; it was an event horizon, the boundary of a grand black hole that transcended the physical universe. It was a black hole not just of matter, but of realities, a singular point of absolute chaos where all existence collapsed into nothingness.

This black hole, the Void Nexus, was the antithesis of creation. It was the opposite of existence, yet in a strange, paradoxical way, it was necessary. The multiverse itself, with its infinite timelines, alternate realities, and quantum uncertainties, required balance. And that balance demanded an end – a final point where everything returned to its source.

Without the void, existence could not endure. All realities, no matter how diverse or infinite, eventually reached a point where they had to collapse back into singularity, into the void. For the multiverse to continue, there had to be something to counteract its constant expansion, its endless possibilities. The Void Nexus was the ultimate equaliser, the place where all realities met their inevitable end.

THE ROLE OF THE VOID: BALANCING EXISTENCE

The multiverse was not infinite, despite appearances. Every quantum particle, every choice, every possibility spun outwards, creating new realities, new dimensions, but they could not expand forever. At some point, every branch of reality, every timeline, would converge again at the event horizon of the Void Nexus. It was a fundamental law, a truth hidden deep within the cosmic fabric: for existence to continue, there must be dissolution. For creation to thrive, there must be destruction.

The void was not an enemy of existence; it was its counterbalance, the necessary dark to every light, the stillness to every movement. Where the multiverse expanded, fracturing into infinite possibilities through quantum entanglement, superposition, and the observer effect, the void acted as the final destination. It consumed everything—matter, time, space, energy, and even consciousness—leaving only chaos in its wake.

The Saint of Duality, in his quest to preserve the balance between light and dark, order and chaos, had understood this on some level. But he had always kept his distance from the void. He had never dared approach it, for he knew that once inside, there was no certainty, no return. The Void Nexus was a place where the very concepts of reality and illusion dissolved, where even the idea of existence faded into a vast emptiness.

A BLACK HOLE OF REALITIES

As the Saint stood on the edge of the temple, the hum of energy surrounding him felt both familiar and alien. He had felt the presence of the Void Nexus across every reality he had touched, but he had never been this close. The air around him seemed to pulse, not with life, but with the opposite, an energy that consumed, that devoured. It was the pull of the event horizon, the threshold of the cosmic black hole that lay beyond the temple.

This was no ordinary black hole, no collapse of stars or galaxies. This was a black hole of realities. Beyond this point, there were no timelines, no dimensions, no quantum superpositions. The Void Nexus consumed everything, every possibility, every alternate reality, every soul. It was a point of infinite compression, where all of existence was drawn into a singularity so dense that even the concept of existence itself ceased to hold meaning.

For the Saint, this was the ultimate paradox. He had spent aeons trying to maintain the delicate balance of the multiverse, guiding souls and realities, tipping the scales between good and evil, light and darkness. Yet here, at the threshold of the Void Nexus, balance did not exist. There was only chaos, pure, unfathomable chaos, where the rules of time, space, and causality dissolved into the endless void.

And yet, he had come. He had been summoned.

THE WHISPER THAT CALLED HIM

The Saint of Duality had not come to the temple by choice. He had been avoiding it for millennia, believing that the Void Nexus was a place of disorder, a threat to his sacred mission of balance. But in recent years—or rather, across countless timelines—the whisper had begun. At first, it was faint, barely audible beneath the layers of reality. But over time, it grew louder, more insistent, until it was a constant presence in his mind, urging him towards the Nexus.

He had tried to resist, to focus on his work of guiding the multiverse, of ensuring that no one force—be it light or dark, order or chaos—ever gained dominance. But the whisper persisted, growing stronger with each intervention he made. It was as if the more he tried to balance the universe, the louder the whisper became, pulling him closer to the one place he had sworn never to go.

And so, here he was, standing at the edge of the temple, the gateway to the Void Nexus. As he gazed into the abyss, the Saint realised that he had been led here, not by his own will, but by something far more powerful, far older than himself. The force that had called him was not an external threat. It was something deep within the fabric of the multiverse itself, something that had been there since the beginning of time.

He took one last breath and stepped inside the temple, crossing the threshold into the void.

THE PUPPET MASTER: RAVANAN

Unknown to the Saint, his every action, every intervention, had been carefully orchestrated by an unseen hand. A force that had existed since the dawn of time, predating even the Saint's conception of balance. A being whose very existence was a rejection of all order, of all harmony. His name was Ravanan, though names meant little in the grand scheme of things.

Ravanan was not a being of flesh and bone, but of pure chaos. In the eyes of those who had encountered him across various realities, he appeared as a trickster, a master manipulator who reveled in disorder. He was a force of entropy, but not of destruction. Ravanan did not wish to end the multiverse, he wanted to unravel it, to watch it twist and turn upon itself in an endless spiral of madness.

Unlike the Saint, who sought to maintain equilibrium, Ravanan sought to shatter it. Where the Saint saw a need for balance, Ravanan saw opportunity. In chaos, there was freedom, true freedom. The freedom to exist without the constraints of morality, of time, of causality.

For centuries, Ravanan had been watching the Saint, waiting for the moment when the cosmic arbitrator would lead him to the Void Nexus. the Nexus was Ravanan's creation, his masterpiece. It was the point where all realities collapsed into one, where every possible version of existence could be consumed and recreated in his image. Ravanan was not a destroyer of worlds. He did not wish to end the multiverse. He wanted to unravel it, to watch it twist and collapse into madness.

The whispers that had haunted the Saint were not random. They were Ravanan's voice, echoing across the multiverse, subtly guiding the Saint towardsthis moment. And now, as the Saint stood at the edge of the Nexus, Ravanan watched with quiet amusement, his plans nearing fruition.

THE BROKEN MINDS CALLED TO THE NEXUS

Across dimensions, across timelines, in realities that should never have crossed paths, sixteen souls were drawn together by the ripple the Saint of Duality had unknowingly unleashed. They were not chosen for their heroism or morality, but for the fractures that lay within them, fractures that made them susceptible to the call of the void. Each of them had reached a breaking point in their respective realities, where the boundary between order and chaos, reality and illusion, had begun to blur. And in that fracture, the void found its opening.

DR. VIVEK – THE SURGEON'S GUILT

Dr. Vivek had spent his life trying to repair what was irreparably broken. A surgeon, hailed as brilliant, now haunted by the faces of those he could not save. His hands, once steady as steel, now trembled in quiet moments, when the whispers of failure crept into his mind. He saw them everywhere, the faces of the dead. "You let us die," they said. "You failed us." And so, when the walls of his reality began to shift and melt, turning the sterile white of the hospital into an endless stretch of darkness, Vivek did not fight it. The void called, and he let it consume him.

ADITYA MEHRA – THE PHYSICIST'S PARADOX

Aditya Mehra was a physicist on the brink of madness, having spent years studying quantum mechanics, only to realise that he had become lost in its paradoxes. The lines between observer and observed had blurred, and he no longer knew if he was studying reality, or if reality was studying him. He had seen flashes, moments where the universe itself seemed to bend under his gaze. But now, those flashes had turned into something more. The walls of his lab flickered like an old film reel, and as he tried to hold onto the equations, they dissolved into dust. The dust reformed into a single point of light, a black hole, not in space, but in his mind. He reached out, and the light devoured him.

RUDRA AHUJA - THE BILLIONAIRE'S GUILT

Rudra Ahuja stood on the terrace of his high-rise building, staring out at the city below, a city that his wealth and power had helped build. But wealth came with a cost, a karmic debt that he could not escape. Every time he looked at the gilded walls of his empire, he heard the cries of those his family had exploited. The guilt weighed on him like an anchor, dragging him down into a pit from which there was no escape. And then, as if in response to his guilt, the city began to collapse. The buildings crumbled, the lights flickered out, and the sky itself split open. A dark void stretched across the horizon, swallowing the world whole. Rudra did not scream. He simply fell.

AARAV - THE PSYCHOLOGIST'S MAZE

Aarav was a master manipulator, a psychologist who saw people as puzzles to be solved, toys to be played with. He had spent years controlling the minds of others, bending them to his will, enjoying the power it gave him. But recently, the control had slipped. His own mind had become a labyrinth of twisted thoughts, and no matter how hard he tried to navigate it, he found himself lost in the maze. The walls of his office began to close in, and the mirrors that lined the walls reflected not his face, but the faces of every person he had ever manipulated. They smiled at him, their eyes hollow. The void called to him, promising new levels of control. He stepped forward, and the walls collapsed around him.

MAYA - THE DARKNESS WITHIN

Maya had been consumed by darkness, not just metaphorically, but in the literal sense. Her village had been swallowed by an eternal night, a night that never ended, a place where the sun had disappeared forever. And though the others in her village had long since accepted their fate, Maya had not. She had always believed that she could control the darkness, that it was merely waiting for her to command it. She had spent years trying to master the night, to make it bend to her will. But now, as the darkness inside her mind grew, she began to lose herself to it. The void offered her the chance to merge with the night entirely. And she accepted.

DEVAN BARUAH - THE REFLECTION'S OBSESSION

Devan had once loved a woman named Lakshita, but she had left him long ago. Or so he thought. Her reflection, however, never left him. Every time he looked in a mirror, he saw her standing behind him, just out of reach. He had spent years chasing her reflection, trying to find her in every glass surface, every pool of water. He had become obsessed, convinced that if he could only step into the mirror, he could bring her back. The void found him in front of a mirror, staring into Lakshita's eyes. It promised him that if he entered, he could have her forever. He didn't hesitate. The glass shattered, and he was gone.

SAMARTH BHARGAVA - THE DREAM WEAVER

Samarth was a dream manipulator. He had the power to enter the dreams of others, to shape them, to twist them into whatever he desired. It had made him rich and powerful, but it had also made him reckless. Over time, he had lost control, slipping deeper into the dream world until he no longer knew where dreams ended and reality began. He had become trapped in his own dreamscape, haunted by nightmares that he could not escape. The void called to him, offering him the ability to control all dreams, to become the master of an endless dream world. But as he stepped forward, he realised too late that the void had turned his dreams into nightmares, and there was no escape.

NAINA - THE FUGITIVE'S RECKONING

Naina had orchestrated her own disappearance. A criminal mastermind, she had evaded the law for years, always staying one step ahead. But now, the ghosts of those she had betrayed began to catch up with her. She saw them everywhere, lurking in the shadows, whispering her name. No matter how far she ran, she could not escape their voices. The void called to her, promising safety, a place where she could hide from her pursuers forever. She ran into the darkness, but the ghosts followed her into the void.

ARJUN MEHTA - THE GENIE'S CURSE

Arjun had once been granted three wishes by a genie. He had used those wishes to build an empire, to gain everything he had ever wanted.

But the wishes had come with a price. Every time he made a wish, the genie would twist it, turning his desires into nightmares. Now, trapped in a cycle of infinite wishes, Arjun found himself cursed by his own greed. He wished for release, but the genie only laughed. The void called to him, offering him a final wish: to disappear into nothingness, to escape the curse forever. Arjun wished for oblivion, and the void granted it.

THE CRICKETERS - A DEADLY GAME

Arjun, Raghav, Kartik, Vikram, Ishan, and Rohit were cricketers, once a team, now bitter rivals. They had been haunted by visions, each seeing themselves as the hero, the one who would lead the team to victory. But those visions had turned them against each other, their camaraderie dissolved into a brutal competition. The void called to them as they stood on the cricket field, the sky darkening above them, the ground beneath their feet turning to ash. It promised them a final game, where only one could win. They stepped into the void, knowing that the game was already over.

ARYAN SINGH - THE INFINITE DESCENT

Aryan was a physicist obsessed with infinity. He had spent years studying the concept, trying to unlock the secrets of the universe. His obsession had led him to Mount Kailash, a place where he believed he could find the answer to the infinite. But as he climbed the mountain, reality itself began to bend and twist. The higher he climbed, the deeper he fell into a loop of time, an endless descent into infinity. The void called to him, offering him the answers he sought. Aryan stepped forward, only to find himself trapped in an infinite loop, falling forever into the void.

IBRAHIM – THE GHOST OF MEMORY

Ibrahim, a man from Lucknow, had killed his girlfriend in a fit of rage and had since suffered from amnesia, unable to recall the horrific event. His mind had fractured, leaving him haunted by flashes of a past he couldn't piece together. Though his conscious memory of the murder was gone, the void in his soul grew larger every day. He felt her absence like a shadow over his life, her presence lingering just beyond his reach. The void called to him, offering to fill the gaps in his memory, to bring him the truth he had long sought to bury.

SIVA - THE TIMEKEEPER'S CURSE

Siva was a clockmaker who had discovered the ability to manipulate time. He could slow it down, speed it up, or even stop it altogether. However, over time, his control over time had begun to slip. The clocks he built no longer obeyed him, and time itself seemed to fracture around him. The void called to him, offering him the ability to control time on a cosmic scale. But as Siva stepped forward, he found himself trapped in an endless loop, where every moment repeated itself forever, with no way out.

KURIAN - THE SADIST'S NIGHTMARE

Kurian was a sadistic farmer who derived pleasure from the suffering of others. He had created potions that induced hallucinations, forcing his victims to relive their worst fears. But one day, he accidentally ingested one of his own potions, and his worst nightmare came to life. He was surrounded by joy, by people laughing and celebrating, and it drove him mad. The void offered him the chance to escape his hallucination, to return to the world where he could control others' suffering. But as he stepped into the void, he realised that his nightmare was eternal, and the laughter never stopped.

ARJUN – THE PERIPHERY OF REALITY

Arjun, a lawyer once regarded as brilliant, had found himself unravelling at the seams. Years of navigating the murky waters of legal battles had left him on the brink of mental collapse. His mind, once sharp and analytical, now struggled under the weight of constant existential crises. Reality, to Arjun, had become a shifting, unreliable construct. He experienced moments where the world around him seemed to flicker, where the lines between what was real and imagined blurred into a chaotic haze. The void, sensing his fractured grip on reality, whispered promises of clarity, offering him a way to untangle the threads of his existence and escape the endless spiral of doubt.

Each of these fractured souls, in their own worlds, felt the pull of the void, felt the weight of the Nexus as it dragged them into its infinite darkness. They had no choice. They were part of the ripple that the Saint had set in motion, and they were about to meet their end.

THE CONVERGENCE

The Void Nexus was not a physical place, not a construct of stone or mortar. It existed outside the realm of time and space, a point where all realities, all dimensions, and all timelines collided, intertwined, and dissolved. It was a black hole of existence, a paradoxical convergence where everything and nothing existed simultaneously, a singularity where the boundaries of existence shattered, leaving behind only chaos.

When the sixteen souls stepped into the Nexus, they did not enter a space as they understood it. They entered the mind of the Nexus, a living, pulsing entity of chaos. The walls seemed to breathe, twisting and bending like the veins of an ancient being. Dark energy coursed through the Nexus, carrying the lifeblood of every reality that had ever been and would ever be. Time itself fractured within its grasp.

At the centre stood **Ravanan**.

He was not human, though he wore the form of one. Ravanan was chaos incarnate, a trickster born of entropy, a force older than time itself. His eyes were endless voids, consuming everything they gazed upon. His smile was thin, sharp, a blade that cut through the fabric of reality with ease. He had been waiting for this moment, for the Saint of Duality to bring the fractured souls to him, to this convergence of chaos.

"You think this was your choice?" Ravanan's voice echoed through the Nexus, reverberating in the minds of those gathered. "You think you had control over your lives? Your choices? Your destinies? No. You were always mine. You just didn't know it."

The Saint, hidden in the shadows, watched in silence. He had once believed that balance was real, that he could maintain equilibrium between good and evil, order and chaos. But now, standing at the precipice of the void, he saw the truth, **there was no balance**. There was only chaos. And Ravanan was its master.

The sixteen souls—Dr. Vivek, Aditya, Rudra, Aarav, and the others—felt their realities begin to unravel. Their minds, already fractured by the burdens they carried, began to crack, and the void seeped in, devouring the fragments of their identities.

THE COLLECTIVE DESCENT INTO CHAOS

The Void Nexus was alive. Its pulse, a low hum beneath the fabric of existence, reverberated through the very bones of the universe. It was not simply a space but a sentient entity, feeding on the minds of those drawn into its gravity. As the sixteen souls stood on the threshold, staring into the abyss, their thoughts began to fray, unravelling like threads pulled from an intricate tapestry.

The temple pulsed with dark energy, its walls seeming to breathe with the lifeblood of every reality that had ever existed. The sixteen souls, standing together at the centre of the Nexus, could feel the weight of the void pressing down on them. Time and space began to warp, distorting their perceptions, blurring the lines between past, present, and future.

As the walls of the Nexus pulsed, the first ripple of chaos spread through the gathered souls. Dr. Vivek felt his mind shatter as the faces of his dead patients surrounded him, their hollow eyes accusing him of failure. He stumbled, his hands trembling, as the weight of his guilt overwhelmed him. The walls of the temple seemed to close in on him, suffocating him with the enormity of his sins.

Next to him, Aditya fell to his knees, his equations unravelling in his mind. The laws of physics no longer held meaning. Time, space, reality, all of it was collapsing into a singularity of chaos. He could no longer tell if he was observing the collapse or if the collapse was observing him.

One by one, the others began to break. Rudra, suffocating under the weight of his wealth, felt the city he had built dissolve into ash. Aarav, the manipulative psychologist, saw his reflection twist and distort, each version of himself more grotesque than the last. Maya, once a master of darkness, found herself consumed by the very night she had sought to control. The shadows devoured her, swallowing her identity whole. Devan, haunted by the reflection of a lost love, reached for her in every mirror, only to shatter into a thousand pieces when the glass broke. Samarth, the dream manipulator, found himself trapped in a nightmare of his own making, where his every desire twisted into horror. And Naina, forever the fugitive, realised too late that there was no place left to hide from the ghosts of her past.

The collective descent into chaos had begun. The void was not content to destroy them individually. It sought to consume them as one, their minds and souls intertwined in a single moment of collapse. The walls of the Nexus pulsed again, the energy growing stronger as the void fed on their fear, their guilt, their despair.

The void did not discriminate. It fed on the darkness within each of them, amplifying their deepest fears, regrets, and desires until they could no longer distinguish reality from illusion.

As each soul unravelled, their thoughts and identities dissolved into the chaotic energy of the void. They were no longer individuals with memories, hopes, or fears. They became fragments, absorbed into the Nexus, where time and space had ceased to exist. Ravanan watched, his smile growing as the Nexus fed on their chaos, growing stronger with each soul it consumed.

The Saint watched, helpless, as the souls around him unravelled. He had spent millennia guiding them, believing that balance could be maintained. But now, standing at the edge of the void, he saw the truth, there was no balance. There was only chaos. And Ravanan was its master.

THE COLLAPSE OF THE MULTIVERSE

The Nexus pulsed one last time, and the final collapse began.

The sixteen fractured souls, once individuals with their own stories, their own burdens, were now nothing more than fragments of chaos, intertwined in the fabric of the void. Their thoughts, their memories, their identities, all of it was consumed, devoured by the Nexus. Time and space fractured, dimensions folded in on themselves, and the very fabric of reality began to unravel.

The Saint of Duality had once believed that balance was the key to maintaining the multiverse. He had spent millennia guiding souls, tipping the scales between light and darkness, order and chaos. But as he watched the void devour the minds of those gathered before him, he realised that balance had never truly existed. There was only chaos, and Ravanan had always been its master.

The Nexus pulsed, a living entity now thriving on the chaos it had consumed. With each soul that dissolved, the multiverse itself began to collapse. Timelines fractured, dimensions folded in on themselves, and the very fabric of existence began to unravel. The void expanded, pulling everything into its singularity, a point of infinite compression where even the concept of existence ceased to hold meaning.

The Saint stood at the edge of the Nexus, his once unshakeable faith in balance crumbling before him. He had been nothing more than a pawn in Ravanan's game, a tool used to bring about the end of all things. The void, once distant and terrifying, now seemed inevitable. It reached out for him, tendrils of darkness wrapping around his mind, pulling him into its infinite depths.

As the void consumed him, the Saint understood that his quest for control had been futile. There was no order to maintain, no scales to balance. The multiverse had always been on a path towards chaos, and Ravanan had simply accelerated its collapse. The Saint's mind fractured, his thoughts dissolving into the blackness, leaving behind only the void.

With the Saint devoured, the collapse of the multiverse accelerated. Ravanan, standing at the heart of the Nexus, watched with quiet satisfaction. He had won. The multiverse, once infinite in its possibilities, now collapsed into a singularity. Every timeline, every reality, was drawn into the void, where it would cease to exist.

The souls consumed by the void were not dead. They were worse than dead. They existed in a state of suspended animation, their minds frozen in the moment of their unravelling. They could not think, they could not feel. They could only exist, trapped forever in the void, with no hope of escape.

The Saint, the last to fall, felt the tendrils of the void wrap around his mind, pulling him into its depths. His purpose, his quest for balance, had been a lie. He had been nothing more than a pawn in Ravanan's game, a tool to bring about the collapse of existence itself.

As the Nexus consumed him, the multiverse collapsed into a singularity. Timelines fractured, dimensions crumbled, and the infinite possibilities of existence were drawn into the void, where they ceased to exist. The souls trapped within the Nexus were not dead. They were worse than dead. They existed in a state of suspended animation, their minds frozen in the moment of their unravelling. They could not think, they could not feel. They could only exist, but they could not exist, trapped forever in the void, with no hope of escape.

THE ETERNAL NOTHINGNESS: THE SILENCE OF THE VOID

Ravanan had always known that there was no balance, no order to be restored. The multiverse had been nothing more than a playground for his chaos, a canvas on which he could paint with destruction. Now, as the last remnants of existence were pulled into the void, Ravanan smiled.

There was no future. There was no past. There was only the eternal present – a moment of pure, unadulterated chaos that stretched on forever. The multiverse was no more. There was only the void.

In the silence of the void, where time and space no longer held meaning, the souls remained trapped. Dr. Vivek, Aditya, Rudra, Aarav, Maya, and the others, all of them had become part of the void. They would never be free. They would never escape. There was no redemption, no final reckoning. Only eternal nothingness.

Ravanan, standing at the edge of the void, watched as the last vestiges of reality collapsed into itself. He had won. There was no balance. There was no good, no evil.

And in the end, there was nothing. There was only the void, and in that void, Ravanan reigned supreme.

EPILOGUE: WHISPERS FROM THE VOID

In the final silence, only the void remains. An endless abyss, it stretches beyond all meaning, swallowing desires, dreams, and identities into its vast nothingness. Each character's struggle, every choice and consequence, dissolves into this darkness, raising the unsettling question: what if everything is but an illusion? The fears, the anguish, the yearnings, were they anything more than fleeting shadows cast by a reality we thought we understood? It feels as though there is no escape from this emptiness, as if the void is the only true destination.

For a moment, despair reigns. The void appears infinite and indifferent, reducing the universe to an illusion of individual moments—disconnected, fleeting, and meaningless. It becomes a mirror reflecting back the futility of every human attempt to define, control, or understand life. In this space, there is nothing to cling to: no identity, no certainty, no answers. The more one seeks to grasp meaning, the further it seems to slip away.

But it is precisely here, in this confrontation with nothingness, that a profound realisation emerges: what if the void is not the end, but the beginning? What if the darkness we fear is not the absence of light, but the place where all light is born? The void, this vast expanse of nothing, is not barren. It is the fertile ground from which everything arises, the source, the origin of all creation and consciousness.

The truth, once hidden by the illusion of separateness, becomes clear: the void is not a place of loss, but of unity. It is the space where all dualities collapse, where opposites merge into one. In this void, the self that we so desperately cling to dissolves, not into nothingness, but into wholeness. There is no distinction between the observer and the observed, the dreamer and the dream, for all are part of the same infinite reality. Each character's journey, seemingly isolated and unique, is a thread in a much larger tapestry, woven together by the same force, the same cosmic dance.

In this realisation, the void no longer appears hostile. It becomes a reflection of our true nature: boundless, timeless, interconnected. The fears and desires that once seemed to define us fade away, revealing a deeper, more profound truth: we are not separate from the universe, but expressions of it. The void is not our end; it is our beginning. It is the space where we return to our true nature, where we see that everything we sought was already within us.

And so, as we step away from these stories, we realise that the void is not something to fear. It is not an ending, but an invitation, a doorway to the infinite. It is the realisation that, beyond all illusions, we are already whole. The universe, in all its complexity, is not separate from us. We are the void, and the void is us, a place where all opposites meet and merge, where all that we are and all that we seek becomes one.

In the end, the void is not empty. It is full–full of potential, full of light, full of peace. In this vastness, you are not lost. You are whole and the only whole. *Tat Tvam Asi.*